The Rabbi's
LIFE CONTRACT

The Rabbi's
LIFE CONTRACT

MARILYN GREENBERG

Doubleday & Company, Inc., Garden City, New York, 1983

TEMPLE ISRAEL LIBRARY
1602 E. 2ND ST.
DULUTH, MN 55812

"MY WAY"
Original French Lyric by GILLES THIBAULT.
Music by J. REVAUX & C. FRANÇOIS.
Words by PAUL ANKA.
© Copyright 1967 by Société des nouvelles Edition Eddie Barclay, Paris, France.
© Copyright 1969 for U.S. and Canada by MANAGEMENT AGENCY & MUSIC PUBLISHING INC.
% MCA MUSIC, A Division of MCA Inc., New York, N.Y.
USED BY PERMISSION. ALL RIGHTS RESERVED.

Library of Congress Cataloging in Publication Data

Greenberg, Marilyn (Marilyn S.)
  The rabbi's life contract.

  I. Title.
PS3557.R3788R3   1983   813'.54
ISBN: 0-385-19003-4
Library of Congress Catalog Card Number 82-45834

Copyright © 1983 by Marilyn Greenberg
All Rights Reserved
Printed in the United States of America

For STA and JRH with affection, admiration, gratitude.

If I am not for myself, who will be?
If I am for myself alone, what am I?

HILLEL

PROLOGUE

"Shoot," he said wearily. "Go ahead, shoot."

"All right, Rabbi," said the lawyer. He sat on the very edge of his desk. "Let me ask you this, Rabbi." He paused. "Rabbi Rosenstock, do you always tell the truth?" Before Shoe Rosenstock could reply, Bobby jumped up from his desk and walked nervously about his office. "Remember, Rabbi," he said tensely, "this is our last chance to prepare ourselves. Remember now," he warned, "I'm *their* lawyer for the moment. So answer me with some caution." He chewed his lips. "*Please* don't answer a question you haven't been asked. That's a bad habit of yours," he muttered, blushing. "And if there's an ambiguity in the question, don't you be the one to point it out. Another bad habit." He stared at the rabbi, a burly, worn man, slouched in his chair. "And if you don't remember something, just say so. You're not expected to have total recall. Nobody is. And," he said urgently, speaking more rapidly, "if you do remember, but not exactly, say, 'To the best of my recollection.' *Not* 'I think' or 'I guess.' They'll make mincemeat of you." He shook his red head and looked troubled. "I hope you understand." He gnawed on his fingertip.

The rabbi's wife yawned enormously and rolled her head back against the wall behind her. Her dress was damp and wrinkled.

"Bored, Myra?" the lawyer asked coldly.

"Of course not, Bobby," she said, sitting up. She tried to

straighten her dress. "I think they turned off the air in here." She rubbed her eyes. "Just get finished with him, Bobby, and we'll all go home."

Bobby bounced up athletically to sit on his desk again. "Okay, here we go." He ran a freckled hand through his red hair and composed his face. "Tell me, Rabbi Rosenstock," he said quietly, "do you always tell the truth?"

The rabbi's lips parted; he paused. Then he smiled gently, reproachfully. "No," he said.

"Yes!" shouted Bobby, electrified. His fair face went dark red. "Yes! Yes! Yes! Oh, thank God I asked him that!" he shouted at Myra.

"What did he say?" she said, blinking.

"The answer is yes!" bellowed Bobby. He beat his palms against the edge of the desk. "What have we been doing here? *Yes*, you always tell the truth! You're a wonderful, truthful person! You're a *rabbi!* You can't go in and tell a judge under oath that you don't always tell the truth! Are you crazy? You want to commit suicide?" He breathed hard and hit the desk.

"Stop, Bobby," said Myra. "It's not the end of the world. He didn't understand. Just tell him what you want."

"Rabbi," the lawyer said, trying to breathe deliberately and deeply, "Rabbi, I apologize. I have said many things to you I never thought in my life I would say to a rabbi."

"Forget it, Bobby," said Shoe with a wave of his big hand. "But nobody always tells the truth. Wouldn't the judge know it was a lie if I said so? Seems like common sense to me. But if you tell me not to," he said hastily as Bobby's face went dark again, "that's the end of the discussion. I take it back. The answer is yes."

"Yes," said Bobby forcefully. "Here's your answer: 'Yes, I always tell the truth.' Oh, thank God I thought of it." He threw himself down into his chair.

"Now, I'm not on the stand now, Bobby," Shoe persisted. Bobby rolled his eyes up. Shoe leaned his bulky body forward and looked at the lawyer. "This is just here in the office. I just want to explain. If I go, say, to visit a dying man and he says, 'Rabbi, I'm not dying, am I?'—well, what would you do? I'm curious. Because I say no. I can see for myself that he can't take the truth, or he wouldn't be asking me. And I lie." He sat back, looking satisfied. He moved his big feet slightly on the tightly woven rug.

"That's not a lie," said Bobby scornfully. "I don't call that a lie!" he said, erupting furiously. "Are you a doctor?" he shouted. "Do you know for a fact he's going to die? Don't miracles occur every day? Come on," he said, slapping the desk. "No, Rabbi! You never tell a lie. I'm not going to let you stand up in front of those suckers—" His face flamed. "Pardon me. But I won't let you, after all they've put you through, and after all the shame they've brought on the Jewish people, I won't sit there and hear you call yourself a liar! *No!*"

"Got it," said Shoe. He pulled a pipe from the pocket of his jacket and bit the stem hard.

"All right, then," Bobby said loudly. "Once again." He leaned back and crossed his legs. "Rabbi Rosenstock," he said mildly, "do you ever tell a lie?" Myra Rosenstock smiled.

"No," said Shoe.

"Do you always tell the truth, Rabbi?"

"Yes." He chewed the stem of his pipe.

"And the truth is," Bobby said, leaning toward him and staring into his shadowed, weary eyes, "that you, Rabbi Joshua Rosenstock, you have faithfully served, faithfully given your all to this congregation for twenty years, under a *lifetime contract*." He stood up and threw out his arms. "And you went on a sabbatical, after twenty years of single-minded devotion, you took a sabbatical in Israel." He drew breath. "And they plotted against you in your absence on sabbatical; and decided to throw you out without warning, with no attempt at mediation; so that you and your wife boarded that plane in Tel Aviv with no bigger worries than to collect your baggage here at O'Hare. And that night," he shouted, "that night, that very night, the very night of your return, they told you you were finished! Isn't that the truth?"

"Yes," said Shoe. His wife sighed.

"Good," said Bobby. He began putting papers in his briefcase. He appeared to have forgotten the Rosenstocks. He looked vaguely around the office for his jacket. His glance fell on Myra, who sat, looking stunned, on the sofa. He grinned at her. "Now if only we could ask questions like that in the hearing, we'd have it sewed up." He laughed. "Let's call it a night."

1

"Rabbi Joshua Rosenstock," said the voice, reaching through speakers all over the airport. "Mrs. Myra Rosenstock," it said. "Rabbi Joshua Rosenstock," the accented voice repeated. "Please join your El Al flight to Chicago."

Shoe stood at the gate. He asked the guard, "Have you seen my wife?"

"What she looks like?" asked the Israeli.

Shoe was taken aback. "Uh . . . tall, I guess . . . a big blonde, as big as me, a good-looking . . . you know—" He broke off. "Say, how do you ask an old married man such a question?" They laughed together. "Hey, Myra!" he shouted suddenly. "Come on!"

Sunburned and peeling, Myra strode in happy confusion out of the booth nearby where she had been searched. She and a female guard clutched each other's arms and balanced Myra's many parcels and shopping bags between them. "Shoe, Shoe," said Myra, "you'll never guess. Nechama here has a daughter in Chicago."

The speaker crackled again. "Rabbi Joshua Rosenstock."

Myra jumped and dropped a small package. "Shoe!" she cried. "They're calling us! Why are you just standing here?"

"Look at this," he said, turning to the guards. "A whole year here, I'm always waiting for her. Now you hear her?"

"So what are you waiting for now, another year?" said the female guard. She picked up the package and gave it to Myra. "Safe journey."

"Oh, I hate to leave," declared Myra, looking around the sunlit terminal. "How I love Israel."

"Bully," said the man. "Why you don't stay with us?"

"But I want to go home," she said, startled. "My children! We have six children!"

"All honor to you," said the woman. "My mother had ten."

"Rabbi Joshua Rosenstock," said the voice, gone sepulchral. "Mrs. Myra Rosenstock. Your El Al flight is departing. Is it yes or no?"

"Good-by," Myra said to the guards. She was tense, disheveled, excited. "Be well, keep safe," she said longingly. It was hard for her to imagine lives that went on when she and Shoe were gone.

"Shalom, shalom," said Shoe. "We'll be back." He turned around. Myra was already striding away in her worn sandals, shifting the shopping bags on her forearms. "Look at that!" he said, exasperated. He ran to catch her. Together, they mounted the burning metal steps that led to the waiting mouth of the plane.

"Rabbi Rosenstock, Mrs. Rosenstock," said the voice, exhausted. "Your El Al flight departs in ninety seconds. Truthfully."

Shoe put his hand on Myra's thigh as she climbed ahead of him. "Here we come, New Saxony," he said. "Coming home. Dust off that pulpit and get your brass band ready!"

Dear Rabbi,

You don't know me, but I met your sister in Omaha and she said you would be home by now from your sabbatical and I could write you about my problem with my mother. We met at a conference on rights for Indian women. Your sister was the Hadassah representative. Anyway, I expect my first baby in December. I know it will be a boy because when you're thirty-eight you get amniocentesis. My mother says I can't make a *bris* in a house with a Christmas tree in it. Could you please write my mother and explain to her about all these ancient rites? Circumcision, the Christmas tree, the maize ceremony: I want my child to have everything. I waited long enough to have him. So if you would tell her they're all really the same thing: an expression of joy and of love and community and of caring and sharing, I'm sure she would accept it. She's of the generation that believes something automatically if a rabbi says so.

I appreciate it very much. I know you must be very busy now after a year in Israel. If your work ever brings you out here to South Dakota, come see us. You'll be more than welcome. I keep a kosher home, if that matters.

Yours,
Shulamith Whitewater

P.S. I did not, by the way, mention to your nice sister that I am not married. I think it's best to leave it that way. Hadassah's doing a fantastic job. We're always proud out here to see what our sisters are into.

2

Down his rolling, graveled driveway drove tiny Dr. Milton Winegarden, rubbing inflamed shoulders against the back of the seat as he manipulated the extensions on the foot pedals of the Land-Rover and guided it into the attached garage of his home. He climbed down off the raised seat, looked about, and saw with relief that his wife was out. Inside the empty house only a small fluorescent light on the stove was lit for him. Milton gazed around the large kitchen and breathed a long breath; good to be home. He scratched his back. Another day done; another day teaching teenage mothers and slashers and rapists, all oozing up to New Saxony from the city for a free education. Another day, another dollar. He wiped a smudge from the stove top with a paper towel. Sunny's note was on the refrigerator stuck to a magnet. And how often he'd warned her about scratching the finish!

Sweetie [said the note],
Gone out to Audubon meeting. Might be late. If Audubon breaks up early, might go on to Friends of Music. Your yogurt is inside on the top shelf and I bought you a very good apple. Don't forget you have a very important synagogue meeting tonight. I love you.

Milton's tight neck muscles relaxed. Ah, really, basically, Sunny was a wonderful girl. One's unconscious directed one to make the right choice at an age when judgment was not yet much developed, and he had chosen Sunny. She loved him. In their large, childless house, they babied one another. They restored antiques and fed each other yogurt and tapioca and soft-boiled eggs. They planted flowers together.

He opened the refrigerator and looked inside. He closed it. What a day! Better not eat yet, too upset. Although, really, basically, nothing was wrong. His skin was acting up because summer was coming on, nothing else. They're not sweeping me out of the college so fast, thought Milton. He walked around the vast kitchen in the glow of the light on the stove with a damp sponge in his hand. He looked for finger marks. Sunny is too negligent, he thought. You have to follow the help around and make sure they clean. He climbed a stepladder and pounced on a faint smear on the knob of an overhead cabinet.

Milton addressed himself rhetorically as he rubbed away the mark. And where was my department chairman back when we first got organized here? Tougaloo College? Picking cotton someplace? Milton's hands itched. He climbed down and rinsed his sponge. Then he scoured the wide stainless steel sink and dried it with a linen hand towel. He set the stove timer to ring in time for his important synagogue meeting.

I've got nothing against the man, Milton went on to himself. He put ointment on his scaling red hands and looked out the kitchen window, through the swelling limbs of the old copper beech outside, down the sloping back lawns to the rose beds whose canes were shining in the twilight. They don't know how to handle authority, he argued. That's all I'm saying. After all, it's only a hundred years since slavery. But give them a taste of power and they start purges. He scratched his mottled heavy neck. Milton giggled in the shadows. "I'll bet he has a dream," he said softly. Sure, Isaiah Summers, Chairman; he has a dream. He has a dream that one day there'll be a community college in New Saxony and the Jews will pay the bills and swindle the government for more; and *they*, they'll sit there like kings and own it. And tell me what to do, how to run my classes. Not so fast, Dr. Boogie Summers, thought Milton Winegarden. He struck the counter with his small, powerful fist. Not so fast, my colleague!

Milton sighed and opened the refrigerator again, looked, closed it again. He felt sticky, his rashes were weeping. I need a bath, he thought. Lie down with dogs, get up with fleas. I'm dirty. He went up the wobbly back stairs.

In this ancient Tudor house, only the kitchen and bathrooms were new, thanks to his income from the college. It brought in just enough for these little luxuries. He held to the rough plaster wall on his way up in the dark. Someday they must put in a light on these stairs, thought Milton. But everything costs money. The builder had the right idea for his time. Let the help break their necks on the back stairs. It's cheaper to get new help than to put in a light. But with help today? Ha! thought Milton bitterly.

He arrived in the main hall on the second floor, a deeply carpeted rectangle with heavy dark doors leading off to the bedrooms. He and Sunny cultivated a flowering winter garden in the window alcove. He went to admire the impatiens and geraniums blooming beneath the leaded glass window. It was getting time to set them outdoors. Soon they would try orchids. They attended a weekly class to prepare themselves. It was a very exciting prospect. All the more reason, thought Milton, scratching in the crooks of his elbows. Get off my back, you Othello. I have a creative life to lead. You don't imagine I must teach remedial English? I'm a Ph.D. in philosophy. I'm a lay analyst. I'm an ordained Orthodox rabbi. I even have an accounting degree. And you're going to tell me how many hours I have to spend in my office? The skin on his buttocks stung and he let his pants fall to the carpet. It's not a time-clock kind of thing, Milton thundered in his head. It's quality that counts. When you've belonged to the middle class a little longer, you'll understand. Milton leaned forward and snapped off a dried blossom half hidden in the leaves. His thumb and forefinger felt like fire. I'm no day worker, you sonofabitch.

He looked at all the closed doors off the hall and felt a stirring below the belt. "Oh, I shouldn't," he said aloud. He looked at his bedroom door. "I don't have the synagogue meeting till nine," he said. He opened the door to the third-floor staircase.

He went up to his study, which he entered with a key. "I'll just take my bath up here," he said. He loved his study. He and Sunny had installed skylights the length of the roof and had knocked out all the partitions of the former servants' rooms to make a huge room, almost royal. The greatest thinkers would have done better work in a room like this: Socrates, Freud, Martin Buber himself. And it had a fabulous toilet and sink and bath, not concealed, no; right out in the open, although with wonderful ferns set about, and mirrors and elegant details like the gold dolphin faucets on the sink and the gilt Greek key motif repeated on all the fixtures. Yes, Sunny was a wonderful girl. She had shopped and painted and curtained; for him. She had worked with the architect to scale this room for Milton somehow, despite its great size. It was his room; he held the key.

He went to the free-standing closet near the tub and undressed. He hung away his clothes and put on a soft, frilly robe whose very touch soothed the angry, sticky rashes on his burning small body. He looked for the matching slippers. "Oh well, it doesn't matter," he said in a motherly tone. "We're going to bathe in a moment." He shook bubble crystals in the tub.

"Better, much better," he sighed. Milton leaned back in the tub and enjoyed the bubbles licking at him and popping and vanishing. He rested his head against the golden trim bordering the tub. He extended his blunt arms along its edges. The crust of the rashes was rinsed away. "No," he said, smiling and shaking his large head. "No, you don't, Milton Winegarden. We're not going to. We have a very important synagogue meeting soon. You just keep your hands where they are."

He wiggled against the hard porcelain beneath him. "You never let me," he said, falsetto. "I never can do what I want." He pouted. "Mean as Isaiah Summers." He laughed and held his small powerful fists aloft for a moment, studied the shreds of bubble foam on the backs of his hairy hands. He put his arms down again. "Why can't I?" he piped. "Won't I be righteous enough to meet with the rabbi?" He curled his toes under water and clenched his strong fists. "I better get out," he said in a normal voice. "I need time for the sunlamp. I don't want to be late for the meeting."

He shivered and wrapped the robe tightly around him. He fastened his towel like a turban to keep his balding head warm. He knelt next to the tub to scour it as the bubbles drained away. There was a presence behind him but he refused to look. These visitations went better if you left them unacknowledged. He hung his middle over the edge of the tub to reach the bottom. He felt the presence against the backs of his thighs. "Go away," he said. "I'm mad at you." He went on scrubbing as though making that tub clean were the only thing in life he wanted. He widened the space between his muscle-bound thighs. He had to move his pelvis to get at the faucets. He pressed himself to the water-warmed porcelain.

"No," he said, moving, rubbing against the tub. "I didn't invite you here."

But he couldn't help it; it wasn't Milton's fault. He hung on the two taps, one hand hot, the other almost frozen, his face hanging above the last warm scented bubbles as they expired in the bottom of the tub. The tops of his stubby chafed feet ached from the pressure of the tiles that surrounded the tub like a lake. He was in a jungle; the steam covered his face; an odor rose around him. He exposed his yellowed, irregular teeth in an appeasing smile and gave himself up to it. The tall blacks appeared and they forced him, it wasn't Milton's fault, they chanted and forced him, and used their great strength, their awful height . . . He cried out, "Isaiah! Isaiah! Isaiah!" and almost fell headfirst into the tub.

The weight at the backs of his thighs fell away. The frilly robe covered his hard buttocks again. He pulled back from the tub and wiped the outside of it with toilet paper without looking. He stretched out, damp beneath the robe, on the fur bath rug, and slept. He slept without dreaming until the timer rang down in the kitchen to remind him of his important synagogue meeting.

My dear brother,

I am just home from a conference on peacemaking in the Church and by now you will be home as well. One of my vestrymen told me of what awaited you—after twenty years here!—and I want you to know you will be in my prayers. Our path is mysterious, Shoe, and sometimes hidden from us, but do please know that our trials may become blessings and disaster our good fortune. I know people whose poor health brought them the blessing of greater sensitivity to the sufferings of others. I'm sure you can think of other examples. So take courage, son of Abraham, be strengthened.

Yours in Christ,
Winstead

Dear Rabbi,
 I need you to fill out this Eagle Scout application in the place where it says Religious Leader. I have two days left to get it in so I know you will do it right away. Thank you.

Brucie Markowitz

3

Blue-eyed, round-eyed, round-bottomed Etta, loving youngest of the six Rosenstock children, unlocked the front door and let the dog leap ahead of her into the house. "Yes!" she cried. "Yes! You came home because Mommy and Daddy are coming! Yes!" The dog turned and threw himself at Etta.

Now that she was here, having cut a late class, she didn't quite know what to do. She went to the dining-room table to make a list. The floorboards creaked as she walked. The house smelled of dust and damp. The dog sniffed in the corners. PUT ON HEAT, she wrote. She got up and turned up the thermostat on the wall and heard the furnace start. Then she turned it off again. She went back to the table. DUST, she wrote. She continued to sit and stare at the paper. What did Mommy do when she made lists? Etta's mind went blank. FOOD, she wrote. She jumped up and went out to the car in the driveway for the groceries on the back seat. A pound of apples, a pound of pears, a pound of bananas. It didn't look like much. Etta reached for the bags. A pound of coffee, a pound of cheese, a bag of croissants from the university bakery for a surprise for Mommy. Etta bit her lip. She might be flunking French.

The kitchen door was warped and Etta struggled to get back inside. She finally pulled it open and the dog cascaded past her to the overgrown space where Myra sometimes grew mint. He twirled in the young weeds and sneezed and jumped back into the kitchen to nip Etta's blue jeans. "I know," said Etta, petting him. "I'm excited too." She put the croissants on the counter out of his reach. She might flunk French and then what would happen? That would make Mommy and Daddy proud! Her blue eyes filled.

The dog was whining and moaning and jumping against the front door. Etta jumped and ran to the front window. There they were! She saw her parents outside in the early darkness, leaning over to talk to the taxi driver, the way they talked all the time, with everybody they ever met. Oh! She ran outside to them.

"Here she is," said Shoe, grabbing her and cutting off her breath with his embrace.

"My youngest," Myra explained unnecessarily to the driver. She smiled tranquilly at her husband and daughter and went about paying the man. All three Rosenstocks, tall, pale even when sunburned, rumpled, blond, walked up the leaf-covered front walk dragging the baggage, the shopping bags, the gifts for friends, the raincoats, while the dog ran in circles around them in the silence of the suburban evening. "These are last year's leaves," Myra said irritably. She pushed back the branches of an overgrown yew at the door. "What a mess."

"Relax, Myra," said her husband. "We're tired."

Etta carried in the shopping bags. Her father came inside and grabbed her again, stifling her against his big chest. "Your mother has presents for you," he said into her wispy hair. "Good thing she loves you. I didn't even miss you." He squeezed her.

"Don't throw your coat on the floor, Shoe," said Myra, coming in.

"She wants me to be a fairy," Shoe said. He pushed his raincoat away with his foot. The dog lay down on top of it with a groan.

"I don't know how I live with him," said Myra.

Etta was happy. "I'll make coffee, Mom," she said.

"Oh, you doll," said Myra. "Oh, you sweetness. How did I leave you for so long?" She kissed her daughter's cheeks.

"I just saw you in Israel at Christmas, Mom," Etta said smugly. "It's only a few months."

"Too long," cried Myra. "How could I be without you so long?"

Etta smiled. "And there's croissants for you."

"Say, how's French?" asked Myra.

"Look at all this mail, Mom," she said hurriedly. She gestured to a row of bulging trash bags on the dining-room floor. "They said it's only two weeks' worth."

Myra moaned. Shoe started toward the bags.

"Leave it, Shoe," ordered Myra. "We're too tired. We'll have a bite and get to bed. Honey," she told the girl, "presents tomorrow, okay? Suddenly, I'm just bushed." She pushed the straggling gray and blond hair off her forehead.

Shoe seized a broom leaning against the kitchen wall. "I'll just see if we have water in the basement."

"No," said Myra.

"Not now, Daddy," said Etta.

"Two of them," Shoe said proudly. "The mother's got an assistant."

The dog put his face between Myra's thighs. She stared at the bags of mail. The phone rang. Etta answered.

"It was next door," she told Myra. "Burglars. Did she think burglars would answer the phone?"

"I was so eager to come home," said Myra wearily. "Now I could leave again." She slumped at the table and opened the first letter. The dog barked. Etta stepped outside to talk to a policeman checking the house. Myra sighed. She lit a cigarette. "What is this?" she said aloud, reading. "What does this mean?" She went to the head of the basement stairs. "Shoe," she called, "you better come up. There's some strange mail here. Come up." The phone rang. "Hello," said Myra.

"Let me speak to the rabbi, please," said the caller. "This is Milton Winegarden. How are you?"

"Fine, Milton," said Myra. "How are you? I'm shocked. We got home two minutes ago. How prompt you are."

"Could I speak to the rabbi?" he repeated.

"Of course," she said. "Everything all right?"

"Just put him on," he said.

"Shoe," she called, "phone for you. Milton Winegarden."

Shoe came upstairs, a dripping broom in his hand. Myra took it from him and whispered, "He sounds bad. Somebody must be sick."

"Hello, Milt," said Shoe heartily. "Just stepped into the house. Greetings from the land of Israel. How's everything?" He leaned against the wall, listening. The dog approached him, looked up at his face, lay down on his feet. "I'm a little tired, Milton," Shoe said carefully. He sat down on the stool by the phone, shifting the dog's inert body. "Could it wait till tomorrow? Can you give me some idea what it's about?" He gestured for Myra to bring him a cup of coffee. She tiptoed to him with the cup. He set it down without tasting it. "If it's absolutely necessary, as you say, I guess I'd better. Can you give me time for a shower? Are there many of you waiting? Just let me clean up and I'll be there. No, no problem. All right, Milton," he said in a reassuring voice. He hung up.

"Why did you say you'd go?" she said. "You're exhausted. Whatever it is, it could wait."

"Sounds like trouble," he said thoughtfully. He unbuttoned his shirt and pulled it off, dropping it on a chair. "What can it be? What's so urgent?" He went upstairs talking to himself. Myra shrugged and returned to the mail.

Etta came in. "Does Daddy have to go out already?"

Myra looked up. "Oh, sweetie, look at this letter."

Dearest Rabbi,

I am sorry to tell you that my husband is terminal. He was fine and then he had a checkup and they found something but didn't know quite what, and then they found the malignancy. It's only two months since then. I don't think he'll be with us another two.

Well, you know Charlie. Always thinking ahead. He would like you to come over and talk to him about the service for him after he's gone. He's still trying to protect young Billy and me and to arrange all the things he can do for me before he has to go. I suppose I should talk to you sometime but it will wait.

I have him at home so you can come whenever it's convenient for you. I hate to take you away from your darling wife and those lovely children. The last I heard, you were going on what promised to be a fascinating sabbatical. I hope it was rewarding but I know you're glad to come home to the children. Charlie and I always admired your beautiful family life. Rabbi, live while you can. That's what I've always believed and now I mean it more than ever.

Come see him soon. There isn't too much time.

Much love,
Lena Bloom

4

"Is that our Dr. Bloom?" asked Etta in a frightened voice. "That used to pull a balloon out of my ear when I got a shot?" She sat next to Myra at the littered table.

Myra stroked the girl's head.

Shoe came downstairs barefoot, hair shining dark with water, laughing at himself. "I figured it out," he said. He stood between the seated women, a hand on each of their shoulders. "It's a surprise party, that's what it is. Get dressed up, you two. The people will probably be here as soon as I'm out of the way. Then I come back with Milton and they jump out of cakes or something." He laughed again.

"I have to go, Daddy," said the girl, standing up. "Early class tomorrow. Here's the car keys. Drop me at the station?"

"Oh," said Shoe sorrowfully. "You have to?"

"I'll be home for the weekend," she said. "All the big kids will be too," she added unconsciously, the perennial youngest.

"Let her go, Shoe," said Myra. She put her long hand over Lena Bloom's letter, concealing it. "Give me a kiss," she said, turning her face up to the girl. "You're my cake. You're my best surprise. You're my party." Tears came to her eyes. "I don't care about anything else."

Etta kissed her. "Well, enjoy it anyway. Act really surprised."

Etta and Shoe went out the back door. Myra heard them laughing as they got into the car. Then the car drove off.

Myra continued to sit and stare at the letters she had opened. She touched them without reading them again. She went down to the basement and finished the sweeping Shoe had begun. Still no doorbell or phone call. She came up and shared a croissant with the dog. "We might as well go to bed," she told him. "It's not a party."

Dear Rabbi Rosenstock,

    All your life insurance and medical coverage will lapse unless we receive a certified check within the week. Our company has been in touch repeatedly with the treasurer of your synagogue to advise him of the above, but we seem to be unable to get a check from him. This is a most serious matter and we urge your immediate attention.

                                              Sincerely,
                                              Al Fortino

Dear Rabbi,

I just want you to know I'm in your corner one hundred per cent. When I think how you married my niece to a non-Jewish boy and how good you were to them, how you explained our religion to him and told him you didn't want any promises from him, except he should keep thinking very hard—he's still raving about you! Count on me and mine, Rabbi. You have more friends than you know about.

Yours very truly,
Shalom Subbotnick

P.S. I'm enclosing a very small check. It's like for a welcome home.

Dear Rabbi,
  Call me right away. Thank God you're coming back. Larry's Bar Mitzvah is not that far off and we need to talk. Here's what's on my mind.

    1. He might have an asthma attack.
    2. He might stutter.
    3. He might forget his part.

These are all things that have happened in the past. I've talked it over with him and warned him. Maybe it would help if your wife gave him a few private lessons. To tell the truth, I wish we could stop now, while he still feels happy about it. What'll we do if he faints up there on the platform? I wish you had come home sooner. We'll get through this Bar Mitzvah somehow, like every other Jewish family, but I wish we didn't have to.

                      Hoping to hear from you immediately,
                      Renee Geltman

5

Sunny Winegarden, squat and buxom, unsmiling, pulled open the massive oak door of her home and said, "Good evening, Rabbi."

"Sunny, Sunny," said Shoe, stepping in. He leaned down to embrace her. "Good to see you." He peered behind her into the dimly lit, long, empty living room. "The Holy Land sends you its greetings." He hugged her. "Isn't Milton here?"

"Up in his study," said Sunny, stepping back. She smoothed her chignon. "Just go upstairs to the third floor."

"Right," he said, puzzled. He started for the staircase. "Myra has a couple little gifts for you. Just mementos," he said. He set his foot on the oriental runner and started up.

"Very kind," Sunny said. She turned away.

"Just keep climbing," called Milton from his study doorway. "We're waiting up here for you."

Breathless, Shoe reached him and took his crusty hand. "I am out of shape," he said, panting. "You've got a Masada up here." Shoe's vision blurred. He blinked several times and saw a man seated in a leather sling chair nestling a pile of papers in his lap. Three other men sat on a small bentwood settee, crowded together beneath Milton's gallery of diplomas on the wall. He struggled to regain his breath. "Shalom, shalom," he said, nodding to the others, gasping.

"Blessed be he who comes," said Milton in Hebrew. He caressed each finger of Shoe's big hand and drew him further into the room. The lights were filtered and had a pinkish cast, making it curiously dim, despite the mirrors and other shining surfaces. Shoe thought he saw a bathtub gleaming at the far end of the room and dismissed the idea. He blinked again. Milton walked him past a group of potted ferns big enough to swallow him up. He went to an oversized brass samovar against the wall. "Will you have a cup of tea, Rabbi?"

"Thanks," he said carelessly. He went to shake hands with the men in the room. The man in the sling chair looked at him without expression.

"Welcome back," he said.

"Oh, it's you, Harry," said Shoe. "Couldn't see that far. Thanks, good to be back." He took a cup of tea from Milton's trembling hand and stood, looking expectant, next to him. "Quite a study," he said.

Milton cleared his throat. "We might as well get to it," he said. He looked up sidewise at Shoe.

"Yes, get to it," said Harry from the leather sling chair.

"Rabbi," Milton began. He broke off and scratched in a circle all around his waist, beneath his belt.

"Get to it," repeated Harry.

"Rabbi," said Milton. Beads of sweat popped out all over him, setting his skin on fire. He took Shoe's hand in his. "None of us ever imagined we'd be at a meeting like this . . . believe me . . . never."

"Maybe I can help you, Milton," said Shoe. He set down the teacup and grinned. "We're going to have to go into phase two in our fund raising, isn't that it? We need more building already, is that what you're so reluctant to tell me?" He laughed gently. "All right, so be it. Shall we start the planning tonight?" he asked patiently.

Milton looked to Harry in horror. Harry looked back without expression on his fleshy face. A delicately built, girlish man on the settee half coughed, half giggled in anxiety.

"I see I'm on the wrong track," said Shoe. "Well, just tell me, Milt, and we'll get to work. There's nothing we can't accomplish together." He waited.

"Rabbi," said Harry in a dry voice, "at the outset, I'd advise you to get a lawyer."

"Why?" said Shoe. "Have I got a problem?"

"No, no," said Milton eagerly. "We don't want you to have a problem, that's just it." He sat down suddenly on a tufted sofa behind him, holding Shoe's hand and pulling him along. He looked into Shoe's eyes as they sat side by side. "In your absence, Rabbi, we made some discoveries. Now, Rabbi, please understand me when I tell you in what high regard we all hold you, how much admiration we all feel for you." His forehead was beading.

"Don't get carried away," said Harry with a cynical laugh. Shoe laughed too.

"Rabbi, in a word, we need someone else as our leader, a more dynamic, younger person, one with a flair for the creative, that will attract the youth," said Milton in a rush. His eyes were glued to Shoe's face. "We didn't realize it till you were gone, Rabbi. We never saw ourselves in perspective before. Because you always fill up everything. We can't see ourselves clearly when you're up there in the pulpit and running everything your way."

"What are you saying, Milton?" said Shoe. He seemed to be short of breath again. The light made it hard to focus. Milton's sweating face was so close.

"Your contract is terminated," said Harry quietly. He sat deep in the sling chair and stirred the papers on his lap. "Milton is trying to tell you that. You're out. Why we're here is to talk to you about a reasonable way to pay you off."

"Wait, wait," said Shoe. He stood up. He made an effort to sound calm. "Naturally, you'll understand if I'm a little slow tonight. The trip and all . . ." He looked at the men on the settee. "Do I understand that you are all here to tell me I'm fired?"

The men nodded, three monkeys in a row, all silent.

"How can you?" Shoe stared.

"We can," said Harry. "We certainly can."

"Look," said Shoe, "you have to talk this over with me, explain this to me. What happened? Milton! You came to see us the day we left! You gave me a passport case for a gift! Milt! What happened?" Shoe was unconsciously backing away from Milton as he spoke.

Milton sprang up and took Shoe's hand again. "Understand us, Rabbi! I beg you! We can't go on with you! It's for the good of the congregation we're doing this. Don't think I would have any part of such a thing for any personal reason. You know me!"

"What good of the congregation?" asked Shoe. "What's wrong with it? I have been building it for twenty years and I'm proud of it. There's nothing wrong with it!"

"See?" said Milton sadly. "That's what's wrong. Not to take away from you, Rabbi, but there's plenty of room for improvement."

"Then tell me what!" shouted Shoe. "We'll work together. We'll make it right. You can't just throw me out! It's immoral. It's base, I tell you. A heartless corporation doesn't do things this way, much less a shul."

"I think that's enough emotional exchange," said Harry dryly. "Listen to me, Rabbi. I have financial proposals here on my lap that I want to discuss. You can take them or leave them. Or some adjustment might be possible," he added. "Maybe. Now here's how it looks in dollars and cents—"

"Have you discussed this with anybody else?" Shoe cut in.

"Certainly," said Milton. "The entire congregation agrees. We can't afford to go on with you. We're giving you one month." He was calm now that the rabbi was not.

"I don't believe you, Milton," said Shoe. Milton shrugged.

Harry said, "May I begin, please? I don't have all night."

"You think you can break a lifetime contract just like that?" said Shoe furiously. "And you don't want to waste too much of your evening at it? This is unbelievable."

"Believe it, Rabbi," said Harry coldly. The girlish man between the two others giggled into his hand.

"This is what I was afraid of," fussed Milton. He went about the room collecting teacups. "I was afraid of exactly this, Rabbi, that your huge ego—it really is overgrown—would not allow you to accept the facts. No." He sighed. He blew a cookie crumb off the table. "Ego blinds us all, but you, Rabbi, you most of all."

Dear Rabbi,

We are not going to sink to the level of these troublemakers. You belong in a small place, whether you like it or not, where the people are all your kind of people. Big success is not for everybody. Bitsy and I are willing to join with a few others and buy a house for you to teach and preach in. We are leery, however, of some of the types you attract. You don't show good judgment, Rabbi, although I admire you for it. People who want to use you can get right past you. Let's form a new group and avoid a low-level public display. We'll screen who may belong and we'll arrange for tax deductibility.

The shock of coming home will be awful for you, I know, but thank God you have people like us who have both the means and desire to help you. Say the word and we'll buy the house and make the changes in it that are necessary. You and Myra can live in the upstairs. The children will have to go on their own, we can't buy you a mansion, but they are old enough. You overbaby them as it is, although I admire you for it.

Rabbi, just ask yourself what life's all about. What's it all about, anyway? It's a ball game, Rabbi, a whole new ball game every day. We don't know what going to be but the umpire is fair. Always. This I believe.

And if nobody else wants to join us, that's their loss. We'll still have long talks about philosophy and religion that we never could have when we had to share you with so many others who didn't really appreciate you. You spent your life the wrong way, Rabbi, like all the saints. I revere a man like yourself but you need a guardian with maybe a little more savvy. Take my advice, avoid getting spattered with dirt and spare yourself a lot of heartache. Let's leave it all behind and form up new. Tell me what you think.

Very sincerely yours for shalom,
Herb Fruchthandler

6

Myra sat up abruptly in bed, unsure of where she was. Was this New Saxony or was she still in Jerusalem? She stared at the blanket and couldn't remember. She heard the door slam downstairs. Shoe was home. She looked at the glowing face of the clock in amazement. Middle of the night. They must be back home, then; and Shoe was back to work at endless late night meetings. She lay down.

He came quietly into the room. "Is the kid asleep?" he whispered. He put his shoulder to the warped bedroom door and forced it shut.

She sat up again. "What is it?" she said. "What's wrong? You know you took her to the station. Why are you so late? You look terrible. What happened?" She pulled the blanket up over her chest fearfully and shivered in the stuffy room.

He stood over her. "It's worse than I thought," he said softly. He looked down at her. "They want me out. They want to fire me."

Myra's heart turned on suddenly like a pump at full power and slammed at her ribs. She put on the lamp. "What?" she said, dazed. "What?" A little polar breeze blew through the limp curtain and hit her in the face. She slid down in the bed again.

Shoe was moving around the room, the dog trailing him. He dropped his shoes in one dusty corner, stepped over to the window, looked outside, and moved his lips while he pulled off his socks and laid them on the sill. He moved against the walls as he undressed and filled the room with his clothing. Myra watched as though she lay in the bottom of a well. She saw the ceiling paint was crackling again.

Shoe's face was contorted. He sat down on the edge of the bed and got up again. "What did I do with my watch?" he said. "What time is it?"

"What happened?" said Myra. "What are you talking about?"

He lay down next to her and whispered. "They want me out. That's what's going on. Don't tell the kids yet. Maybe I can nip it in the bud."

"Who said this? How can they fire you?" She gripped the binding of the blanket. "What went on here? Who told you this?"

But Shoe was fast asleep next to her on top of the blanket. His mouth was open and he snored. Myra flipped her part of the blanket across him and got up. Sitting on the radiator under the window, she smoked two cigarettes in succession and waited for her heart to quiet. Her hands shook. She went to the bathroom. "I don't understand," she said in the bathroom. She got back into bed and dropped into sleep as though into a pit. She awoke a moment later and looked around in the dark bedroom, wondering where she was. Had she just dreamed that they were home and that Shoe had said . . . ? She fell asleep again.

"Winegarden says they'll give me a month," said Shoe in the dark.

"What?" she said groggily. "What?"

He was asleep again. She put a pillow over her head and pressed her face into the mattress. The dog lay on the backs of her calves. There were bursts of light beneath her eyelids. She turned over and sat up. "Who was there?" she said. But he slept. She smoked another cigarette.

Shoe stirred and sat up. "What should we do?" he said, looking at her wildly. "I don't know what to do!"

"Go to sleep," she said, blowing smoke at him. "Get some rest." He fell back to his pillow and closed his eyes. Myra looked out the window from her bed. She could see the very first faint signs of dawn coming, streaks of lemon light filtering through the treetops at the window. It was not the blaze of morning in the Middle East. I must be home, she thought. I have to think of what to do. But maybe it was a dream. She concentrated very hard on what she thought her husband had said and fell asleep.

Shoe got up and looked through every drawer in his dresser but he couldn't find it. He forgot what he looked for. He went back to the bed and slept.

Myra moaned in her sleep. "But I told you . . . we must have this flight." She rolled back and forth against Shoe. The dog jumped off the bed to the floor. "We have to," she said very clearly. "My husband is a rabbi." The dog licked her face and woke her. He whimpered.

Myra tiptoed out of the room with the dog. As she pulled the door shut behind her, she could see Shoe stretch out to fill the whole bed, looking slain. "I might have dreamed it," she said. She went down the creaking stairs. She fumbled stuporously with the coffeepot in the kitchen. She said, "How can it be true? Maybe it's Milton's idea of a joke. Maybe Shoe was too tired to get it." She found an old jacket belonging to one of the boys and went out barefoot in the dew with the dog. The early suburban stillness was total. In only an hour the street in front would be choked with cars and pedestrians rushing to the station; and the milk trucks and the diaper service would be coming; and the gardeners and the garbage man would be at work; but for now the living world consisted of Myra Rosenstock, shivering and confused and barefoot, and her dog, and a lone, fanatical jogger who went down the dividing line in the middle of the deserted street in perfect safety. The dog barked at the jogger and Myra pulled him back into the kitchen. She smoked and drank leftover coffee as she stared out the back door. Who could she speak to? Who would know? Why tell people who might not know? Shoe slept on and she wanted him to. He must rest. She smoked again. What was a lifetime contract? Could this happen when you had a lifetime contract?

She walked restlessly through the dusty rooms of her old house, flicked on the television, turned it off. She looked at the piles of mail without touching them. The dog followed her closely. She looked in the front closet: the hockey sticks, the tennis rackets, the shabby running shoes, and a single boxing glove; she wanted her children.

Dear Rabbi,

Well, you know how bad news travels. I want you to know you will always be my idea of what a rabbi should be. I'm in law school here in Berkeley now, but even after all these years, I remember the way you talked to me in private before my Bar Mitzvah about what it is to be a Jew. I try to live by it.

Say hello to your kids for me. Maybe they still remember me, I hope. It's a long time since my parents got divorced and we moved away from New Saxony. Tell them they have a wonderful father and I hope they appreciate what they have. Good luck, Rabbi Rosenstock, whatever happens. You're too good for those people. I never was happy there. You'll be happier away from there too.

Love,
Shane Kaplan

7

Myra called her friend Suzy.
"Warmflash residence," said the maid.
"Hi, Gladys," said Myra. "This is the rabbi's wife. Suzy home?"
"I'll call Mrs. Warmflash," the maid said with dignity.
"What do you say, Suzy?" said Myra. "What's new?"
"Oh, don't ask," Suzy drawled. "I'm just disgusted."
"What is it?"
"Oh, did you ever have one of those days? In the first place, I lost my diamond cocktail ring yesterday. Gladys and I took apart the garbage looking for it and then we searched in all my coats and jackets and nothing. Nothing! I was petrified."
"Are you insured?" asked Myra.
"Oh, please, you can't insure jewelry today, are you kidding? The rates they want today? Anyway, we finally did find it, in a pile of girdles in my bureau. It must have slipped off my finger while I was dressing. And I was in such a hurry, too, because my mother was waiting to meet me in the Loop, and I know her, she doesn't let the cab go till she sees me, so I had this picture of her in my mind, with the meter running. It just drove me crazy. And Gladys got so upset, she vacuumed the living room in all directions. I thought I'd die. I came home and I saw the pile of the carpet going this way and that way. I said to her, 'Gladys, have you gone out of your mind?' She

probably wants a raise, *entre nous.* So listen, what's new with you? Recovered from your glorious wanderings?"

"Well," said Myra slowly, "you must know what's doing. Do you? We may be the last to know."

"Honey, frankly, that was for your sake," Suzy said promptly. "We didn't feel somebody, some stranger, should just waltz up to you in Hebrew school or someplace and tell you just like that. For your own dignity, we decided to keep it quiet and let the men tell Shoe in the proper manner."

"You say 'we,'" said Myra. She pushed the hair off her forehead. "I'm a little taken aback."

"Now, Myra, don't get the wrong idea. You know how I feel about Shoe and you. In fact, there wasn't one person on the Board who would say one word against you. I wouldn't have let them if they tried. But the fact is, everybody loves you both, has all the respect in the world for Shoe. But it's not working out, that's all."

"What? What's not working out? After twenty years?" said Myra, her voice rising. "The whole Board is in on this? Did everybody agree? What's different from the day we left? Explain it to me, Suzy. Tell me what happened."

"Now, Myra, you know there's absolutely no money," said Suzy in a confidential voice. "You know it as well as the next girl. There are months where we can't even pay the utilities."

"What's that got to do with it?" asked Myra. "When were we ever caught up with the bills? Suzy, what happened? I can't believe you want to pay the light bill and destroy what we spent a life in building. You'll have paid-up bills in a dead synagogue."

Shoe crashed past Myra in the kitchen in his underwear. He tried to snatch the phone from her. She turned her back to him and pressed the phone to her ear. She covered her other ear and closed her eyes. He shrugged and went to the coffeepot.

"You're wrong, Myra," said Suzy gently. "The place won't die without Shoe. I suspect it may be just that attitude that people can't tolerate. You think just a trifle too much of yourselves. We can run our own house. We're adults."

"Oh boy," said Myra. She sat back. "And you're his friend. I hate to think of his enemies."

"No, you're wrong, Myra," said Suzy warmly. "I hate to keep correcting you but you're absolutely wrong. We're all your friends. And hope to go on being friends. It's up to you. Naturally, if you get ugly, you'll have to expect people to defend themselves. We're not saints. Just ordinary human beings," she said happily. "Doing our best. We want to serve but we're giving a lot of money we can't see any end to. There's just too much unhappiness, Myra, honey. Shoe will have to understand it."

"The hell with Shoe," Myra blazed. "*I* don't understand it."

Shoe laughed into his coffee cup.

"Honey," said Suzy, "I wish I could talk to you more but I am absolutely so rushed today you wouldn't believe it. But *please*, whatever happens, don't you turn on your husband. And listen," she said lightly, "you know better than anybody, he's so brilliant, he's so gifted, he could write books or run a university or anything. That man could sell refrigerators to Eskimos! He doesn't really want to be a rabbi. I think we've all gotten that from him in recent years."

"I can't believe this," said Myra. "I called you for help. I see I don't even know you. After all these years."

"Myra," Suzy said chidingly, "if you go away from this bitter, then I'll know we must have done something wrong. Not you, Myra, not you. Don't get angry. It's not you, honey. Dear, I'm sorry, but I really have to go. I'll call you tomorrow. I have to get things ready for this masquerade we're attending tonight. It's a benefit for this new Jewish Life Center at the college, Milton Winegarden's starting it, or I wouldn't bother, but we've become friendly this year. You know, I couldn't think how to dress. Then I thought: We'll go as a little old Jewish couple! Won't that be funny? I'm wearing an old rag of Gladys' . . . Come on, Myra, let me hear you laugh. Don't ruin my day."

"Will you call me tomorrow? Please? Is that a promise?"

"I'm a little hurt that I have to promise when I already said so, but I promise. Now listen, Myra, you want some advice? Get one of the kids' baseball bats and go up to your room and hit those pillows and that mattress with all your might. Get rid of some of this rage. Have a good cry. It's therapy."

"Certain people, maybe," Myra said tonelessly. "What harm did my pillow ever do me?"

"Oh, shame on you! Really, this is not like you at all!"

"Good-by," said Myra. She hung up. To Shoe she said, "She's part of it. She'll never call me back."

Shoe pulled on his chino pants in the kitchen. He walked out to the backyard in his socks without answering her. He absently coiled the garden hose he stepped on, then dropped it again. Myra went out to him in her nightgown.

"I was trying to tell you," he said. "Harry Warmflash was there last night. He's one of them. He's a prime mover."

Myra was shocked. "It seems like a dream, doesn't it? A bad dream?"

She looked at Shoe. "I guess it's true," she said in a tentative way.

Shoe said nothing. He put his arm around her neck, let his hand dangle into her nightgown. She looked over her shoulder at the neighboring house.

"Oh, what a show we're giving. Stop." She made no move to stop him as he stroked her breasts. "You ought to go to the office. There must be plenty for you there."

"Yeah," he said with a strained smile. "I might get fired if I don't, huh?" He urged her back inside, pushing her with his chest and stomach, keeping his warm hand on her. "Come back upstairs," he said. "Just a little while."

The doorbell sounded. The dog started a furious barking and jumped against the door. Shoe bounded upstairs, out of sight.

8

Myra took a coat from the closet by the door and put it over her nightgown. "Coming," she called, grasping the dog's collar. She opened the door a crack and saw a young Buddhist, head shaven, in a toga of muslin, his bare shoulder goose-pimpled in the cool air.

"I'm sorry," she said. "You've caught me at a bad moment, young man. I don't have time." She closed the door.

There was a pounding on the wood. "Mrs. R.," cried the Buddhist. "Mrs. R.! It's me, Kevin! Don't you recognize me? It's Kevin Nussbaum!"

"Kevvy?" said Myra. She reopened the door. "Kevvy? Come in, honey, I'm sorry. Here, come in and sit with me in the dining room. Maybe you'd like a cup of tea, honey, or a Coke. There's not much in the house. We've been away."

The Buddhist stood by one of the dining-room chairs. "No, I can't eat or drink here, Mrs. R. Is that seat leather?" he asked, staring at the chair.

"No, it's plastic," said Myra. "You can sit down, honey." She looked across the table at him. "Kevin, I'm not going to ask you any questions. I'm very glad to see you again. I don't think we've sat here together since we worked on your Bar Mitzvah lessons, remember? It's still the same dog, too. Remember how he used to try to sit in your lap?" The dog licked the Buddhist's fingers. "Oh, Kevvy," she said, lips trembling, "you were so sweet. How old are you now, nineteen?"

"Twenty," said Kevin with a faraway look. He touched the tuft of hair in the middle of his shaven skull. "Is the rabbi home?"

"Yes, darling. I'll call him. Wait right here. Maybe you can accept an apple, Kevvy?" she said doubtfully.

"I remember once, you gave me a baked apple," said Kevin dreamily. "Right at this table. With cinnamon, I think." A trickle of saliva appeared at the corner of his mouth. "You meant well. Your intention was pure."

Shoe walked in, white shirt half buttoned, hand extended. "Look who's here! Welcome, Akiva, welcome to our home. You make us very happy by coming over."

"Rabbi," said Kevin, staring at the floor, "I won't shake hands. I can't. It's not disrespect. I know you're a holy man in your way." He looked at the tabletop. "I came to warn you, you and Mrs. R. There's a plot against you, people strive and contend; you're in danger. I had to tell you." Kevin threw Shoe a distressed look. "An unclean love muddies all waters. We are told that the stream of life flows on but I was home because my grandfather is very sick and my folks sent me a ticket and my guru said I should, and that's what I heard and I lost my self-control and I came to tell you."

"We'll take a walk, Akiva," Shoe said softly. "We'll let Mrs. R. get dressed and get the house together. We'll walk and discuss everything. Come." He led the weeping boy outside.

Myra watched them walk side by side, within the hedges of her backyard. They gestured, they pointed at the sky, at the house. Shoe picked up the handles of the wheelbarrow left standing by the dormant flower bed and unconsciously pushed it before him. Then he set down the handles. Kevin picked them up and pushed the wheelbarrow around the yard several times, talking, talking. Myra saw that he wore no shoes, that he stepped indifferently on stones and gravel. Kevin bowed to Shoe. Solemnly, Shoe raised his hands over the boy's shaven head and blessed him. Kevin left.

"This is not a religious problem, Myra," said Shoe, coming inside hurriedly. "I better call a doctor. I didn't feel too good letting him go, but I was afraid to set him off if I argued with him about it."

She handed him the phone book. "You're wrong," she said. "His problem is that he's not a vicious nature. He's a good, sweet boy, always was. He's naturally upset that people want to hurt you. He doesn't want to be like them." She waited for Shoe to refute her.

"I'll call Gabe Becker," said Shoe, ignoring her. "He doesn't belong to the synagogue. The kid's privacy will be protected. But I have to do something." He shouted into the phone. "Service? Tell the doctor to call Rabbi Rosenstock fast." He turned to Myra. "I couldn't get what he was talking about. Unclean love. Poor kid." The phone rang. "Gosh, thanks, Gabe," he said. "That's really fast."

"I'm going away tomorrow," said the doctor. "Just clearing off my desk. No patients today. What's the trouble?"

"You acquainted with the Nussbaum kid? Kevin? Twenty or so?"

Gabe Becker sighed. "Nutty as a fruitcake, Rabbi. I could use fancier language but you wouldn't be any more informed. Don't get involved."

Shoe laughed. "It's too late for that. You've seen the boy?"

"Not professionally, thank God, if that's what you mean, Rabbi. But who hasn't seen him the last few days? He's been agitated, on the move day and night, all over New Saxony like a ghost in a white sheet. He's been hanging out of trees, climbing on his parents' roof. I hear he tried to break into the junior high. Says he left something there ten years ago." The doctor chuckled. "Didn't we all leave something behind in our youth? Ah well, it's a pity. A pity on the parents." He sighed. "You know, someday we'll understand it. There'll be a pill as simple as an aspirin to compensate for the enzyme deficiency or whatever it turns out to be. People will wonder how we could have been so ignorant, so primitive. Ah well, I won't be around to see it."

"Personally, I plan to live forever," said Shoe.

"Interesting, Rabbi. Who knows? Maybe you're onto something else I know nothing about. But I'll tell you one thing: stay away from the Nussbaum kid. The parents will have you crucified for interfering. They have a crowd of malpractice suits going already and a suit against the School Board. It's a common enough response. They'd love to find you or the synagogue at fault, too. I pity them, as I said, but you can spend valuable emotional energy defending yourself."

"I'll have to see . . . ," said Shoe. He watched Myra kneel before the refrigerator to sponge out the bottom.

"Actually, I'm glad we're talking. I felt you might perceive it as intrusion if I were to call you. There's something I want to say that might prove useful . . ." The doctor's voice trailed away.

"Don't stop," said Shoe. "I need all the help I can get. I came home last night and got hit with an atom bomb. Everybody knew but me. Even Kevin Nussbaum."

"You don't mind then? I realize that not belonging to the synagogue and not really taking part in the Jewish community . . ." He paused.

"All Israel are responsible; one for the other," said Shoe.

"Interesting," said the doctor. "Well then, it's obvious I know you're in trouble. They want to throw you out. They cooked it up while you were away. I can't help knowing; half my patients are dreaming about it. The other half can't sleep."

"Can't they just have sexy dreams and leave me in peace?"

"There's more wisdom in what you say than you know, Rabbi. But what I specifically wanted to discuss must be totally confidential. I'm sure you understand. You know that I am employed in a visiting capacity at the New Saxony Community College?"

"Yes."

"Good," said the doctor. "Now, you know of someone else who is employed there full time? A prominent member of yours? The extremely little fellow?"

"Yes."

"Very good. Now, what I want to say is that I have known this person socially for very many years. In the first place," the doctor said with contempt, "I never knew him to be such a big man in the shul."

"There is hope for a man till his last hour," Shoe said with a little laugh.

"Interesting. Yes, I never knew of his involvement till recently when I got involved myself in the Jewish Life Center he's organizing on the campus. But it struck me as completely uncharacteristic, all this obsessional attention to organizing. Now the striking thing is that I think there is a real character change, a deterioration, taking place. There's been erratic behavior, absences from the school that are highly inappropriate, sudden tempers, grandiosity; particularly with reference to this Jewish Life Center." He sighed. "We've all been cowards on the staff. Nobody wants to take up a matter like this with a colleague. All of us at the mental health department think he should try lithium to moderate his mood swings. So who's going to tell him? In fact, it might even give him some ease with that skin problem, who knows? But you see, I'm not gossiping for the sake of gossip. I think there's a very real relationship between his disorder and your problem. I am no politician. I don't know what you should do with this information I'm giving you. But it might be a help."

"Thank you," said Shoe thoughtfully. "It might be. I'll let you know. I may call on you to explain a lot of people to me."

"They're crazy," the doctor said simply. "Nuts. Good luck, Rabbi. We'd hate to see you leave. My Rose would truly miss your Myra. I'm sorry we've not become friendlier, but where's the time these days?"

"I'm not going anywhere," said Shoe firmly. "You can relax on that score. I hope you'll have a good time on your vacation."

"Actually, I'm checking into the hospital. But never mind—me, I'm always happy."

Shoe laughed. "Would you want a visit?"

"No, good heavens, no. I'm not ready for any last rites. It's just for a bit of rest and contemplation. And a review of certain symptoms. Nothing at all. Lots of luck, Rabbi."

Dear Rabbi,
 I'm sorry for your trouble but I must tell you there are two sides to every story. You carry on all the time how we are the Chosen People and we shouldn't marry out. Well, how do you think people feel that have intermarried relatives listening to your sermons? It's very embarrassing. I think you belong someplace else. Wait till your children get married and it happens to you. Then you'll know what I'm talking about. I won't sign because I know you. You'll make remarks.

A Member

Dear Rabbi,

I took the liberty of bouncing your problem off my lawyer before you even got home. I had hoped to be able to stop this thing before it got off the ground. But he told me he doesn't want to touch it. He says you never know how much potential business you may be losing with so many people involved, it's like a ripple effect. I don't give him enough from my operation to be able to push him. But it's my impression you need a lawyer. Sorry, I wish I could help.

Sincerely,
Velvel Fox

9

It was clear they needed help. They delayed, opened more baffling letters, made more discoveries that led to new mystery. What had happened while they were gone? The rabbi decided to make cautious inquiry about his legal position. He invited Norman Dorfman for a drink at the house.

"So you see, Norman?" said Shoe. "I came home and I was fired. Actually, they told me to resign, which I won't, but I'm so confused! Where do I stand? I'm asking you as a lawyer, Norman. It's not that I want to run around and complain to people. Just the opposite. This has a terrible, demoralizing effect on the synagogue. But does a lifetime contract mean nothing?"

Norman Dorfman ran his hands through his thick hair and slouched in the worn armchair. He exhaled. "I never go to services, Rabbi," he said wearily. "I'm an ignorant man." He rubbed his eyes. "My children will all marry goyim. What are you gonna do?" He sat up. "But I'm a Jew, Rabbi, and I'd like to help you. The thing is, Rabbi, I'm in criminal law and I'm not so sure I should advise you." He sighed again and picked up his glass of cream soda.

Shoe made a gesture of impatience. He got up and walked around the small living room. "Just tell me what you think, Norman. Please! We're staggered. We don't know where to begin. Some people don't even know about it and some people are already boiling mad because

I didn't drop dead and resign on the spot. And I have work to do at the synagogue, and weddings, and a list of Bar Mitzvahs piled up that they scheduled for my return. What should I do?" He took his seat again on the sagging sofa and faced Norman.

Slowly, Norman said, "Well, as I see it, based on what you been telling me, they simply have no right to do it. You're a normal man, you do your work, so who are they kidding? Unless, Rabbi"—his voice grew grave—"there's something you're not telling me." Shoe stared at Norman. "Lookit," said Norman. "I repeat, I'm a criminal lawyer. Nothing you might say is gonna shock me. And nothing you tell me is going outside this room. Is there something I should know?" Norman looked away from Shoe, through the archways of dining room and kitchen where Myra was working at the stove. "I'm on your side, Rabbi," he said. "Whatever you tell me. That's a given. But I better know."

Shoe was mystified. "Like what? I don't know what you're asking me."

Norman looked at Shoe. "Like, I mean," he said very softly, "is it a . . . ?" He mouthed "woman" without a sound. "I'm a big boy, Rabbi. You wouldn't be the first. But I gotta know what we're up against."

Shoe snorted. "Oh, for heaven's sake," he said scornfully. He sat back. "I'm supporting a wife and six children. Where would I even get the time?" He laughed. "No, Norman, I told you they said they can't afford me. I'm creeping up on my pension and I make too much right now. And I'm not the man I used to be. They want the Joshua Rosenstock of twenty years ago. I told them," Shoe said ruefully, "that so did I. I'd be twenty years younger."

"So that's *it*?" said Norman. He shook his head in disbelief. "And I had myself all braced . . ." He scowled and scratched his head. "Oh, Rabbi, these little people . . ." He looked through the archways at Myra. "Listen, as far as I can determine, nothing at all has happened. Some people called you over and fired you? They didn't. Maybe they think so, but they didn't. They can't. You know what it's like? It's like me and your wife." He pointed through the arches. "We had a meeting, me and her. And me and your wife, we decided at our meeting that the President of the United States can't be the

President no more. See? It has no meaning. They don't have the power to tell you to go."

"What did I tell you?" called Myra from the kitchen.

"Oh, Jeez," said Norman, hunching his great shoulders. "I didn't know you could hear me."

"I'm no lawyer, Norman," called Myra, "but that's exactly what I said. Who are these men, anyway, to arrogate all this power to themselves?"

"Come in here, will you, please?" boomed Norman. "Why do women always have to be chopping something in the kitchen?"

"They don't," said Myra, coming in. "Only if you want to eat."

"Now, I didn't say you don't have a problem," warned Norman. "What you have, you got a political problem. You want to sit down?" he asked her testily. She sat next to Shoe on the old sofa. "You don't need a lawyer, if you ask me. But you do have to organize support, get people to fight on your account. Now I know nothing, zero, about the people in this congregation. I pay my dues and leave me alone. But if you have all the friends you say you have, Rabbi," he said seriously, "now's the time to call them out. They don't know what's going on any more than I did. You gotta tell them, like you told me. And you gotta holler. Say, 'Help!' You don't want to be shy and modest. The situation has gone past that point. You gotta remind them they owe you. Things you've done for them, like that. . . . That'll settle these little guys down." He sat back and patted the arms of his chair. "Jeez," he said in a wondering voice. "That little putz, Winegarden. What got into him? You have any idea?"

"None." Shoe shook his head. "He's my friend. We've been friends for years."

"That putz," said Norman, thinking. "What is he, a sawbones? Proctologist?"

"Ph.D.," said Shoe. "Jewish studies at the college. He likes you to call him doctor, though. Harmless enough."

"Putz," said Norman again. "Well, get out your real friends and put 'em to work. If you got rich friends, so much the better. Don't yell at me, Mrs. Rosenstock," he said, holding up his large hand and grinning. "I know you don't like that. But I didn't make the world. That's your hubby's department." He laughed to himself.

"Oh, Norman," said Myra unhappily, "I hope you don't regret getting into this." She twisted her hands together in her lap. "There are some really big lawyers in this, like Harry Warmflash. They may give you trouble, professionally."

"Yeah?" said Norman. "Never heard of 'em."

"Well, there are," she said. "We'll understand if you want to think it over. There are really big people in this congregation."

"Yeah?" He smiled hugely. "Like how big? Six feet tall? Seven? Eight? Don't worry about me, Mrs. Rosenstock." He stood and began a bearlike walk to the door. "Take my advice and start lining up your friends. I'll make a few calls myself. My wife will know who our friends are. I don't."

"Thanks, Norman," said Shoe, following him. "I value your advice."

"My pleasure, Rabbi," said Norman. He picked up his hat from the bench by the door. "I'll tell you something else you should do. Sniff around. Find out whatever you can about the little putz, Winegarden. You never know what can come in useful."

"It's not a question of personalities, Norman," said Myra stiffly. "I'm not looking for gossip and scandal."

"Do what I say, Rabbi," said Norman, ignoring her. "Talk a little to the guy who took your place. See what he knows. He's been on the spot the whole year. Maybe he knows what's eating the little putz. You never know what you'll uncover. Jeez, that little putz, Winegarden. Something so disgusting about him. . . . I don't just mean the leprosy . . ." He popped his small hat on his large head. "I don't really know him . . ."

"No, you don't," said Myra severely.

"I should have advised you to have an uglier wife, Rabbi," he said, staring at Myra and grinning. "And your kids are doing too good in school. But would you have listened?"

They laughed. Shoe patted Myra's behind. "No, I guess I'm stuck with her." Myra pushed his hand away. "Thank you for coming, Norman."

"Listen," he said with a dismissing wave, "I better start racking up a few good deeds for myself. It's time to worry about getting admitted to the great country club in the sky, assuming there is such a place." He laughed and pointed upward.

"I guess," said Shoe with a sigh. He opened the door for Norman.

"Don't get me wrong," he said. He pushed aside the yew crowding the doorway. A boyish expression passed over his seamed face. "I want to stay in this vale of tears as long as I can."

"Me too," said Shoe.

The Rosenstocks went into their kitchen. Myra peeled an egg.

"Shoe," she said, "take out the garbage, will you?"

"Yes," he said thoughtfully. "Myra," he said, "I'm going to my study. I'll make a draft of a letter to the congregation. You'll tell me what you think of it. Then I'll get you some envelopes and you can address one to each member. I think Norman is right. We have to go public. And I'll speak to Rabbi Yossel and see what he knows."

"Could you take out the garbage first?" said Myra. "The children will be coming on the weekend. I'm *trying* to get ready."

"Right away, yes," he said. He went to his study, a glassed-in sun porch. She heard the typewriter. She took out the garbage. She came in and went to the phone.

"Norman?" she said. "Me, Myra Rosenstock again. I'm having more thoughts. I'm not happy about letter writing and running to people. What about a suit, Norman? Is there something we could sue about that would be so threatening they would give up this idea?"

"Who're you gonna sue, Mrs. Rosenstock?" he said. "Where's the money?" She heard the sound of a televised ball game behind his voice. "None of these guys is personally liable for any damage that I can see. So how much has the synagogue got? Where's the money?"

"I don't know," she said stupidly. She pulled down the door of the dishwasher and rubbed at a rust mark inside.

"See, you don't just go suing. I can win you a five-million-dollar settlement on anything. Anything. Just give me the case. But where's the money? I can get you ten million dollars. But who'll pay it? It has to be there. So who's in charge of the money at the synagogue?"

"I guess the money's in the bank," she said. She bent over the dishwasher door. "I suppose so. I suppose nobody would want to keep it in a mattress. But I don't know. Shoe might know, but I doubt it."

Norman laughed. "Their money's in the bank?" he mimicked her. "Oy vay, Mrs. Rosenstock. Look, let your husband write a letter to

THE RABBI'S LIFE CONTRACT   49

his friends. Don't let him get too poetic. He should holler, 'Gevalt!' And if that won't help," he said, quiet suddenly, "then I'm afraid he's going to have to find another place to do his work in, much as I would regret it."

"You mean they *can* do it?" Myra overruled her sudden fear. "But what about the facts, Norman?" she argued. "He didn't do anything, Norman, he wasn't even here, and all the while they're plotting and planning, and then they just drop it on him the night he gets home from a sabbatical? Norman!" she said frantically. "You have no idea! It was like falling out of an airplane, like getting shot with a cannon! You can't imagine! Norman!"

"Yes, yes," he said quietly.

She controlled herself. "Norman, can't we just tell what happened? It's a matter of right and wrong. Why should friendship be a factor?"

She heard him sigh.

"I think," she said slowly, "I'm going to tell the children not to come home just yet. I can't face it. Shoe won't be able to take it. Maybe after the Geltman Bar Mitzvah. . . . Maybe that'll patch things up . . . maybe people have forgotten what a fine rabbi they have . . ."

"Mrs. Rosenstock," he said soberly. The crowd behind his voice on television was cheering. "People get raped, people get robbed. . . . Greater injustices are committed every day. I'm sorry. You really want to help your husband? Knock it off with the outrage and get busy. Write letters. Make phone calls. Have people over, give 'em cocktails. You're sitting on your trouble like a hen on an egg. Get up and fight! Defend yourselves! There are bad people in this world. Get busy and quit sympathizing with your husband. I'm really sorry, but where's the money? Either he'll hang on here with the help of his friends or he'll be on his way."

Dear Rabbi,

My husband and I feel strongly that you should do nothing in your own defense. It's just too undignified for a rabbi, and besides, you haven't done anything you need to defend yourself about. My husband and I are going to speak to Milton Winegarden and to the president and the rest of the officers and lay down the law to them. Milton seems to be heading a runaway committee and we are going to stop it.

Please rest assured, Rabbi, that you have nothing to be concerned about other than going on with your duties in the wonderful way we have all come to expect from you. Maybe we needed this to shake us up and stop taking you for granted. But the one thing I couldn't stand would be if you and Myra would lose even one wink of sleep over this. We will take care of it. I repeat, do not worry.

Your friend,
Faigy Greenwald

Dear Shoe,

You ask what I know about what's going on and the plain answer is: not a thing. I hope you'll believe me when I tell you that I did my best to keep my nose clean and simply take your place, not that I ever could, while you were on sabbatical. Sometimes I got the feeling there was whispering that suddenly stopped when I approached but I never gave it a thought. I didn't want to know, to tell you the truth. They weren't paying me that much that I should get involved. It seems like a normal congregation, the usual misfits and nudniks along with the everyday people. For Jews, they were all right. Let me know what transpires and if I can be of any help.

Yossel

Dearest Rabbi,
　Your visit with Charlie was the best medicine he's had. I hate to ask it of you, but if you would come again, we should be most grateful. Come whenever you like. By the way, my son Billy found the reading you suggested for him most consoling. How will I ever thank you for your many kindnesses?

　　　　　　　　　　　　　　　　　　　　Love,
　　　　　　　　　　　　　　　　　　　　Lena Bloom

10

Milton Winegarden needed to plan; he needed help. The best generals knew how to delegate authority, he told himself. Top people needed expert advice on small aspects of their plans. The President of the United States had a cabinet, didn't he? Of course, if the rabbi had simply resigned, as he had suggested to him, this would not be necessary, this spreading around of unease, this rising excitement in the congregation, this lack of respect. Rabbi Rosenstock would have a lot to answer for someday.

Meanwhile, Harry Warmflash sat here in Milton's third-floor study, bored and impatient, alternately staring at Milton and around the room with a certain hostility and catching up on some paperwork of his own. "Can we get down to business?" said Harry in an even voice. He looked at his watch. "I have things to do."

"I'm busy myself," said Milton, setting down a spray can with which he had been polishing the leaves of an old and very large philodendron. "I promised Sunny a day in the field, bird watching. But let's give Irv Seltzer a few more minutes to get here, okay?" He looked seriously at Harry. "It's my fault, I accept the responsibility, that I forgot all about him. I want his support, see. It shouldn't be too hard. I want him to see it's important to you too, Harry." He smiled, showing his irregular teeth. "You can be a role model for him. He was a poor boy and he needs some guidance." He smiled again, slyly. The men looked up as Irving came in.

Milton sprang to Irving's side. "Thank you, good of you to come. Need your counsel, you know." He gestured to the leather sling chair. "Take a seat, Irv. Good to have you aboard."

Irving Seltzer, wiry, gray, with a tendency to a middle-aged belly, almost disappeared into the chair. "What's going on?" he asked aggressively. "Do you guys think it's right I should hear for the first time from the rebbitsin? Is this a way to do business? Any kind of a business? That the poor rebbitsin has to call me up and cry and I don't even know what she's talking about?" Irving's body was tense but the sling chair almost doubled him over.

Milton sat next to him and touched Irving's knee with a blotched, crusty hand. "Irv, I want to say, once again, as I told you on the phone, how much we regret our oversight. Harry and me." He glanced for a second at Harry, who did not respond. "You're perfectly right. We should have sought you out first thing. But we're only human and we overlooked it. I know you'll find it in yourself to forgive. Am I right, Irv?" He cocked back his balding head and looked at him.

Irving pushed his glasses up on his nose, mollified. "Doc, don't talk about forgiving. Who's mad? I know you have the welfare of the shul at heart. So do I. It was just like such a shock, Myra Rosenstock calls me up out of the blue that he's fired, and will I help them, will I call other people for them. . . . I didn't even know they were home yet! Anyway," he said, moving his knee from Milton's heavy hand, "I'm in on it now. So!" He tried to sit erect in the sling chair. He pressed his golf shoes against the floor. A beautiful spring day waited downstairs and outside of Milton's overwhelming study. "You two feel we could bring in somebody else for less? Is that correct? And you'd be satisfied with the quality? Did I get what you said on the phone right?"

Milton nodded. Harry said, "Yes," and looked at his watch again.

Irving gazed at the etching of Maimonides on the wall. An Einstein signature was framed in real gold. There were portraits of famous Hebrew writers. "Well, you're the doctor," he said with a laugh. "I sure wouldn't want to judge." He stood up with difficulty and looked around the room. His eyes fell on the bathtub and sink and toilet, all shining, all gold trimmed. "Never saw anything like it," he said. The other men rose. "Listen, I'll go along," Irving said reluctantly. "The way the shul's books look . . . What else *can* I do? I didn't go to college but I can read numbers," he said, grinning. "I can see the bottom line."

"Exactly," said Harry without expression.

"Ech," said Irving, moving slowly to the padded study door. "It's really no job for a Jewish boy, is it? Poor Rabbi Rosenstock. Nice man, good family man. I assume you'll pay him off some way that's decent?"

"Irving," said Milton reproachfully. He looked at Harry.

Harry said, "What did you think, Irv?"

Irving flushed. "No offense. Just wanted to satisfy myself. Six kids is no joke."

"It's no joke to us either," said Harry, flaring up. "We can't go on carrying them. The rabbi understands. He said he'll cooperate fully. But, for God's sake, we're not throwing the man in the street. What did you think?" He looked at the gilt wall clock. "Leave it to me. I'm an attorney and I will be responsible, gentlemen, to work out what is fair."

"I'm glad he's not going to fight it," said Irving, shifting his feet. Milton averted his eyes from the scratches he was creating on the polished floor and kept silent. "I'm relieved to hear you say that," Irving said. "I guess he didn't explain it right to his wife."

"I must leave," said Harry officiously, looking again at the clock.

"Okay by me," said Irving. "Well, you have my support, Doc. I hope we can put things in order fast?" He sneaked a last look around Milton's eccentric study. "You hold meetings here often?" He suppressed a smile.

"I wish it were possible," Milton said stiffly. "But academic life . . . and now with my new Jewish Life Center over there . . . But what can you do? We Jews are brought up to have a sense of social responsibility, even to our own cost . . ."

Sunny's voice elbowed its way in. "I'm getting in the car," she screamed from the kitchen. "I've got your binoculars. I will wait just one more minute!"

The men smiled in mutual understanding and walked to the staircase. Milton turned around and locked his room behind him.

Dear Rabbi,
Just a note to wish you luck in your fight. Please, Rabbi, if there is anything self-destructive in you, you can be helped. Let me know and I will refer you. We have only one life, so far as I know, and we don't have the right to throw it away. And things look different the next day. Call me, I am really your friend. Leave your message on my machine.

Fondly,
Aviva Shapiro, M.S.W.

11

In the early evening darkness a redheaded man with a briefcase stood on the Rosenstocks' doorstep. Myra looked out warily, thinking, A salesman; no, a missionary.

"Mrs. Rosenstock?" he said. "My name is Robert Etkind. I don't know if you remember me, we're members of the congregation . . ."

"Of course," she said. "Come in." She held the door open. "We're a little untidy this evening. . . ." She looked around helplessly. "I can't seem to pull myself together. . . ."

Bobby stepped into the front hall. "Don't apologize, Mrs. Rosenstock." He gave her a sympathetic glance. "I should have called." She took his topcoat, stared around herself, and dropped it on the cluttered bench against the wall. "But I haven't been home yet. I'm still on my way from the office. See, I saw my friend Norman on the train home. Norman Dorfman? The criminal lawyer? He told me a little about the situation. I want to talk to you and the rabbi."

"Come inside and sit down," she said tiredly. "I'll call my husband. He's a little worn out, though. I hope it won't take too long. It must be jet lag or something. . . ." She collected herself. "But of course he's at your service. I'll go get him."

"Wait a minute," said Bobby. He held Myra's sleeve. "I came to help. I'm a lawyer. Don't look so bad. Norman and I don't see eye to eye on how to go about it, but we're both on your side."

Myra smiled bleakly, a faded smile. "I didn't know. Thank you for coming. I'm sorry the house is such a mess."

"Mrs. Rosenstock," he said.

"Myra," she said.

"I'm Bobby," he said.

"And my husband is Shoe."

"Oh, I couldn't call him by name," said Bobby. "But I would like to talk to him. I need to hear it from him, what's going on; and then Norman and I want to work together, and a number of other people, attorneys, want to get in on it too." He let go her sleeve and took her hand. "You're not alone, Mrs.—Myra. You're not alone."

Myra's eyes filled. "I'll call Shoe. Go in and sit down."

Shoe came down the steps into the dark front hall. "Talked to Norman, you say?" he said. He extended his hand to Bobby. "Welcome. Myra, have we anything to offer Mr. Etkind?"

"It's Bobby. And I don't need anything. Please sit with us, Myra. I want to speak with you both."

Myra emptied an armchair of newspapers for Bobby. He sat down and looked at the Rosenstocks, who seated themselves side by side on the old sofa facing him, sagging toward each other, gray-faced. "Tell me what happened, Rabbi," he said gently. Through the archway into the dining room, he saw the table stacked with mail and crumpled balls of paper. Suitcases stood in the corners. The dog lay beneath the table in a mass of dust, chewing a ragged towel. "Norman didn't quite . . . describe . . . your obvious distress," said Bobby slowly.

"When Norman came . . . ," said Shoe. He hesitated. "We didn't really know yet. Didn't understand yet what we were in for." His voice trailed away.

"What does that mean?" asked Bobby.

"The synagogue treasurer paid the household bills for us while we were gone," said Shoe. "Out of my salary. So he stopped. Three days after we got home, the phone company cut us off," he said quietly.

Bobby reached for his pen and a tiny pad.

"My kids could have been needing me," Myra said, growing tearful. She blew her nose. "The lights went out; same story. Till I could make them understand it was my phone and my money. . . . The treasurer told them to turn us off. It's like you're not a human being." She scoured her eyes with a tissue.

"Go upstairs and compose yourself, Myra," Shoe said in a low voice, looking at the floor.

She looked at Bobby. "I'm fine. I'm just a little upset. And we had to borrow money to pay his life insurance." Her lips trembled. "They didn't pay it and they're holding the money we left to pay it with. A father of six children!"

"I begin to appreciate how you feel," said Bobby carefully. He had paled and his freckles stood out. He made another tiny note on his pad. "Well." He leaned back. "Go back to the start, Rabbi."

"There's not that much to tell," said Shoe aggressively. "I'd been away on sabbatical, a gift after twenty years. They gave me a farewell party, personal gifts. I came home and I went to his house and he told me I was fired." He chewed on an empty pipe and stared at the lawyer as though he expected a challenge.

"Yes," said Bobby. "Could you tell me a little more about it? Who, for example? Whose house was this?" The lawyer considered how to proceed. The rabbi and his wife were not young. Their color was bad. I hope he's in good health, thought Bobby.

The rabbi bit his pipe. Myra said, "Tell him. Describe how happy we were to be home again," she said bitterly.

"You tell me, Myra," said Bobby. He thought, I guess I have two clients.

"Well, our youngest daughter, Etta, God bless her, well, she came home to meet us for a surprise; and she brought the dog home and he was so happy . . ."

In the next room the dog thumped his tail on the floor. Bobby grinned.

"And Shoe right away had to look and see if we had water in the basement," said Myra. "Of course we did, and he starts right in with the broom. I yelled at him because he was too tired but it never helps." She smiled at her husband. "And I started to look through this ton of mail waiting here and I just couldn't understand it. People were sending him their prayers and people were angry and some people sent him little checks. . . . Why? I said. And then I was just floored to see that insurance notice. We were about to lose it all."

Shoe sighed and interrupted. "And then he calls me to come right over. It's urgent. They didn't wait five minutes." He sighed again. "They must have been watching the house."

"Who?" asked the lawyer.

"The hatchet committee," said Myra.

"I told him I was more dead than alive from the trip," Shoe went on. "But he really insisted." He laughed. "I thought I had to."

"Tell me about it," said Bobby. "Tell me what they're like." He glanced covertly at his wristwatch. "I'm trying to get a picture of what happened."

Slowly, thinking aloud, Shoe said, "Well, I thought I knew him pretty well. I was glad he wanted to serve. He's good with people despite his appearance, the skin thing, and he's almost a dwarf, but still; and he has a good Jewish background . . ."

"Oh, stop," said Myra. She lit a cigarette and smoked impatiently.

"You want to say something, Myra?" said Bobby.

"This is very hard on her," said Shoe abruptly. "She doesn't eat, just smokes. Doesn't sleep."

"I'm fine," she said, inhaling smoke. "You want to know what happened, Bobby? I think about it all the time." She looked quickly at Shoe. "I can't bear it. That he had to face it alone." She rubbed at her eyes. "He was mugged, Bobby," she said, low. "I'm always thinking about it. It's like an attack in the dark. You know, everybody thinks about it sometimes; how you'll be alone late at night and you'll be assaulted; well, so he was mugged. And he called for help; and the lights came on; and he looked around; and it was his friends. His friends who hurt him!" She looked incredulous. "I keep thinking about it." She scrubbed her eyes with her shredding tissue handkerchief. The men looked uncomfortable.

"Myra," said Shoe.

"Bobby," she said. She did not look at her husband. "Every rabbi has his battles. Don't think I don't know that."

"I wish I knew more about it," said Bobby.

"Well, I know," she said. "I know that a family will join because they like the architecture of the building and another one goes away mad; the windows offend them. The rabbi should have put in better windows."

"Is she joking?" Bobby asked. Shoe smiled wearily.

"Or a couple is ashamed because their daughter went and became a Bahai, so they quit and blame it on the rabbi; he didn't pronounce their name properly. Don't I know all that?"

"My goodness," said Bobby. "I had no idea."

"Well, ordinarily, I wouldn't be telling you. Because it's not what's really important." She lit another cigarette. "I just want you to understand that I'm used to crap and pettiness and people not admitting what really bothers them. And even so, this—this is so beyond that kind of problem that I . . ." She wept.

"Enough, Myra," said Shoe miserably. "Go upstairs. I'll tell him whatever he needs."

"So Shoe comes home from this urgent meeting," she continued. "Very late. And I was damn mad at him for sitting around telling jokes when he knew I'd be worrying about him, he was so tired, but he always does that . . ."

Shoe cleared his throat. "Myra, I have to."

"And then he came in and told me. He's fired. Be out in four weeks. After twenty years! Do you realize that? Do you understand?" she demanded. Bobby nodded. "My heart started pounding and my first thought was, He's going to have a heart attack." She shot a look at Shoe. "Not really."

"No," said Shoe.

"Yes," said Bobby slowly. "But tell me what happened. Rabbi, what was said?"

"Basically," said Shoe, standing up, "they told me my presence was killing them. The synagogue wouldn't survive with me as rabbi. Nice, isn't it?" He paced the room. "I said, 'This is crazy, this is impossible. Tell me what's wrong,' I said. 'We'll work out a solution.' But no, their decision was made. They said the whole congregation wanted me to go. I said I didn't believe it. I don't, by the way." Shoe took out a pipe from his pocket. He looked at it, confused. "Was I smoking this?" Wordlessly, Myra took it from his hand and gave him the lit pipe from the ashtray. She lit a cigarette.

"So then," said Shoe, sucking the pipe and continuing to pace, "Winegarden—you know him? Calls himself doctor? The little guy I was talking about before?" Bobby nodded. "So then Winegarden says, 'Denial is not the good way to handle this, Rabbi.'" He flung himself down beside his wife again.

"So I said—I was so bewildered, I may not be getting that across to you, how astounded I was—I said, 'But I have a life contract.' Not, Bobby, that I ever expected to need a contract to hide behind. I was just pointing out to them the step they were taking, its implications. And so another one said, 'You'll have a life contract and no congregation and what good will that do you?' But why should there be no congregation, Bobby?" Shoe said. "'*You* leave,' I told him. And I meant it, Bobby," said Shoe, simple as a child. "Why don't they leave if they don't like it? Why such a brutal act instead? I can't comprehend it!"

"Go on," said Bobby. "Then what?"

"So he puts his arm across my shoulders and says, 'For your own good and the good of your family, I advise you to resign. Don't make a fuss and we'll do our best for you.' They'll raise me a purse and give me a little something till I get on my feet. But why should I take charity, Bobby?"

Myra got up abruptly and walked to the kitchen.

"'I don't want any goddamn purse of yours,'" cried Shoe, oblivious. "I said, 'I'm employed and I'm doing a good job and I have a life contract. I founded this place, I have more in it than anyone. If you're not happy, you leave. Not me.' So then Harry Warmflash, the lawyer, he says, 'We'll see about that life contract.'" He stood up.

"I know it's hard, Rabbi," said Bobby softly. "Is there any more?"

Myra returned, carrying a bottle of kosher wine and three paper cups. Bobby and Shoe waved away her offer, keeping their eyes fixed on each other. "Well, I said," said Shoe, trying to regain control of his voice, "'I'm not resigning and you can't fire me. I have a lifetime contract. It takes a full congregational meeting to make this decision and they never will.'" He picked up an empty cup and set it down.

Bobby held his pen above his pad. "Is that a fact?"

"That's the law," Shoe said gloomily. He sat down near Myra. She sipped wine from her full cup. "He told me to get a good lawyer. And to keep in mind I'd need a lot of money for that. Get it?"

"I don't understand people," said Myra. She drank.

"And at that time I didn't know," continued Shoe, "that they were holding my money. All these unpaid bills. No salary . . ."

"Shameful," declared Myra to the wall next to her.

"Go ahead," said Bobby grimly. His face was tired and pale.

"That's it," said Shoe. "They talked and laughed. It was a social evening for them once they broke the ice and told me. And that little Winegarden had the gall to stroll over to me and tell me, 'Be wise like our sages. Resign and go devote yourself to study. Other people aren't going to be so gentle with you.'"

"You should have walked right out," Myra said to the ceiling. "Oh, when I think of you all alone against them . . ."

"I'm not resigning," said Shoe. "Why should I?"

"Yes, why should he?" said his wife.

"You shouldn't," said Bobby. "If you resign, you're giving up your claims under the contract. Of course, Warmflash is a lawyer; he knows that."

"Don't worry," said Shoe. "I'm not and they're not firing me, either."

"We have to be prepared for everything," Bobby said soberly. "We'll get to work."

Dear Rabbi,

There's two different things in this world. There's law and there's justice and I say this as a lawyer. Get rid of these parasites that have attached themselves to you and come in and talk to the president of the shul like a man. More will be accomplished than with all the legal committees in the world. A legal aid committee for the rabbi? It would be funny if it wasn't so sad. You think they're looking out for you? Wait till you get the bills. I know lawyers. I know the profession. Let me say you are naive, telling me they are serving you without fee. There ain't no such animal as a free lawyer. Cheap is cheap. They'll sell you out first thing when they understand there's no money coming from you. But first they'll talk you to the sky and encourage you to look for huge settlements. Where's the money going to come from? You're not fighting IBM or General Motors. You're talking about a smallish congregation with leading members of the community in it as volunteers. You think a judge wouldn't give that consideration?

I'm writing as a friend, one who respects you and wishes you nothing but the best. But we all have to face reality. We all live under the hammer. Rabbis are not excepted. You might wish it to be otherwise and so would I but this is the real world. In the real world, you must go to the president and tell him you're sorry for anything anybody's got against you, and ask him to take into account that you have a big family to support. I'll go with you. I'm your friend. I had to go on my knees to my father-in-law many years ago and I'm the better for it. We all have to humble ourselves sometime and rely on God.

I'll do what I can for you. I'm willing to donate my fair share. But you must get rid of your lawyers. I can't tell you that too often. A militant stance will get you nowhere. And your lawyers in particular are street fighters. They belong in the gutter. They have no place in this business, which is a religious matter. It doesn't look nice. I'm an older man like the president. I could talk to him for you. You know I have nothing to gain by interfering. I want only your good name and the good name of the Jewish people.

Rabbi, don't take us through the mud in public. The Jewish community isn't all that safe yet. And you don't have to go through this, yourself. Let me help you.

Very sincerely,
Isidore Le Bowitz

12

The Rosenstock living room was papered in tan with small circlets of faded roses repeating themselves across the walls. The paper had been there when they bought the house, when Joey, who was now finishing medical school, came in and licked his forefinger and tried to taste the roses off the wall. At that time they had only Joey and Nathan, and thoughts of law school and medical school bills were far away. Instead, they thought of redecorating, new paper on the walls, matching bedroom sets for the two boys, a washing machine.

Now they had six children. Etta, the baby, was in college. And the faded paper, miraculously, still hung on the uneven walls. They sat in the faded living room on the sagging sofa and looked at Bobby, hair flaming, serious-faced, disturbed.

"We'll get to work," Bobby said soberly. "I'm going to represent you and Norman Dorfman's going to; and we'll work out the route we'll be going." He paused. Delicately, he said, "But you must tell me, Rabbi, what are the reasons? You haven't told me why they want you to go."

"I don't know!" shouted Shoe. In exasperation, he jumped to his feet again. "Really, I do not understand. Pederasts, thieves, drunks, adulterers, they keep their jobs; and me, me, they want to throw out." He walked in a circle around Bobby's chair. "I said so to them. I said, 'Even if I wanted to resign, say to spare myself and Myra, I couldn't. It looks as though something awful happened. Twenty years and out? How could I ever get another pulpit? The next congregation would naturally want to know what I could have done to be treated like this.'"

"Did they have anything to say to that?" said Bobby. He craned his neck to look at Shoe behind him.

"Yes," said Shoe. A strained expression came to his face. "More nonsense. Nothing important. I got fed up, finally, and came home. My knees were buckling. I was really very tired from the trip."

"He's still tired," said Myra.

"Well," said Bobby softly. He leaned back in the old armchair in thought. "Well, we have our work cut out for us. You think we'll be going to a congregational meeting, Rabbi? It sounds like we may be too late to avoid it."

"My friends delayed me," said Shoe. "They told me to wait, they'll talk it over with Winegarden and fix me up. And I'm still sitting. I've been a fool."

"Now," said Bobby, preparing to make another tiny note. He blushed. "I must ask you. Was Norman correct? You don't get actual raises? You have a cost-of-living provision in your contract?" His face burned.

"It's not a secret," said the rabbi. "Cost of living is fine with me. But money is not the issue here," he said. "I don't care about that. There's principle involved. Covenant. We made a pledge to one another, the congregation and me. I haven't looked for a job in twenty years. I devoted myself to this synagogue and these people and I'm willing to go on doing it. This can be resolved," he said sternly.

"Yes," said Bobby, carefully moving his briefcase over a threadbare place on the rug. "Maybe it can be resolved. But, Rabbi, don't say anything about not caring about money. Money may be all we can salvage. And you'll need it. In fact," he said with decision, "the less you say from now on, the better. I'm your lawyer. Let me do the talking."

"You don't know him very well," said Myra.

"And I must stop a moment and use your phone," said Bobby. "I wouldn't but it's a four-million-dollar deal and they won't know where to find me."

"Phone's in the kitchen," said Myra. "Don't mind the mess."

The Rosenstocks heard Bobby's voice in the kitchen as they sat together in silence. "Four million dollars, Shoe," she said after a time. "Shoe, what are we getting into? Who is he?"

Shoe studied the roses on the wall. "I don't care if it costs us every penny we have."

"It may not be enough," she said.

"Myra, please," he said irritably. "One thing at a time."

Bobby returned cheerfully. "The deal's progressing," he reported. "It's only money, only a game. Who can actually relate to that kind of sum?"

"Yes," said Shoe. "The rabbis knew that. There's an interesting discussion in the Talmud . . ."

"Excuse me, Rabbi," said Bobby gently. "But before I forget, I'd like a copy of your contract, to start with. And a copy of the constitution of the synagogue."

"Where are they, Myra?" said Shoe.

"You think I know?" she said without stirring.

"You don't have a copy of your contract?" asked the lawyer. "You must."

"Listen," said Shoe offhandedly, "I don't sit around evenings, reading it. I got it twenty years ago. Myra, go look where you keep the seder plate. I might have put it there."

"I think it may be in the linen closet," she said. "With all your diplomas."

"Well," said Bobby. He picked up his briefcase.

"But, Bobby," she said from her seat. Her voice rose. "Why? Why must we show anything? You know he has a lifetime contract. Everybody knows. You understood that when you joined, didn't you? He's the reason people join. They want to hear him speak. He's a wonderful speaker and he has something to say."

"I know," said Bobby. "I know."

"So I don't see why we have to lift a finger," she said rebelliously. "We don't have to do anything. We didn't do anything wrong. They did."

"Myra—" began the lawyer.

"We'll find the contract," interrupted Shoe.

"But I don't have the feel of it," said Bobby, standing and thinking. He wrinkled his brow. "I should go home to my family. But I'm not sure who's who yet, except for the little guy, Winegarden. You didn't make it clear. . . . Let me ask you something else. Do you think there may be a bride in the wings?"

They stared at him.

"I mean, is there somebody else lined up? Could that be what it's all about? How about the fellow that took your place, for instance?"

"You mean Yossel?" asked Shoe. He was incredulous. "Oh no, Bobby. There isn't anybody. I even asked him. Norman told me to talk to him. Did you ever meet Yossel?"

"No," said Bobby uncomfortably. "We never happened to attend services while you were away. . . . I don't know where the time goes. . . ." He blushed.

"I just mean . . . Yossel? No, Bobby. He's a very nice human being. I arranged for him myself. He needs the money badly and he does a very capable job. But charisma? Oh no, Bobby." He touched Bobby's arm. "Yossel's been a candidate for a Ph.D. about fourteen years, get the idea? He's hung up on the dissertation, something about pain and grief, God knows. And there are family problems . . . he's sort of a stunted person, emotionally. Oh, but blameless, I'm positive. What makes you ask?"

"Norman," replied Bobby. "But you probably know. Norman told me on the train that he's been doing some snooping around. He seems pretty sure there's some kind of . . . relationship . . . between this Rabbi Yossel and little Winegarden."

"Oh, Norman," said Myra scornfully. "I *told* him not to do that. I guess it comes from dealing with criminals. You always look for shmutz." She took a long swallow of her wine.

Bobby looked away. "Well, we'll see what else he can come up with. And now I must go home. My eyes are closing." He blinked. "Listen," he said, "here's what I want you to do for me. Do it right after I leave. Just give me a list of the enemies and a little characterization of each one. It might be easier for you to do it in writing. I don't know these people, see. I can't get a picture of the big battlefield. Will you do it for me? It's like a game, like assembling a puzzle. I need to see the picture better."

"We'll try," said Shoe.

"I want input from each of you," said Bobby, stifling a yawn. "It doesn't matter if you disagree. It will still help me."

"We never disagree," said Myra.

Shoe was concentrating. He looked up abruptly. "Bobby, I think I have an insight that might be helpful. It struck me yesterday when I was reading about Jacob and Esau. One of our enemies is a twin!"

"And?" said Bobby, leaning forward.

"Well, I thought it might be significant," Shoe said weakly. "In terms of a kind of mind set. Because she certainly can have nothing against me. I've been trying to understand what's gotten this woman into this plot."

Bobby sighed and looked at his watch. The phone sounded in the kitchen. "If it's for me, tell them I've gone home, please, Rabbi," said Bobby. Shoe went to the kitchen. "I must go," Bobby told Myra.

"Thank you for coming," she said, walking him to the door. "It's a strange way to get acquainted, isn't it?" She smiled tiredly. "I haven't been much of a hostess, I'm afraid. I don't feel capable of much of anything. He's such a really good person and look what happens. . . ." She looked into Bobby's light eyes. "Don't get the wrong idea about him because of me. He's a much better person than I am. I don't want to bring him any harm. Any more harm," she said, eyes reddening.

"What harm are you doing him?" he said angrily. "Jesus, are you brainwashed by these people? Just do what I asked." He rapidly strode through the door and down the front walk.

Dear Rabbi,

Just what is going on with our Jewish People? It's not enough they bomb us and kill us all over the world, but we have to fight among ourselves? I am getting calls from everybody, people I didn't even know, for my support. We are in a mess, Rabbi. I hold you responsible. The place reflects the Rabbi. That's what I say to these people. After all, years ago, when my son was getting ready for his Bar Mitzvah, I ran from pillar to post looking to see who was going to teach him, what was going to be. Could I get an answer?

And also, why do you and the cantor not wear the beautiful white robes which I donated a goodly sum to see? Who do you think you're kidding? What happened to the money? And also, I personally told the cantor if I wanted to hear opera, I'd go to the opera. But nothing helps. And also, our new prayer book is a Chinese menu as far as I'm concerned. I can't make heads or tails out of it. And that kitchen and that ladies' room, they are so dirty that I paid a fortune to hold my parties elsewhere when I should be able to use my own synagogue for my simchas. Not to mention the landscaping we were promised years ago we have yet to see.

Get things straightened out and then we'll talk about my support. I want a synagogue that I can hold my head up.

Blossom Kelbanowsky

13

She returned to the living room to find Shoe lying on the sagging couch, one foot dangling to the floor. "I guess we have a lawyer," she said. Shoe threw his arm across his eyes. "You look like a pile of old clothes," she said. "Take your feet off the couch."

"I only have one foot on the couch," he said, motionless. "God, I'm exhausted. Decent of Etkind," he said sleepily. "But it takes a lot out of me."

"Do we have to have a lawyer?" she asked quietly.

He sat up. "I think it will help. It gives the impression of strength. Winegarden'll probably fold right off."

She reached for a blank envelope and sat near him. "Let's start, then. Our lawyer wants a list."

"Start with Milton's buddies," he said, yawning. "Remember that psychiatrist who wrote a rhymed funeral for his father? Write that down, that he's a mixed-up guy, religiously. In a lot of conflict. The father was a rabbi."

Myra wrote: The heavy breather.

"And Milton himself," said Shoe. "I'll leave that to you."

She wrote: Milton.

"Hey, about the friend, My," Shoe laughed. "You'll love this. I once asked Gabe Becker, 'What does this mean, eclectic psychi-

THE RABBI'S LIFE CONTRACT

atrist?' And Gabe said, 'Would you go to an eclectic surgeon?' " He laughed again.

Myra said, "You want to list any women?"

"There's Mimi Seltzer," he said. He rubbed his eyes. "No, leave her out of it. I don't feel too good picking on women. She's just a woman who overeats. It's an occupational hazard for a caterer."

Myra wrote: The fatso castrater.

"Put down the bandleader, Myra," said Shoe seriously. "And that fellow who teaches third grade. It's significant. Bobby should know about that. It's rough to be a failure here, living alongside the brokers and the doctors. Maybe he'll see a way to use it."

Myra wrote: The Bobbsey Twins Are Jewish.

"My wife," he said abruptly. He stood up, dropping his jacket on the old rug. "Write what you want and call Bobby with it. I'm beat. Maybe tonight I'll be able to sleep."

"You know what your jacket's going to look like?"

"Like I stepped on it," he said hotly. He walked across it to the staircase and snapped his fingers for the dog to follow him.

Myra considered her paper. Her mind flooded with names. Enemies? Bobby wanted to know about the enemies? He should have asked for a list of friends. Then she could finish in a moment and go to bed, she thought bitterly. What a privilege it was, what delight was hers, to know family secrets, stories of quarrels breaking out over open graves, children rejected, the aged alone. New Saxony, Jew and Gentile, struggled to be peaceful, uneventful. Problems existed elsewhere, never here. Only an ineradicable Kevin Nussbaum lurked behind a tree, always threatening to come out in the open and expose them. Could Myra compile a list for Bobby? The question was: Could she ever finish it? She wrote rapidly.

> The beauty
> The orphan
> The Algerian
> The bore with heart trouble
> The faggot
> The gun collector
> The Peeping Tom on probation thanks to Shoe
> The rat face
> The one with his hands on my daughters

She phoned. "I hope I didn't wake you," she said.

"What is it, Myra?" Bobby yawned.

"I just wanted to tell you we can't seem to come up with anything. I mean, I'm so angry now, but they've all been my friends. I couldn't be friends with monsters, could I? No, they're all plain, ordinary people. This isn't going to lead anywhere."

14

The guests all said even the heavens smiled on the Geltman Bar Mitzvah. The synagogue was full. Sabbath morning sunlight streamed across the faces of the congregation. The fresh-cut baskets of flowers glowed. Tiny particles of dust floated upward in the clear light between Shoe, on the pulpit, eyes shadowed, big shoulders drooping, and the people seated before him.

Mimi Seltzer, the caterer, stood at the kitchen door to the rear of the building, keeping one eye on the cook and the other on the hallway, guarding Suzy Warmflash, who was in the office searching through the confidential financial files.

The rabbi touched the microphone lightly and inhaled to ready himself for the conclusion of his talk. Suzy Warmflash came in and stood in the aisle at the rear. She bent to speak to her husband, showing him something in her handbag. Shoe blinked to rid his mind of this distraction. He turned to the seated boy at his left.

"Know, Larry," he said to the boy, "that every time a young person comes up here to pronounce the blessings over the Torah, and to read from the Torah, he's done something for us all. The Jewish people takes on new life and strength. Because, Larry, our own lives are limited. Our own lives are short. But our people has a great life, a long life, one that is extended by every celebration like yours, and by every birth and marriage. We say that the Torah is a tree of life to those who hold fast to it; that its ways are ways of pleasantness and all its paths are peace." He looked at the boy. "Have you thought about it, Larry? About what it means?" He sighed. "We hope, dear Larry, that you will have a long and happy life. That's no more than any parent wishes for his child. I know that as a father. But as a man, an adult, I know it may not be so. You may know unhappiness. Frustration and failure may come to you. We hope not. But they may come. The loss of loved ones comes to each of us. No man may live to the end who has never known that sorrow. And we are told, 'Yea, though I walk through the valley of the shadow, I will fear no evil, for Thou art with me.' What does that mean, Larry?"

The boy was winking and wiggling his fingers at his friends in the first row. He stopped abruptly at this sound of his name to look at the rabbi. He swallowed his cough drop.

"Look at it," said the rabbi intensely. "Read it for yourself. 'Thou art with me.' That doesn't mean you won't have to walk through the valley of the shadow, Larry. It's no guarantee you won't know suffering. But not alone! 'Thou art with me.' That means your friends may betray you," growled the rabbi. He kept his eyes on the boy. "Friends may let you down. Maybe they were never your friends. Promises will be broken. Oaths may not be kept. You may find yourself like Job, afflicted and visited by false comforters. God doesn't promise you won't have to go through that. But 'Thou art with me.' That is our shield and that is our hope." He looked out into the filled pews.

"We Jewish people know that life isn't easy. We know that our material possessions won't protect us; although we bless God for food and wine and raiment, we don't scorn the good things of the world. But, Larry Geltman," he said, raising his voice, "they are not the world. The world is a mother and father who love you, teachers who teach you, a goal in life that is worthy of a Jewish boy and of a God who cares about us and what kind of life we build. It makes a difference, Larry, it matters. Because 'Thou art with me.'"

"And if this is so for one boy, one Larry Geltman," he said softly to the congregation, "then how much more so for the Jewish people. How much more vital for us, as a people, to remember that it matters what we do, how we live." He paused. "We all know 'It's hard to be a Jew.' Our mothers told us that in the cradle. It's hard to be a

Jew, it is. It's *hard* to be a Jew, it's *hard* to try to follow God's commandments, to resist the everyday pressures from other people, to fight the urge to go along, the desire to do what we know we should not do. It's lonely to be a Jew," he declared. "We are so tiny and the nations are great. We are weak and the nations are mighty. We complain, we cry out: 'It's *hard!* We are the chosen people.' For what? How many of us have cried, in agony, 'Chosen for what?' The gas chamber? The crematory? But we held fast," he said, voice trembling. "We clung to the tree of life, our Torah, God's word for us, and in truth we found its ways were ways of pleasantness—its ways, not the world's ways; its truths, its ethical imperatives, which call on us to do justice, to love mercy, and to walk humbly with our God—even when we feel all alone, when there seems to be no hope." He paused. "'Thou art with me,'" he said once again. "There's a demand implied in that statement. 'Be worthy of Me. I am with thee.'"

Shoe took a deep breath and wiped his eyes. "So mazel tov, Larry, this is the beginning for you." He picked up his prayer book. "And now," he announced, "we will rise for the returning of the Torah to the Ark as the cantor chants 'Etz Chayim Hee, It Is a Tree of Life.' Please rise."

At the close of the service, as the congregation filed out to the social hall, Faigy Greenwald made her way over to Myra. The women embraced. "Wherever he's going," Faigy said, "I'm going. What a man! That sermon! Whatever happens, you're lucky to have him." Myra nervously pushed the hair off her forehead. "But nothing's going to happen," said Faigy. "This is temporary. You'll see, Myra. Someday we'll look back at this time and we'll laugh." She looked more closely at Myra. "How are you taking all this yourself? I forgot to say welcome home."

"We're okay, we're okay," Myra said tensely.

Harry Warmflash stood at the base of the steps leading to the platform. "You're a real pro, Rabbi," he called up to Shoe.

Shoe moved about on the carpeted dais, putting books inside the lectern. "Good Shabbes, Harry," he said, preoccupied.

"You really know how to put on a show," said Harry. "We may even miss you." He smiled to himself.

Shoe came down the steps holding his robe over one arm. He

shook Harry's hand. Within the door of the social hall, Mimi Seltzer and Suzy Warmflash manned a hospitality table set aside for the worshipers not specifically invited by the Geltmans.

The people coming in were met by a blast of heat and music. Most passed by the paper cups of wine and the sugar biscuits offered by the women and made their way directly to the big buffet. "I've Gotta Be Me" issued in a hollow voice from the bandleader. "This is for your dancing pleasure," he announced. The waiters began to circulate, moving fast, trays high. "Hey! Mr. Basketball Star!" snapped an old lady. She yanked the waiter's arm down. She gazed at the tray of brightly colored hors d'oeuvres and said, "Feh! Take it away!" She swept a garnish of red grapes off the silver plate into her beaded purse. "You see something interesting?" she jeered.

Suzy Warmflash spoke seriously to a woman in the crush. She handed her a paper cup. "I have a list," she said in an undertone. "You'll call A to G. Just get everybody to realize we're not kidding. It's time for a change," she declared.

"I agree," said the woman, handing the cup straight back. "He's getting to be an old man. 'It's hard to be a Jew!' Who wants to hear that old stuff? And at a Bar Mitzvah?"

"That's what I'm saying," said Suzy.

Larry Geltman, dark cheeks imprinted with lipstick, his peach satin shirtfront already smeared with pizza, thrust a pile of envelopes at his mother. "Hold them, Ma," he whined. "There's so many."

His mother and aunts, sallow women in peach and pink dresses like so many withered bridesmaids, surrounded him, pinching the backs of his hands, his neck. "The image of Poppa," sighed Renee Geltman. The aunts threw back their heads to study the boy.

"Larry," boomed the bandleader. He waved the microphone. "Mr. Wonderful, where are you?" The children hissed and cheered. Bottles of orange soda were splashing on the floor at the children's bar and the girls were screaming. "Get Mother, Larry," said the bandleader. "We all want to see the Bar Mitzvah dance with his best gal."

Lena Bloom came into the social hall, distracted, accompanied by Sharon Gitlin, a shy young neighbor who shrank from the noise and the crowd. Sharon reminded herself it was a good deed, a mitzvah she was doing, to stay with Lena, a woman whose husband was about to die.

"I'm all turned around, it seems," Lena said to Mimi Seltzer. "Which way is it to the ladies' room?"

Suzy Warmflash leaned across the table and touched Lena's thin arm. "I've been meaning to call you, Lena. I hope Dr. Charlie will be better soon."

Sharon tried to signal Suzy with her eyelids that this was not to be. "Glad we ran into you, Mrs. Warmflash," she said. "Can you explain about the rabbi? My phone doesn't stop. But I don't understand what the trouble is."

"They should move, the Rosenstocks," Mimi replied, looking over her shoulder. She leaned forward with an overweight exhalation to nip an ant on the table between her heavy fingers. "There's too much commotion going on. It's better for the community not to have to see them all the time."

"I can't agree with that," Lena said sharply. "This is where they belong. The man has a lifetime contract."

"Does he?" asked the timid neighbor.

Suzy fingered the gold chains at her throat. "He doesn't want to be a rabbi anymore."

"He visits Charlie," said Lena. "And that is not my impression."

The bandleader tied on a baby bonnet to sing a song of the Bar Mitzvah boy's life, from the start. Sharon winced.

"But does he have a life contract?" she asked Lena.

"Be realistic," said Mimi Seltzer, wiping her hands on her skirt. "How can there be such a thing? Life is too long."

"He does or he doesn't have a life contract?" Lena's companion asked her.

"He does," said Lena calmly. "This is an attempt to break it."

"Wow," breathed the young woman. "I'm impressed. Think of the, like, *stress* and all, preaching and everything, while people are trying to get rid of him." She rolled her light eyes. "So what's wrong with him, then?"

"There are many problems," said Suzy, staring up and down at the young woman, assessing her. "Some are better not discussed in public."

"Really, Suzy," said Lena, straightening her back. The children were arranging themselves on the dance floor for a group dance. "Innuendo. And such haste. Such discourtesy. A rabbi! Firing a rabbi who's away, not having a single good talk with him."

Mimi thumped down a gallon wine bottle. "Haste?" she exclaimed. "Don't you know we've only been talking about it since the day he left?" Suzy stepped on her foot. Mimi ceased. "Why don't you ladies come to the lunch?" she suggested. "The food is good. I should know."

"Thank you," said Lena. "But I will be leaving. My husband is very weak. . . ." Her face grew slack. "I came to pray and receive the comfort of the service. My husband insisted I go out and I wanted to hear the rabbi. . . ." She wiped her eyes.

"So you won't dance," said Mimi. "You still have to eat, don't you? Try it."

"I wasn't invited," said Sharon. "I don't know the Geltmans."

"They'll never know the difference," said Mimi.

"You're very kind," said Lena icily. "I think I'll wait and use my own bathroom." She took her neighbor's arm and turned to leave. "Good Sabbath to you."

"Mrs. Yiffniff," sulked Mimi. Her chins wobbled as she stuck her nose in the air at Lena's back. "What should we do, Suzy, fall down and grovel because Charlie Bloom was the first Jewish doctor out here? What are we, nothings?" Mimi's swollen face seemed to grow even larger.

"Oh, don't excite yourself," said Suzy with a wave of the hand. She served another paper cup of wine. "I have a list," she said quietly to the man who took it from her. "You can handle H to K."

Norman Dorfman stopped Shoe. "I only got a minute," he said, taking Shoe's arm. "Can we talk in private in your office?" Their exit was slow; Shoe shook hands in all directions.

"Don't go, Rabbi," said Larry's father in excitement. "Rabbi, Rabbi, have a drink, at least!"

Norman Dorfman said, "He'll be right with you," and steered Shoe out of the social hall.

"Cold fish," muttered Larry's father.

Myra stood alone at the edge of the dance floor, stiffly smiling at the children dancing in a circle around her.

"You know who I feel a little sorry for?" said Mimi in a wistful voice. "Her." She pointed with her chin to Myra. "See how bad she looks, Suzy?"

"I see she's here," said Suzy, compressing her lips. "Which a little more frequent attendance in the past we might have taken into account today. But done is done." She fetched her purse from under the table and took out a gold compact. She pulled down an eyelid, looking in the small mirror. "I'll tell you what else I saw." She snapped the compact shut. "She smells like a saloon! What an honor for us! Nine A.M. in the morning and she's got whiskey on her breath. It almost knocked me down when I kissed her."

They began to clear the special table. "I hear Rosenstock's putting up some fuss," Mimi said anxiously. "That wasn't supposed to happen. He might get vindictive. I have a business here to think of."

"Stop worrying," said Suzy over the noise of the band. "He's broke, we're holding back his salary; that's number one." She looked up from the paper cups. "And number two, I've got the name of every delinquent member now. A whole lot of them are old-timers like the Blooms, they pay whenever they happen to remember. But if Rosenstock demands a congregational meeting, we'll give him one, I promise! Nobody's getting in who isn't paid up." She swept the cups into a plastic trash bag.

"I guess," said Mimi moodily. She went to the kitchen door. "Get a move on in there!" she called. "The Geltmans paid good money for this."

The bandleader held up his hand. "Your attention for just one moment," he implored. The roar diminished. Larry Geltman rode past the bandstand on his brother's back, whipping him like a pony. "Our own beloved cantor," cried the bandleader, "our cantor has graciously consented to do a little number for us today, in honor of our Larry. Will you give him a hand, please?" he begged.

"Remind this little character where he eats," said Harry Warmflash between his teeth. He gripped Milton Winegarden's powerful shoulder. "He does a lot of business here. Tell him we expect his cooperation."

"You mean the bandleader's a member?" asked Milton, sweating.

"You better believe it," said Harry soberly.

The cantor strode out of the kitchen, wiping his lips and unwrapping a white silk muffler from his throat. "Thank you, thank you," he said, smiling and bowing as he made his way to the bandstand. He stopped in front of Myra and fingered her collar. He stared at her throat. The cantor was an actor who dominated amateur theatrical life throughout the county. And now, as he stood touching her collar, a transformation began. His elastic, well-fed, well-cared-for body changed; he became a stooped, elderly Jew. "Nu?" he rumbled. "We're all in the hands of God." He looked sorrowfully at her throat.

"He's going to sing for us!" cried Renee Geltman in a strained and happy voice. "Slip him a hundred, Victor," she said out of the corner of her mouth to her husband.

The cantor strode to the bandstand. "I never refuse a beautiful woman," he said, bowing to Renee. He tucked the bill into his sleeve, pulled out a handkerchief, spat into it, put it away with the bill. "I don't usually do this," he said in a clear voice. "But the Geltmans have been more than kind." He ran his polished hands through his hair. "Now what would you like?" He winked at a nearby woman.

"Oh, is this hysterical," said the woman in deep appreciation. She turned to Myra, holding a champagne glass in each hand. "Care for one?"

"Thanks," said Myra, "I never can get at the bar."

"Say, did you see how the rabbi rushed out of here before with that big guy, Norman Dorfman?" said the woman. "What do they do together?" She looked suggestively at Myra and sipped from her glass.

Myra laughed. "*I hear the rabbi's a married man.*"

"Oh, please," said the woman. Her stole was sliding off her shoulders. She bent her face to the floor and hooked the stole into place with her teeth, hands occupied with food and drink. "My ex-husband," she said through the lace in her mouth, "he could swing both ways. These men . . ." She spit out the lace, looking grim.

Myra was afraid to let the conversation go further. "I'm just kidding around," she said. "I'm Myra Rosenstock, the rabbi's wife. Don't be embarrassed," she said, touching the lace. "I'm so glad to laugh a little."

"I'm not embarrassed," said the woman. "I'd introduce myself but my foot's in my mouth." She turned away and fled.

Myra saw the woman pointing at her and talking to Renee Geltman.

"How about *Ayshes Chayil?*" asked the cantor, grinning. "Our favorite old-time number about the woman of valor? Shall we dedicate it to our rebbitsin? For old time's sake?"

Someone threw a broken flower across the small dance floor to the cantor. He knelt for it, grinning, and picked it up in his teeth to wild applause. "To Myra, then," he said, gesturing with the broken stem.

A man standing alongside her turned and said, "You're the rabbi's wife? Say, do you know our rabbi in Duluth? I forget his name."

"I'm sure we do," she said. "How do you do? And you are . . . ?"

The cantor sang and gestured. The audience swayed and hummed. The man from Duluth was giving Myra the names of each of his children and the Jewish name of the relative each had been named for. She interrupted him.

"Could you get me a glass of water?" She felt very sick.

"Certainly," he said, startled. He left her at once for the bar.

Myra sat down rapidly in a tiny golden chair rented especially for the party. She held the champagne glass against her forehead. "We're going to need that chair in just a sec," warned a waiter. She watched Larry and a group of his friends trying to make a human pyramid. They crashed.

"Here," said the man, returning with a glass full of ice cubes. He took the champagne glass from her. "This stuff could make anybody sick," he said under his breath. "At my son's Bar Mitzvah we had nothing but the finest of everything. This . . . isn't." He bent to look at her face. "A little green," he pronounced. "But you'll be okay. I'll distract you," he said in a friendly way. "You like jokes?"

"Sir," Myra said abruptly, "I'm sorry. I have to go outside."

"Let me help you," the man offered. But she was too quick for him; she was out the door, so fierce-looking in her concentration, her determination, not to be sick in public, that he fell back, intimidated.

"Unusual woman," he remarked to Renee Geltman. "She's got like an electric fence around her. Does she always act so afraid of people? Who the hell wants to hurt her?"

"It's a long story," said Mrs. Geltman. "Listen, are you having a good time? Did you get yourself some champagne?"

"The best, Renee," said the man sincerely. "I take my hat off to you. And that sermon! Your rabbi's the best, too."

Milton Winegarden broke in. He had been standing, unnoticed, at Renee's elbow. "I wonder if I could have just one little instant of your time," he said. "Oh, but my manners! First, my dear Mrs. Geltman . . ."

"Renee," she said, pleased.

"Renee, then," he said. "But I insist you call me Milton—I'm Dr. Milton Winegarden," he said to the man. "Renee, congratulations to you on what must be the happiest day of your life, not including your wedding day, of course."

The man walked off.

"Renee," said Milton, smiling up at her, "can I speak to you for a tiny moment? About priorities and, for that matter, *proprieties*, we'd like to see observed here? Especially on a day like this, the most important day in your boy's life." He smiled warmly. "I'd like your input . . ."

The band was playing a hora. The outer circle of dancers were the grandmas and great-grandmas and old aunts, tipsy on tomato juice, moving in their stockinged feet. Inside their ring, a smaller circle went the other way; little girls still young enough to accept hair ribbons and large taffeta dresses. The college-age cousins stood or sat about morosely, chewing celery sticks, avoiding one another. One young man had brought his calculus textbook with him. His grandmother shouted from the dance floor, "Come here and give me a kiss! Come dance with me! How long will I live?" He opened his book and stared at the page.

Irving Seltzer went to the kitchen, where he trailed behind Mimi like an orphan. "I wish to God we could get out of this," he said quietly. He sipped a soft drink and dodged her heavy step as she crisscrossed the room, inspecting pots and platters.

"What's the matter?" She stopped her pacing.

"It's like an ego trip for him, Winegarden," Irving said. He held her soft, heavy arm for a moment. "You should see him out there, working the crowd like he's running for office! At a Bar Mitzvah!"

"What's wrong?" she said.

"Mimi," he sighed, "he talked me into it, Winegarden, on the basis it's for the good of the congregation. We can't afford the rabbi anymore. This I understand. I'm a businessman." Two waiters came in to refill their trays. Irving waited till they left. "I know anyway management is better off without a contract, right?" Mimi nodded curiously. She looked at her watch. "But did we want to hurt the rabbi?" said Irving. "Do him harm? No!" he said loudly. "We just wanted to get rid of him. We got the right." He rubbed his eyes with his knuckles, scratched his nose, shifted his shoulders uncomfortably as though his jacket were too heavy. "But it might not work out, Mimi," he said warningly. "The rabbi's got friends we didn't figure on, they're out there, and the way we're doing it, you'll see who'll be left out front with egg on his face if Rosenstock stays. It won't be little Miltie. It'll be us. He's going around quoting us. He'll say *anything*, depends who he's talking to. He's a real bastard. He's got some kind of a *feeling* against the rabbi he don't admit to. It's sick! And Warmflash ain't a lot better. I want to get out of this and I don't know how." Irving fell silent again as the kitchen became busy.

"Come with me," said Mimi, a ferocious look on her large face. She led him out to the adjacent cloakroom. They stood between two empty racks, the wire hangers jangling. "I wish," said Mimi, quivering, putting her face to his, "I was married to a man. Don't you know how to fight? Don't you want to win? What are you, a Girl Scout? Oh, God," she breathed angrily, short of breath, "I always have to do everything."

Larry and his friends snaked through the cloakroom, a noisy human chain, holding each other at the waist. "A forward and a backward and a bump, bump, bump," they shouted, falling on each other. The empty coat hangers vibrated and rang.

Myra stood outside near a blooming forsythia. She breathed the gentle air deliberately. In the unsparing sunlight she became aware of how she looked among all these gorgeously arrayed people; how seedy, linty, unpressed, stuck about with dog hairs. Her daughter's cast-off corduroy suit looked all right in the house this morning, but here . . . She had no place here. The forsythia moved in the light breeze. Looking at it made her seasick. She decided to wait in the car. She was ashamed to go back inside.

The cantor was headed for the kitchen again. Mimi usually had a parcel for him. The band was back on the bandstand after its break.

Renee Geltman ran to the cantor urgently. "I can't find the

rabbi," she whispered. She put her hand to her peach satin décolleté. "People will think the Geltmans don't count," she whispered. "I have out-of-town guests; *non-Jews*," she said with a significant look. The cantor shrugged. "One day in my life I want him," said Renee furiously, eyes scanning the social hall. "One day. . . . Where is that rabbi?"

The cantor calmly entered the kitchen. "Mimi!" he sang. Mimi stood in a cloud of oily steam at the stove, her hair dank. He took her damp fleshy hand and kissed the palm. "What does a woman like you do in a kitchen?" he demanded melodiously. "*Ah, che gelida manina!*" he sang, spreading wide his arms. "A woman such as you . . ."

Norman Dorfman and Shoe left the office. "You're right, Rabbi," said Norman. "More I think of it, your way is smart. Sure, you keep on with the Marquis of Queensberry and I'll deal with these shmucks my own way." He leaned against the push bar of the hall door. "How are *you* supposed to know what every little shit is doing? You got some very unethical friends." He rushed outside, grinning.

The dancers in the social hall were laughing and cheering as Larry Geltman was borne past on a chair raised high above the heads of the strongest waiters. "Mazel tov, mazel tov," they cried out. The women blew kisses at him. Shoe searched the crowded room for Myra. He was hungry but all the food was gone from the ravaged buffet. Only garnishes of parsley and the nibbled remains of radish roses were left scattered on the wine-stained white cloth.

"And now," the bandleader crooned, " 'The end is near . . .' " He unconsciously touched his hairpiece, his fly. " 'The end is near . . .' " he sang. He twirled an imaginary partner at the microphone. His knees gave him pain. Milton Winegarden had spoken to him. He had no choice.

Shoe touched a waiter's elbow, unaware of the music, the dancers, the raucous children, his mind on Norman Dorfman's proposals. "Anything to eat?" he asked.

"Only a whole lunch coming," said the waiter with hatred, already exhausted. "Only meat and fish and cake and booze," he said wrathfully. "Will that do ya, mister?"

The bandleader laid the microphone on the floor and bent over it tenderly. Then he lifted it up and kissed it. " 'The end is near . . . ,' " he sang. " 'The end is near . . . the record shows . . . I took the blows . . . ,' " he sang. " 'I took the blows,' " he quavered. He depended on this work. He had an old mother. He was the only one. Milton Winegarden gave him no choice. Rich people pushed you, kicked you, right to the wall. He had no choice. " 'The record shows . . . I took the blows . . . and did it . . . my way.' " He tipped back his head with a worried thought for his hairpiece and stretched his mouth to its widest. The spotlights blazed on the gold in his molars. " 'I did it . . . my way!' "

Dearest Rabbi,

Young Billy told me of your visit. He was in charge of his father overnight till I got this silly back spasm under control in the hospital. He seems changed by the experience, more of a man. Rabbi, I'll come right out with it and confess that Billy told me how you cared for Charlie, the needles, the bedpan and all, when Billy was all at sea over it. Charlie never mentioned it, of course. He simply told me that you are a saintly man. We all know that. Billy is talking about becoming a rabbi, God help us. You'll have another task before you, talking to him. Charlie is very weak. I think it is only a matter of days now. We are looking forward to seeing you. Your visits are the most important thing in our lives.

Love,
Lena

Dear Rabbi,

Till now I was so busy with the invitations and the food that I had no time to listen to Milton Winegarden. But now I see for myself what's wrong with our synagogue. How did you dare to put your arm around my Larry when he was reading from the Torah? You wanted to make sure everybody knew he couldn't do it alone? You always have to be the star? In my opinion, the boy should be the star, not the rabbi. And why couldn't you have written him a nice speech to give instead of giving one yourself? I've seen it done in other places. But I guess those rabbis know what's really important. I am completely disgusted. It was supposed to be Larry's day. Instead, people gave me compliments on your sermon.

I understand what's really behind it. Even your wife, who acts like she's so nice with the kids, she plays with them and lets them play with the dog, when they go to her for help with the Bar Mitzvahs, it's just an act. She couldn't be bothered even to eat a little bite with us. If we were rich, she would have. She fooled Larry but she doesn't fool me. I'm proud to tell you that Milton has put me on his committee and we look forward to the day when the children can get what they're entitled to on the most important day of their lives. I'm going to be on the Rabbinical Selection Committee, too.

Very disappointed,
Renee Geltman

15

"But we're depending on people like you, Diana," pleaded Myra. It was the fifteenth call of the morning. "Don't say you're not important in the synagogue. You think only the troublemakers are important?" She dug a toothpick into the small greasy crevices of her kitchen stove while she spoke. "You want to side with people like that? Because that's what it is. If you stand aside and act neutral, you're helping them."

Diana spoke.

"In the first place," said Myra impatiently, "you're not so old. But what difference does that make in any case? I'll tell you who's too old! Shoe's too old. What's he supposed to do, fired like a thief at his age? Have you looked at it that way?" She listened. She rubbed the flat of the stove with a sponge and sighed. "All right, Diana," she said wearily. "The best of everything to you too. There's no need to apologize. I mean it. You don't owe the rabbi a thing. I just thought you'd want to help." She lifted a burner ring and put it in the sink.

"Diana, I'm with you," said Myra. "I don't know why he wants to fight it, either. I hate it. I wish we could do like you say and move and do something else. I'd like a clean business for a change, like a liquor store. Or I could peddle dope. You know what they want; you provide it; they're happy. They'll pay you for it. But Shoe and I are not twins," she said, voice trembling. "We're only married. We don't agree. He feels that people shouldn't do wrong. He says the victim should at least make it tough to get away with it. So what can I tell you? I have to help him." She took a breath and pulled the dog to her. She hung up and burst into tears.

At noon she phoned her husband at the synagogue. "Come home," she said. "Lunch is ready. And don't talk on the phone over there." As he walked in a few minutes later, she said, "I'm not going to make any more calls. Don't ask me to do it anymore."

"What happened?" he said. He was looking at the mail.

"I'm no good at it, that's all," she said. "I'm not getting anywhere. I'm no salesman." She was afraid to tell him all of it.

"Oh, go ahead," he said carelessly. "Lots of people don't even understand what's going on. A lot of people will be glad to help once you've explained. Once you ask them. You're not selling anything. This is information you're providing." He looked at the table. "I wish, Myra," he said, "you could dream up something else for lunch. I've got cottage cheese coming out of my ears." He sat down and helped himself.

"I don't have time," she said resentfully. "These people are all on the phone to me, crying how much they love you; and they're going to let you get the ax. Don't you understand? They don't want to fight with their friends. You're disturbing the peace. They think if you really cared for them you'd go away." She looked at her plate, pushed it away. "I'm out of control," she said quietly. "Don't let me make phone calls. You won't believe what I said this morning. I told someone I wanted to sell dope."

"Got any better bread?" he asked.

"I can't be trusted to talk to people!" she cried. "Let me off the hook! I'm doing you harm! Can't you guess how fast the news is traveling? The rabbi's wife says she wants to sell cocaine."

"Who knows?" he said with his mouth full. "Maybe we'll get some good connections."

"Don't you hear what I'm telling you?" she said sadly.

"I hear you," he said. "But what should I do? We'll keep trying."

She took to her bed. That afternoon she watched him leave. She turned her back on the dust and the laundry, let the dog outside on his own, and carried up cigarettes and a bottle of beer to keep her company. Fully dressed, she lay splayed out on the double bed. The phone rang. Myra didn't move. A bed jacket was on her mind. Baby blue, she daydreamed. Lace buttons, those little handmade buttons. The phone rang again. Myra didn't move. A satin pillow, maybe pale pink. She felt very tired, a heaviness in the belly. . . . She heard the kitchen door slam.

Shoe came in. He stood at the foot of the bed and pulled her feet. "Feeling okay?" he asked. "What's wrong, My?"

She swallowed a mouthful of beer. "My period, I guess," she said. "At my age," she said in disgust. She lit a cigarette. "Shoe," she asked, "would you like a baby?"

"My," he said cautiously. "And pay for college from Social Security?"

She put her hands on her belly. "I didn't really mean it, I guess." Tears slid down her cheeks. Shoe fell heavily alongside her on the bed. The phone rang. "Please unplug it," she said. He sprang up and ran downstairs to answer.

"No," she heard him say, "that is not the case. No, if you'll just let me explore that a little further with you . . ." Myra looked at the worn coverlet, at the marred night table to her side. She tried not to hear Shoe's voice. A little satin pillow, she daydreamed. She began to drowse. Shoe fell down beside her again, jarring the bed. "You want anything?" he whispered. "That was just—"

"Don't tell me," she said. "Just for a couple hours. Could you make me some tea? I'm deadly thirsty."

The phone rang again.

"I'll get it in the kitchen," he said, rushing out.

She heard his voice. "That's a damn lie! He better be ready to prove it!" She closed her eyes again.

Shoe entered the room like a tightrope walker, his eyes fixed on the cup he was carrying in a soup plate. "Here we go," he said with false cheer. He set the cup down, already half empty, the soup plate awash in tea. He lay next to her again. "What is it, My?" he asked softly. "Tell me."

"I'm thinking about my mother," she said. Tears rolled gently into her hair. "Peculiar, isn't it? I was thinking about us at home in Flame Lake. In that freezing bungalow we lived in. It could never be a real house. Oh, honey," she wept, "it was so cold! I was so lonely! Even when everybody was home, it was just me and my mother."

He put his arm across her. He had heard this many times before. He hid his face in her upper arm.

"I never thought about it before, Shoe, I swear," she said. "But today I thought, I wronged her. I *wronged* her, Shoe. Such a selfish kid. I was mad at her because I was so lonely." She wiped her nose on the pillow. "Till today, I swear, till today, I never thought—she was lonely too! Oh," she said miserably, "I *wronged* her. I wronged her and she's gone and there's not a thing in the world I can do to make it right." She cried. "Used to light the Friday night candles and just stare over at me, the only two Jews in Flame Lake, Wisconsin. And all I could think about was how we didn't have a house, just a freezing summer cabin, and we didn't have a father and she always had to work and she made me work . . . and I blamed her." She put her arm over her eyes. "I'm so ashamed of myself. I couldn't wait to get away and get married. I wanted to have a hundred children and be warm and happy. . . . I don't know what's wrong with me. I just keep dwelling on sad things I can't do anything in the world about."

"My," he said gently. He put his warm face to hers. "Let go. Let go of it. It's over. I'm here." He put his arm and leg across her and let his bulk weigh on her. "Let's just rest a little." The phone rang. With his free hand he jerked the telephone cord from its plug. "We'll rest," he said, closing his eyes.

Dear Rabbi,

As a member of a caring community, the psychiatric community, I address you as a member of another such, the synagogue. We share a common concern: that good come from what we do and not evil, as far as we can bring that about. I don't know, incidentally, if I ever shared with you the fact that my father was a rabbi. He was not like you. He was Orthodox, with all the strength that implies, not much of a speaker. Your rhetoric he never had. But he was a saint.

What I want to get at is that this can be a learning experience if you open yourself to it. Losing a pulpit is nothing compared to the benefits your experience is offering you. We need a man who will walk humbly and who loves mercy, not a judge. Perhaps you will learn to still the intellectual arrogance that clouds your emotional understanding of us. We don't come to services to be told how we're wrong.

Will you take advice from a friend? Don't be vindictive. Go away from us and don't fight us. Go to some little place, learn from little people. You'll be a better human being for it.

I wish you all success in your new undertakings. All good wishes to your lovely wife and family.

> Best from our house to yours,
> Shelly
> Dr. Sheldon Vitz

16

There was a noodle casserole with spinach and mushrooms in it. "It's better with fresh parsley," Essie Ringel said. She was there on her own behalf and to represent her husband, who was at a funeral. "But I couldn't get any." There was a platter of sliced bagels with cream cheese oozing out on the picnic table and a tray of oily smoked fish alongside it. They had brought thermoses of coffee and containers of cream. It was the LIARS group, the Lakeshore and Inland Association of Rabbis, brunching in the Rosenstocks' backyard. Not everyone could make it, explained Ben Martin. The men had such hectic schedules.

"You don't have to tell me," said Shoe. "Nice of you to take the time."

"It's like a condolence call," said Myra. She viewed the wrapped plates of cookies and the marble cake, Essie Ringel's specialty, through a haze of cigarette smoke.

"I'm not taking anything home," warned Essie, chewing. "Let the kids eat up whatever's left. Let them live and be well," she added.

"They'll love it," said Myra. "They keep coming home, and I don't know why, but I can't seem to keep house anymore." She looked at the overgrown backyard strewn with broken lawn furniture. She sighed at the weed-filled flowerpots.

"You have a lot on your mind," said Essie. She patted Myra's shoulder.

"Maideleh," said Pinny Fleischman, staring at her across the table, "*corpses* I've seen that look better."

"Just speak your mind, Pinny," said Essie. "Don't hold back." Myra laughed. Plump Essie smelled of fresh ironing. Myra leaned against her on the bench.

"Exile," muttered Pinny. He slumped forward on his elbows, risking his silk suit on the dry, splintering tabletop. "Oh, exile; hard and bitter." Beads of cream cheese stuck to his full mustache. "What do they want from us?" He ate another bagel. "You give to them with all your heart. They say, 'I want a piece of your lung; give us your liver.' Oy, oy, oy."

A youthful rabbi in shorts brandished a Frisbee. "Let's play," he said. He got off the sagging picnic bench and grinned at his colleagues. "Get off your butts, you guys. You're depressing them more." He plucked his University of Chicago T-shirt away from his damp chest. "Who wants to play?" No one stirred. Myra lit a cigarette and dropped the match in the dry grass. "You wanna sing?" asked the young man. "How about a round? How about it?" he persisted. He looked eagerly around the redwood table.

"Till I see you," said Pinny Fleischman sourly, "I feel young. Oy," he moaned. "Exile. Sodom and Gomorrah. Where's the coffee I brought?"

"What's the latest, Shoe?" asked Ben Martin. He was the current president of the LIARS group.

"Nonperformance," said Shoe. "They claim I haven't done a thing in years." He smiled with difficulty.

"Nonperformance, nonperformance," exclaimed Essie irritably. "It sounds like an actor who didn't show up."

"Sounds like a potency problem to me," said Pinny. "Present company excluded."

"If you feel like discussing strategy, Shoe, we're ready," said Ben Martin. "We can run through some scenarios."

"It's not a matter of strategy, if you'll excuse my saying so." A soft-spoken elderly man stood at the table. "You have to make them feel you care about them. It's not just technique. They need to know you are indispensable to them."

"Apparently I'm not," said Shoe tersely. He unwrapped a plate of cookies. Essie Ringel hurried over to his side where he dropped the foil to the ground.

"Oh, let it go, Essie," said Myra hopelessly.

"Was it your civil rights stand, you think?" asked the young rabbi.

"Nah," said Shoe scornfully. "What do you think these people are?"

"Anyway, you can get away with anything in the pulpit," observed Pinny, "as long as you take care of them as a pastor. These sonsabitches, they should all be struck with rare diseases."

"Ma," called Etta from the back door. "Phone."

"Take a message," said Myra without turning around. To Essie she said, "After this congregational meeting, I'm having every phone in my house torn out by the roots."

"I know, I know," said Essie. "You have a lot on your mind."

Etta approached the table shyly.

"How's life?" cried Pinny at the girl. "Everything's good with you? Of course," he answered himself, top volume. "What should be wrong? They're young, they're healthy . . ." He reached for a pickle. "No cholesterol, the kidneys function. Why should they worry?"

"Hey, man," said the young rabbi softly, "you're embarrassing her. Don't you see that?"

"What I see," said Pinny, rising, bristling, surprisingly tall when he straightened his round back, "I see you are a graduate of a fine sensitivity training experience." He grabbed suddenly for the young man's throat. "Don't tell me how to talk!" he shouted, lunging. "Twenty years ago she shat in my lap and she wasn't embarrassed!"

"Hi, Uncle Pinny," said Etta. She blushed and smiled at the young rabbi. "That's just how he is." She put her hand on Myra's arm. "Ma, it was the neighbor phoning. Too much noise. I told her we'd hold it down."

"Certainly, we'll quiet down," said Shoe.

"In a pig's ass, we will," said the young rabbi.

"This is how they talk today, with the hot tubs, with the Rolfing?" asked Pinny.

"A Jewish neighbor?" asked Essie. Myra nodded. "That's what I thought," she said. "A goyish neighbor, they have a little respect."

"Respect, I think, is the missing ingredient today," said the elderly rabbi quietly. "The tone of daily life has changed. In my day, a certain form governed the way people behaved. But this is a time for iconoclasm. Tear down the symbols of authority," he said. "The idea of free speech and equality perverted to—"

"The rabbi was never equal," broke in Pinny. "I hate to tell you this, but my father suffered in Minsk, and then in Godforsaken, New Jersey, and then in the end they kicked him out to Bedroom Slipper, New Mexico, so he could die of TB there and still earn a little piece of bread from a bunch of outcasts, criminals. Iconoclasm! Listen to him! The Jewish people is a rabble, still in the desert making golden calves. . . . Exile, exile is what it is. What are we doing here? Why don't we all earn an honest living instead of this?" He looked at his watch. "Who has the right time? I have an unveiling this afternoon."

"You must reach out, Joshua," the elderly man continued calmly. "They have to understand that you are their representative to the world. How it reflects on them if they mistreat you."

"What will the goyim say, he means," explained Essie. She served Shoe a fresh cup of coffee.

"I appreciate your advice," Shoe said quietly. "But I'm not a green kid. I'm aware of these things. But something went on while I was gone that I can't figure out. I'm stymied," he said in frustration. "By now, even my supporters are starting to think if there's so much discontent there must be something behind it. What happened here? That's the key."

"If they gave us a sabbatical on a silver platter now," said Essie, "I think I'd be afraid to go. Does Yossel know anything?"

"Oy, Yossel," said Pinny. There was an uncomfortable silence at the table. "Poor Yossel. Hey, kid," said Pinny, brightening, "they give you any advice in school for a situation like this, like Rosenstock here has got?"

"Sure," said the young man eagerly. "See, you have to think of it like chess. You take your king's men—" Myra snorted. "Well then," he said with resentment, "go to work on the Options Exchange if you don't like the rabbinate, Mrs. Rosenstock. I used to make my way there well enough. But it was empty. I chose to become a rabbi," he said coldly.

"Don't get mad," said Myra. "I wasn't laughing at you. It's just the idea of manipulating people like chess pieces—well, it seems impossible. People who know damn well how he built this congregation from the ground up, and people that he's really gone out of his way for, they don't want to get involved. So how are you going to manipulate the rest of them?"

"Ach, I don't know the answer," sighed Essie. "Do you know the answer?"

"The answer is," said Ben Martin, scooping up a scattering of crumbs, "that the Association takes a dim view of congregations playing around with lives of rabbis and cantors. That we may have to take a stand if this congregational meeting is not to our satisfaction."

"Great," said the young rabbi. "But you have to put some teeth into it. Like we'd have to agree not to let anyone else come in. Until rabbis develop some consciousness of themselves as labor," he declared, "we're all potentially up shit creek."

"They love you, they love you; they'll turn on you in a minute," said the mild Essie in agreement.

"I'm all for it," said Pinny. "But don't use my name, whatever you do." He glared at the young man, who laughed. "It's very funny to you, I realize. But my buddy, Shoe Rosenstock, will be the first one to understand. You get a little cardiogram, you get a little rupture . . . I can't take any chances. I'm going on pension in a couple years and that's that. You can all come to me and my rebbitsin in Israel." He groaned. "Exile, that's what it is. Bastards, cholerias . . ."

"We're adjourned," said Ben Martin impatiently. The LIARS group rose. "Shoe, let's go inside the house and talk," Ben said. "I think perhaps I ought to have a meeting with Yossel—"

"Leave him alone," said Shoe. "It's not his fault. He's a frail guy. You'll knock him into a depression." The two went inside.

Myra and Essie cleared the table. Etta tossed the Frisbee with the young man as the dog raced between them, barking madly. The others stood aimlessly in the disorderly yard.

"Well, the cemetery is waiting," said Pinny. "One thing, they stay there and you can go home." He kissed Myra.

The elderly rabbi took her hand. "God loves you," he said. "Life is more than our jobs."

Another man said, "You know, seriously, New Saxony is a good position. The competition's going to be fierce."

"Please!" said Essie. "Let the body get cold." Her plump hand flew to her mouth. "I'm sorry, Myra dear."

"No, he's right," said Myra. "This nonperforming Rosenstock, he built them a building, a good school. They own a cemetery now. All that stuff. Somebody will want it, Essie. It's a good job now. Why should we hold it against some new man? It won't be his fault." She made a stack of paper plates.

"Don't run ahead like this," said Essie. "Nothing happened yet."

Myra poured out coffee on the dry ground. "Ess, we know that even when somebody actually dies, the living don't miss a beat. Won't somebody come?"

"Wait a minute," said one of the rabbis. "What's all the talk about dying? You'll be a rabbi or you'll be something else, like the young fellow said. It could be options, shmoptions, do I know what it is? But whatever you like!" He put his arms affectionately around the women. "What would you like, sweethearts?"

Myra smiled sadly at the ground. "I'm a wife," she said. "Let Shoe be all right and then I'm all right." She began to cry.

"Myra," said Essie earnestly, "don't get carried away. You've got a lot on your mind, but you'll see, the meeting will turn out how you want."

"I guess so," said Myra. She moved away to pick up some fallen napkins. "I wish I knew what I wanted."

17

On Sunday, Shoe preached at All Souls. The Reverend Winstead Pegg, his friend, had invited him to talk about Israel, "to inform us of the condition of God's people today."

In the shade behind the stone church, Myra shivered. "Fine talk," said the pastor, taking her hand. "He's a fine man, Myra, my dear. Try not to worry. He'll overcome this."

"I can't tell you, Winn," she said, "how much it means to us to have you invite him here." She shook with cold. "Even doing like he is now, standing out front to greet everybody, he needs it. It brings him back to life."

"And not you?" Winn said soberly.

"No," she said. She rubbed her eyes. "No, it doesn't help me. He gets something from people that I don't get."

The pastor looked at his watch and sighed. "I'd better get up there with him. I'll be missed. Take care of yourself, my dear, and look after your husband. See that he eats and gets enough rest. Maybe vitamins. It's little things like that which only you can do for him that might make the difference. He needs all his fortitude for your congregational meeting."

"Yes," said Myra. "Yes. There are meetings for everything. . . . We'll have to go to court if we lose . . . of course, we'll win."

"I suppose you have some skills?" said Winn. "Just for the time being? Weren't you a teacher? Or was it a librarian? I seem to recall it was one of the caring professions."

"Oh, sure," she said. "Tell him I'll be waiting in the car. I just don't feel like seeing people." She unlocked the car and got in to wait, watching Winn climb the slope to the front steps of the church, which lay in sunshine. The two men stood together in the spring breeze in their robes, Winn's with elongated silver crosses embroidered on the full sleeves. They shook hands with the Sunday morning worshipers. Skills? she thought. What are my skills? Raising a family won't do it. You can't raise somebody else's. I can make great packages to send to college. Probably not too profitable. I can sit all day in the hospital hallway till they tell the family the verdict. But what good does that do me? It only does good for everybody else.

Now Winn and Shoe shook hands with one another and went in the front door of the church as Winn unfastened his splendid purple stole. Myra supposed Shoe would be out the back door in a moment. Winn wouldn't be able to wait much longer for his drink. From Sunday afternoon till the following Saturday, he floated lightly above his duties, cared for his people, attended meetings and wrote letters and sermons, all supported by alcohol. Shoe and Myra were in awe of his ability to do it. And from his alcoholic cloud Winn reached out and offered them his friendship and his jokes and his time. Now he searched for new ways to help Shoe. And who's helping me? thought Myra, eyes stinging. Why don't I have a friend? I'll have to learn to drink more. "Goddamnit," she said aloud. She wiped her eyes. I don't want to suffer like this. I hate being fastened to all these troubles, to watch him be insulted and robbed of all his work. Nonperformance! They want to take away his past, they'll go to court if they have to, to prove he never was anybody. Taking the future away from him isn't enough.

I don't need it, she rebelled. I won't go on with it. And the children phoning, six children phoning, because there was no way to keep it quiet. Six children phoning from all their campuses, where there always seemed to be a boy or girl from New Saxony to tell the children about their father's troubles. They phoned, while she feared the bills. How is Daddy? Take care of Daddy. Look out for him. Even the alcoholic Winn, the celibate, presumed to tell her her duty. Take care of Shoe. Cook hot meals. Take care of him. This is hard for him.

How do you think it is for me? she shouted, her mouth shut tight. I don't even count. I just sit there with the damn mourners and make the coffee and answer the phone. She's so nice, the rabbi's wife. What's her name?

Nobody did it to me, thought Myra. She watched the back door of the church. I did it to myself, because I wanted to be good, as good as Shoe. She moved about on the car seat. I lost the sense I was born with. And now he asks me if I have any skill. Yes. I have the skill to starve. I have the skill to cry. I have the skill to hide my feelings. We'll see how much they pay for that. Shoe was coming toward the car.

"Hey, aren't you cold?" he said. He slid next to Myra on the car seat and kissed her cheek. "You should have come out in front in the sun. You'd have liked meeting Winn's people. Nice bunch."

"I'm sure," she said. "Can I start the car? Are you ready to leave? Can you tear yourself away?"

He leaned back. "Go ahead," he said. All the liveliness was gone from his face. "Don't think I like it, Myra. I'm just trying to be courteous to Winn."

"You like it," she said, with murder in her voice. She pulled away from the church and headed for home. "Don't do me any favors. Don't lie to me. You like it. At least admit it." She rolled up her window. "Close your window, Shoe. I'm so cold. Just admit it and allow me not to like it, can't you?"

"Nah," he said. He closed his eyes and put his head back. "It's a pile of shit."

"Please!" she cried. She strained to see the familiar road. "Shoe, please. It's all right, it's fine. You're a rabbi. Just leave me out of it from now on. You can like it and I can go some other way. . . ."

"Myra," he said, eyes closed, "if I had some other skill . . . But it's late in life and I had no warning. . . . We've got kids in college. . . . If I had another skill . . ." He looked over at her.

"I'm just a little tense, I guess," she said quietly.

She entered the driveway, watched Shoe go to the back door and open it, watched the dog bolt outdoors. She eased the car into the cluttered garage. I'll never clean out this garage, she thought. It's hopeless. She sat in the car. If I had the strength, she thought, I'd do the carbon monoxide thing. She got out of the car and went inside to make lunch.

Dear Rabbi,

Most assuredly you are a Man of God! Pardon what may seem a girlish effusion but after hearing you speak at my church I couldn't sleep. Your wide experience of life and your manly and vigorous responses were too thrilling. Truly, Abraham's seed lives in you and all the prophets are within you as well. If you'll permit me, I would like to visit with you and get to know you better. I feel you could help me broaden my horizons, or what's a heaven for? (Just my little joke!) Come to tea at my home next Thursday. We can walk in the garden and speak about the Old Testament I love so well. There were giants in those days.

Affectionately,
Bev Heimerdinger

18

The moths beat at the screens on the kitchen windows. An exhalation, compounded of the neighbors' lawn sprinklers, the honeysuckle climbing the telephone pole, the flagstone path to the back door giving up its daytime heat, arose peacefully from the Rosenstocks' backyard. Bobby Etkind, attorney, strolled cheerfully enough through several adjoining backyards in the dark, stirring up the dogs, wearing only a pair of shorts and carrying a briefcase. He noted that he was wearing a path in the lawns that led to the Rosenstock house. He stopped at Myra's screened door and looked inside the enameled yellow kitchen. He gasped. He burst in. Myra's head and shoulders were in the oven; her bare feet turned their black soles to the ceiling. She screamed and bumped her head on the roof of the oven as she tried to jump up. She turned around on the floor and laughed, pale around the mouth.

"Sorry, Bobby, you frightened me to death."

"Sorry," he mumbled, blushing. He had sneaked a look at the electric oven. He felt like a fool. "Sorry, I forgot to knock. Thought I might catch your husband. Do a little work."

"Have some of that chianti, Bobby," she offered. She gestured with a dirty rubber glove to a bottle on the counter. "The glasses are right above it. Shoe will be back soon. He told me you might be over. He's at the Blooms'. Charlie Bloom died this morning. Did you know?"

"I'm sorry," said Bobby. "I guess they knew it was coming, though." He poured himself a glass of wine. "You want some more?" He poured for Myra, squatting by her glass on the floor.

"Yes, they knew it was coming," she said. She drank, sprawled on the floor, holding the stem of her glass with the greasy glove. "Even Charlie knew. He knew right along. I guess a doctor can't fool himself. But they're devastated over there, just the same." She sighed. "Shoe's been back and forth to them all day. Funeral's tomorrow."

"You have to be ready," said Bobby, looking at the ceiling. "I well remember your husband's sermon once, to that effect. We have to be ready. I'll never forget it."

"Yeah," she said. "Well, he's out of it now." She peeled off her gloves, stood up, and threw them in the sink. "Pure masochism. Nothing I hate more than cleaning the oven. Just killing time. The kids all went out. They came up to see Shoe but he couldn't stay home. They can't stand the constant phone calls. Come on in the living room, Bobby. Take your glass." She wiped her hands and picked up the wine bottle.

Bobby took the armchair familiarly. He looked at the side of his glass. "How's his health, Myra?" he asked.

"I told you," she said, coming in. "He died this morning."

"Your husband's health." He studied the side of his glass.

"He's fine," she said. She looked frightened. She sat on a footstool by Bobby's bare knees. "What are you thinking about?"

"I was thinking about an EKG, Myra." He looked into her eyes. "This is just the start of a long battle. I think neither of you appreciates that yet. There's a lot of stress in store for him. He keeps talking to me as though he's on the verge of straightening it out. But, in my judgment, there are harassments ahead, and meetings before we ever get to the congregational meeting. And who knows how that will come out? You just never know, Myra. And officiating at the synagogue, at the Bar Mitzvahs and all, is going to seem like the easiest part." Myra rested her forehead in her hand. "He doesn't understand that yet. And if it goes further, if we have to go to court, Warmflash already gave me to understand he's going to ask for an inventory of all your personal possessions. To see what you've stolen," he said earnestly. "I won't let him, don't worry," he said. "But you see what may be coming? If we have to go to court, I wouldn't want to put him on the stand, if it came to that, without an EKG." He wriggled in the chair. "How Winegarden could do that, how he could give a man such a shock, not the youngest man in the world or a man in the best of shape; he could have killed him! I keep thinking about the story your husband told me. Unbelievable! Hitting him like that the night he comes home. That's a doctor, an educated man? Might as well say Hitler was a doctor. I saw no reason to emphasize this to the rabbi, by the way."

"I understand," she said quietly. "He's not a real doctor," she added, "you know. He just wants to be called that."

"But I think we need an EKG, Myra," said Bobby, looking at her. "I'm a little afraid to go ahead without it."

"No," she said. "If I tell him now to go for that, it's as good as killing him. I'm not going to do it."

"It's just a reading, Myra," he said. "Maybe you don't know what it is. . . . Or I could suggest it. . . . Or your son Joey, he's a doctor, for all practical purposes . . ."

"No," she said harshly. "Just tell Joey that, he'll leave school tomorrow. No, I'll be responsible, Bobby, not you. It's my decision. I know my husband. It's not the thing to do." She stared at the carpet. "It might scare him into something, just doing it. Don't say anything about it to him."

"I didn't," he said. "I won't. I'll do as you say."

She looked up at him emotionally. "I feel like you're my son sometimes, Bobby. And the funny part of it is, I feel like my son, I mean you, are going to pick us up and wheel us home in a baby carriage. I feel safe with you." She touched his bare ankle. "Freckles even here." She sipped her wine. "Actually, I feel incestuous."

Bobby blushed deeply and looked at his legs. She laughed. "Don't get worried. I'm an old lady. I'm old-fashioned. I don't know how else to express my feelings when I'm so grateful." She laughed at his red face. "But don't get scared."

He cleared his throat. "I've been hearing about the women's group," he said, attempting a businesslike tone. "I've been hearing they had some role to play. Would you say that's right?"

Myra laughed loudly. She got up and went to the old sofa, carrying the chianti bottle with her. "I'm a target for the women." She drank from the bottle. "I like my husband too much. I liked having kids. Not allowed." She looked at Bobby. "I hear women want to be rabbis now. Did you know that?"

Restraining his impatience, he answered, "I've heard about it."

"I think it's a good idea," she said, stretching her legs. "Wait till the Board sees the rabbi cry, right in front of them. Then they'll know what bums they are. Instead of the rabbi putting up a big front, and at home his wife is wetting her pillow and phoning her mother. Let's see how they feel about themselves when they're cheating and lying and stealing from the rabbi and the rabbi is a girl!"

"Probably no different, Myra," he mumbled.

"You think so?" She was startled.

"Tell me about the women's group, will you, Myra?" he asked patiently.

The dog bounded into the room in an aura of urine and old leaves. He jumped into Myra's lap. She kissed his nose. "Shoe's coming," she told Bobby. "He can always tell."

Bobby looked up as Shoe came into the room. "We were just talking, Rabbi, about the women's group."

"Yes," said Shoe distantly. He looked tired and remote.

"Sit down, honey," said Myra. "I'll get you a drink."

"Get me some club soda, will you?" He sat down and stared at Bobby. "We lost Charlie Bloom today."

"I'm sorry. Myra told me."

"Interesting thing," said Shoe from his distance. "He was not afraid of death. That wasn't it. But, oh, how he hated to go. He loved being alive." He took his glass from Myra. "Well, of course," he said, impatient with himself. "This is not such a great insight. I feel the same way. There's so much to accomplish . . ."

"Yes . . . ," said Myra. "But sometimes it's so tough. . . ."

"Could we talk about the Sisterhood a moment?" said Bobby gently. "I can't stay too late."

"You know what they say," said Myra with a grin. "Sisterhood Is Power! Etta's got a button like that." She sat down between Shoe and the dog on the sofa. She drank her wine. "Well, they meet once a month. And they always start off about spirit; we don't have it. And how we could attract more people by snappier social events. It's an old story; Shoe tells them there has to be a Jewish rationale for whatever we do in the synagogue. And they agree and then they're mad. They wanted a fashion show or a disco night. Every year. He won't understand it."

"I understand it," said Shoe grouchily. "What do you want me to do?"

"You don't like Sisterhood, Myra?" asked Bobby. "Is that what you're saying? Excuse my ignorance. I really don't know."

"I don't *dislike* it," she said. "I go to a lot of meetings. PTA, the Mothers' Hot Lunch Committee, the hospital auxiliary; they're all the same. They gossip. They're mad at the ones who don't come. They have to do higher math to calculate how much coffee to make and how to divide the cost."

"Myra," said Shoe tiredly. He covered her hand with his.

"He asked me to tell him, Shoe."

"Let her tell, Rabbi," said Bobby.

She filled her wineglass again. "You know that big woman, she's got these eyelashes like a rodent?"

Bobby grinned and shook his head.

"Myra . . ." said Shoe. "This is trivial. Bobby's a busy man."

A look of anguish came to her face. "Why I went up against her, I'll never know," she said. "After all these many years. But I did. She wanted a belly dancer for entertainment at a dinner dance and I objected. I said belly dancing's degrading to women. I tell you, it was better than refreshments! They could go against the rabbi without even confronting him! I gave them their chance!"

"I don't think there's anything important here," said Bobby, thinking aloud.

"It is," she said eagerly. "I'm trying to explain—"

The lightest snore came from Shoe's mouth. Shocked, Myra turned. Shoe's mouth was the least bit ajar; his eyes were closed. Bobby and Myra looked at him.

Shoe's hands twitched and his eyes snapped open. "Oh!" he said. "Was I sleeping? Oh, Bobby, I'm very sorry."

"You're tired, Rabbi," said Bobby thoughtfully. He looked at the side of his glass. "It's perfectly all right. You know," he said regretfully, "I'm really sorry I don't know more about these things. I wish I had been active in the synagogue. I'm embarrassed, but you know how it is. I put in a pretty long day at the office and my wife puts in a pretty long day herself."

"Bobby," said Shoe. He put his head back and covered his eyes with his hand. "You're apologizing?"

"I'd have to be called a Yom Kippur Jew, I guess," said Bobby, blushing. "I'm ashamed to say it but it's true."

"But that's ridiculous, Bobby," said Myra. "To apologize for missing a dance with a belly dancer? Or you're sorry you aren't buddies with Milton Winegarden and his psoriasis?"

"Myra," said Shoe, sitting up, "if God can stand the Jewish people, so can you." He patted her thigh. "She's upset."

"I'm just trying to get a better feel for all these undercurrents," said Bobby, thinking. "That's why I asked about the women. I don't know most of these people. But I'm just outraged by the situation. I mean, I don't know you two all that well, but still! A clerk you give notice. A cleaning woman, a gardener. So a rabbi? A rabbi you tell without notice, to take his life contract and shove it?" He blushed deeply. "Excuse me. But I'll tell you the truth, I'm not sleeping over this. I get up and walk around my house all night."

"No kidding," said Myra with maternal interest. "So do I."

"Maybe we should take turns," said Shoe wearily. "Why should all three of us be awake?"

"Myra," said Bobby slowly, "would you say some of these women you've described are behind this ouster?"

She drank more wine. "They killed their own husbands. Castrated their sons. Now they want fresh blood."

"Myra," said Shoe angrily, "you're too damn sensitive. It's too bad if some woman was rude to you, but it's not at the bottom of this. Don't tell me my life hinges on these trivialities." He touched her arm.

She shook off his hand. "I thought it was good to be sensitive."

"I should go home," said Bobby. He stretched his bare arms and arched his back. The small tan room was stuffy. "Tomorrow's a busy day for a change."

"I have a funeral," said Shoe. "We have to bury poor Charlie."

"You know, they're crazy when you get down to it," said Bobby, getting out of his seat. He pushed aside his briefcase with a bare knee. "I can't uncover a single, defensible reason. This proposal is a nullity," he said loudly. "I'm not going to let them terminate you."

Myra laughed nervously. "Please," she said. "It's terminate the contract, not the rabbi."

Shoe guffawed. "No, the lawyer's got it right."

They walked to the door. "Once more, quickly, Rabbi," said Bobby. "Just run over the events of the evening you came home. I know, I know," he said, holding up his hand. "You've told me dozens of times. Humor me. Just do me the favor of running over it once more."

"Sure, Bobby," Shoe said patiently. "I came in the house. He phoned within a couple of minutes and told me to come over—"

"Winegarden," stated Bobby.

"Right, and I went, I had to, and Sunny Winegarden greeted me very civilly and sent me upstairs to this weird room of Milton's, and . . . the rest of them. . . ."

"Who, again?"

"Sunny Winegarden, Milton's wife."

"No, no. Who else was there?"

"A few guys," said Shoe. "And they told me; and we argued back and forth," said Shoe, shifting his feet. "And Winegarden was talking relationships and jargon like that; and somebody else was calling the synagogue 'management'; I guess I'm labor—"

"You guess," put in Myra.

"And somebody told me to get a lawyer." He smiled at Bobby.

"Go on," he said, blushing.

"I told them I didn't need a lawyer, and then I brought out the point that I couldn't resign if I wanted to. It would look as though I had done something unspeakable. I'd never be able to get another pulpit."

"Go on," said Bobby. Myra stood by, bored, drinking from the bottle.

"And then Harry Warmflash—" Shoe's face went red. He cleared his throat. "And then that bastard, Warmflash, he said . . . he said . . . 'Maybe your days as a rabbi are over . . . maybe you ought not be a rabbi . . .'" His eyes filled. He turned and went quickly to the kitchen.

Myra and Bobby stood in silence together in the hall. They heard

Shoe taking deep breaths and blowing his nose. He became quiet, then cried a moment longer.

"Maybe I should leave," said Bobby.

"No, don't go," said Myra. "Come in and sit down again. Just a few more minutes. He'll be all right. This is overdue. I never heard that part myself."

Shoe came back to them. "Pardon me for getting upset there," he said, wiping his eyes. "I don't know what came over me. It wasn't even an emotionally significant part of the story . . . just how Warmflash told me to quit being a rabbi . . ." His voice broke. He shook his head in bewilderment.

"Let's have a drink," said Myra firmly. She went to the cabinet beneath the bookcase and pulled out a bottle and three glasses, all covered with dust.

"I'm not letting them terminate you," said Bobby loudly. He took his glass from Myra. The dog lay on his foot.

"Myra," said Shoe, looking awed, "you opened the Courvoisier?"

"It's very good," said Bobby.

"Why should I save it?" said Myra rebelliously. "For what? Let the future buy its own brandy! L'chayim." She tipped back her glass.

"Myra," said Shoe angrily, "that's enough. I want this drinking to stop. Drinking is not going to replace eating. You're as thin as a rail and I don't like it."

"Don't scold me in front of company," she said fondly. Her face was flushed. She touched the stubble on his chin. "Your beard is going white. You look like my little doggy." The dog heard her caressing tone and thumped his tail on the floor.

Bobby laughed. "I'm sorry we've got acquainted under these circumstances," he said, raising his glass to them. "But I feel lucky to know you."

"Next time, 'auf simchas,' " said Shoe, relenting with a small smile. Bobby was puzzled.

"That means, next time we'll meet on a happy occasion," she explained. "You say it at a funeral. It's his idea of humor."

Shoe seized the bottle and the glass from Myra's hands. "She keeps me from self-importance," he said, suddenly furious. "Thank God for her, otherwise with all this love and adulation from the congregation . . . Good night," he said abruptly. He walked away to the kitchen, holding the bottle under his arm.

Myra took Bobby to the door. "Once again, thank you for coming," she said quietly. She held his fingers. "I'll walk you outside," she said. She closed the door silently behind her. "Don't be impatient with him. He's in such pain. And losing Charlie Bloom today . . ."

"Jesus, Myra!" said Bobby hotly. "What do you expect from him? I'm not *not* patient!"

"You're mad at me too," she said sadly.

"Oh no," he said, embarrassed. He shuffled his feet on the front walk. "It's just you don't always stick to the point. . . ." He blushed in the dark. "No, you're both very tired."

"He's tired and he's touchy," she said, almost to herself. "But I stick to the point all right, Bobby." Her voice became stronger. "*He* doesn't. *You* don't. You two think the point is all about winning." She became short of breath. "But is it? Is it worth dying to win? Isn't that what you just warned me about? That he could die from this? Why should he die? Bobby, why should anybody die to be right? I can't see it. I can't. I try but I can't. And if I tell him our life has been trivial, why can't he see it as a chance to change? Why must we go on being trivial? The hell with these people!"

"I'm no marriage counselor, Myra," he muttered, greatly embarrassed.

She laughed. "Did you think I was asking your advice, counselor?" She stroked his bare arm. "No, bubeleh, we'll still be married. Don't be frightened. We have a lifetime contract. A real one." Tears came to her eyes. "I love him. I really do love him."

In an agony of embarrassment, Bobby moved a step away from her in the darkness.

"And I admire him!" she cried. She pursued him, staggering a little, and clutched at his arm. "Do you know what a privilege that is, to admire your husband?" She breathed in his face. "Are you old enough to understand how privileged I am?" He tried to steady her with his bare arms. "I hear him yelling in the shower," she said hoarsely. "Shakespeare." She shook his arms. "Take a walk with him in the woods, it's Psalms." She choked. "I've never envied any woman."

"Please, Myra," he said desperately.

She steadied herself and stepped back. In a changed, quiet voice she said, "Every day I expect something tragic to happen. I see him dead. It wasn't just your idea. Or I see myself falling down the cellar steps and breaking all my bones. Or drinking Drāno." She moved her bare, dirty feet among the old leaves littering the walk. "Maybe I want it to happen. So I won't have to live through this. A congregational meeting? Like a public flogging or a public trial, no matter how it comes out? How can I live through it? Why do you think I drink so much?" He shut his eyes. "Huh? Why? You don't know me, but I just discovered drinking. I went into a liquor store myself last week, for the first time in my life. I finished the scotch. We must have had that bottle five years. . . ." She laughed. "It doesn't help, really. I'm poisoned, poisoned, I'm sick, but I'd rather be sick than face this!" She crossed her hands on her chest. "I just would rather die."

"You shouldn't talk that way," he said in a shocked voice.

"I keep frightening you." She smiled. "Bobby, I can't even get my house clean. I just talk." She looked up at the sky. All the surrounding homes were dark. "Listen, Bobby," she said. She looked at him. "I've wanted to say this . . ." She moved near him again and stroked his bare chest. "Now I know how an angel looks." She paused. "A redhead comes down from heaven with a briefcase, in a pair of shorts." She drew the back of her hand slowly across his stomach. She laughed as she felt his muscles contract. "I've asked myself," she said, "where did he come from? Who is he?" She put her palm to his bare nipple as he compelled himself not to draw away. "God sent you," she said simply. "He saw how much we needed you and He sent you." Bobby stepped back. "You can thank the brandy for this," she said, voice breaking.

"Myra, slow up," he said hoarsely. He blushed deeply. "Wait till I help you, at least. Don't be grateful yet," he said, armpits stinging. "This is just the start. We've got a long way to go. I hope you understand that," he said anxiously.

"You still don't understand," she said, looking at the stars. "It doesn't matter if it helps. As long as I know you exist." She touched his naked belly lightly. "Good night, I won't embarrass you any further." She went inside and faced the wall, leaned on it, and cried quietly.

A red-faced Bobby tapped on the door. "Myra? My briefcase?" She handed it to him without speaking. "I'll be back tomorrow night, Myra," he said softly. "Have him ready to spend the evening with me. We have a lot of work to do."

Dearest Rabbi,

Charlie loved you. Billy and I love you. What more is there to say? Billy and I must try to go on without Charlie, knowing that he would not want us to grieve too long. I thank you for reminding us of that. If one can say that a funeral is beautiful, then what you did for Charlie at his was beautiful. You recalled him for all of us in the days of his strength and with all his hope and idealism, which he never lost, not to the last moment. We are very grateful to you.

There have been some bad moments. I ran up to his room after I got back from the cemetery—to give him his medicine! I keep forgetting. But I suppose it will get better. Please don't forget us now. I think we still need you.

Much love,
Lena Bloom

19

Milton was seeing Harry to the front door. "So you feel the meeting won't take place, then?" he asked.

Harry was preoccupied. He looked at his watch. "I didn't say that," he said without emphasis. "We may well have that damn congregational meeting, even though it's a terrible waste of time. I'm just saying I'm not impressed with the legal talent he's got going. I think we've got the rabbi on the ropes. It took longer than I thought, as it is."

Sunny called from the kitchen. "Telephone, darling!"

"Take a message," said Milton brusquely. He tore at the skin between his fingers with his close-trimmed nails. "You know Dorfman and Etkind personally? I don't."

"Dorfman," said Harry, becoming animated. "You could worry if it was a negligence case. Let him talk to a jury and show them pictures of a burned baby or some goddamned thing, and it's good-by Charlie. He gets awards! Like you never heard of. But this is entirely different." He puffed out his chest. "This takes a bit of close contract reading, a dash of brainpower. He no got." Harry often fell into dialects to make a point. "He no got uppa here." He tapped his skull.

"Like a shvartzeh," mused Milton. He rubbed at his mottled neck. "If you think Dorfman's bad, come spend a day with my chairman at the college." Milton was drifting into his own professional difficulties.

Harry was not interested. Harry stared without expression at the filling pustules on Milton's cheeks and put his hand on the brass doorknob. "I have an appointment," he said.

"And Etkind?" said Milton, not noticing. "How would you describe him professionally? I need to get a fix on these men. They're getting between me and the rabbi in my talks and I have to handle them a little more forcefully, I'm afraid." Sunny called him again. Another phone call. "Take a *message*, I said," he shouted. "Can't get any support from her," he said, annoyed. "Every little thing, she calls me."

"Get out of the house," advised Harry. "Go to the office."

"My office," said Milton. He rolled his eyes. "Liberia. Wait till I get this Jewish Life Center rolling," he said. "They'll sing another tune. I'm not going to have them teaching Swahili, not while I'm there," he declared. "That's all I need. That's why I went into teaching, you know, to knock bones together and learn voodoo."

"Good-by," said Harry.

"Wait! Etkind?" Milton stood on the front step now with Harry. The bright sunlight lit up his flaring spots and highlighted the indoor pallor on Harry's face.

Harry laughed. "Etkind's a knight," he sneered. "He's going to save the world, the shmuck. Has he got a wrong number."

"Oh," said Milton in surprise. "Somebody told me he's a corporate man."

"He is," laughed Harry. "These types, they get little fits of conscience. He wants to make up for what he's missing. What's he going to do? Lose money? Tell his partners he'll be absent while he goes to march for nuclear disarmament or some goddamned thing? Just try it in one of those firms. You'll be out on your ass in five minutes. No, he's just using the rabbi to make himself feel good. He doesn't worry me. I'll take him on any day. Overage flower child," he said contemptuously.

"It's been good talking to you," said Milton. He extended his crusty hand. Harry pretended to busy his hands with his papers and briefcase and went to his parked car. Milton went back into the cool, dark house. "What were the calls? Sunny?" he shouted. "Sunny? Where are you, Sunny?"

She put her smooth head over the banister. "Don't scream at me," she said coldly. "Take your own calls and do not scream at your wife. I'm not your servant."

"What was it, Sunny? Just tell me." He craned his neck to look up the stairwell at her. "Then we'll go out together and work in the peony beds like I promised. And we'll get some annuals today."

"Listen to this," said Sunny. She glared at him. "What a homebody! What a devoted husband! I can't get your attention for anything."

"Sunny," he said, very dignified, "I believe you are being unfair to me." He began to climb the stairs to her. "I am juggling many very complex tasks. I am maintaining an important position," he said as he plodded up, "at the college as well as"—he stooped to rub at his instep, itching and burning—"trying to create something new there. It amounts to creating a new synagogue on the campus, Sunny, one that's just the way it should be."

Sunny was bent over the flower box in the hall alcove, pulling off dead leaves, moving soil with her fingers at the roots of all the plants she could reach. Milton came up beside her.

Shoulder to shoulder with her, he went on. "And I've taken on this task here with Rosenstock." He looked over his shoulder into the empty hallway. "It looks good. I think we won't have that congregational meeting at all. We can"—he lowered his voice—"have Yossel in place by fall."

"Something has to give, Milton," she said bossily. "I require some of your time too. Let Warmflash do this. You've done enough. Summers is getting very impatient. He wants you for that curriculum revision meeting in the worst way. Those calls: the first was his secretary, the next was Summers himself. I had a hard time making excuses for you, darling. You must at least appear to be interested."

"I'll call him," said Milton. He smiled amorously, exposing his irregular teeth. "As long as mah sweetie ain't gwine be mad wiv me."

"Oh, Milton," said Sunny, pleased and aroused. Her voice went higher. "Let me . . ." She reached for him. "Let it wait."

Milton laughed happily. "No, no!" he said gaily. He backed away. "You'll wait, you minx! I have phone calls!" He lightly ran up the next flight of stairs to his study, whistling under his breath. He looked down and saw Sunny smiling up at him. He blew her a kiss. "Just you wait!" he called. He went into his room and shut the padded door.

She's quite right, he said to himself. He began absentmindedly to pull off his clothes to let his skin breathe. Something's got to give. He went in his underpants to an ornate Italian walnut dining table with a concealed panel behind it. The panel swung open at the touch of some buttons Milton loved to operate and the electric typewriter came out and rested on the table. He got out his finest, thinnest paper and began to type.

Dear Dr. Summers,
This is to confirm our telephone conversation earlier relative to my leave of absence from the college. I expect to be absent from my duties for a period of not more than two weeks. A matter of a private nature has arisen which necessitates this. Thank you for your understanding.

       Fraternally,
       Milton Winegarden, Ph.D.

Milton laughed to himself and inserted a new sheet of paper.

Isaiah,
Just file the enclosed re my leave, will you? I didn't have time to call you. I'll be back before you can say Jackie Robinson.
       Milton Winegarden, Ph.D.

There was still something to do. What was it? Milton scratched his scalp, picked off some scabs, thought hard. Oh yes!

Dear Rabbi,

In glancing through the books, the treasurer and I happened to notice a certain confusion surrounding the dues status of your lawyers. Accordingly, I am directing the treasurer to suspend the family memberships in our synagogue of Robert Etkind and Norman Dorfman. They may clarify their good standing by stating their position(s) in a registered letter to the president and the treasurer with a copy to me. Please inform them of this at your earliest convenience.

Milton Winegarden, Ph.D.

20

Myra snored lightly, body bent on the sagging sofa, twisted to accommodate the dog, who lay beside her asleep. She dreamed her purse had been stolen at some customs barrier. It was a dark and threatening country she was in and her purse held all their money and their passports and their tickets home. She begged the customs official to help her find her purse. The man spoke a language Myra couldn't understand. He was impatient and angry. "But I have nothing!" Myra pleaded. "Nothing!" The man laughed and invited his colleagues to look at Myra. She was growing disheveled and shabby. They all laughed. She was helpless.

Faigy Greenwald appeared. "I'll help you," Faigy said. "Here's money. Don't be frightened."

"No, Faigy," Myra said. "I don't want you to give me anything. Just help me find what's mine. Just help me."

"Here's money," said Faigy.

"No," said Myra, beginning to cry. "How can I take money from you?"

"Of course you can," Faigy said soothingly. "Why shouldn't I give my rabbi money?"

"No," moaned Myra. "Don't do it for that. Help me because I'm a fellow human being on the planet."

"But you're not," said Faigy. "You're married to my rabbi."

Faigy's purse made a loud rattling sound as she reached into it and Myra, sweating, in confusion, half woke to see Milton Winegarden closing the screen door behind him in the front hall. He came quietly into the living room. Standing over her, he seemed to pluck a faded wreath of roses off the wall. He offered it to her. Myra and the dog sat up, coming fully awake. Milton stood there.

"I knew I'd find you alone this evening," he said softly. "Your husband's with his lawyers tonight. You really should lock your doors, you know," he said.

She was conscious of her bare feet, the dusty furniture, the bottle and the glass next to her. Her gums felt sticky. She said nothing. She was dazed with sleep.

"I've got a problem, Myra," he said gently. "Maybe you can help me."

She stared at him. The dog got behind her on the sofa, rubbed his tail against the roses on the wallpaper, and looked at Milton.

"You know I never want to hurt you or the rabbi," said Milton in a cajoling way.

"I know," she said. She felt paralyzed.

"Don't force me to do it, Myra," he said. "I don't want to do it and the suffering for you will be very great. What shall we do, Myra? Let's have a conference."

"Do you want me to make coffee?" she said. A headache was settling on her eyebrows like a fog. She wished she were more sober or more drunk. Something terrible was coming and she was unprepared, defenseless.

He shook his large head. He remained standing. "There are things that you don't want known, Myra. You really don't."

"Like what?" she said stupidly. Her tongue was thick.

"You're better off never knowing," he said sincerely. "I have facts, damaging facts. I have names, I have dates. I have specifics. What should I do about it, Myra?" He looked at her curiously. "These matters should not be discussed with anyone. Certainly they should not be discussed at a public gathering. I'm thinking of you, you know." He smiled gently, showing his teeth.

"I know," she said. She believed him.

"So what shall we do?"

"I guess you should tell me," she said simply. "Because, honestly, Milton, I can't think what it is. I wouldn't want anybody to know what an awful housekeeper I am, I guess, but honestly, Milton, that's about the worst thing I can think of that I'm guilty of." She pushed the hair off her forehead, beginning to feel awake at last. "Why don't you sit?"

He continued to stand over her. "Marrying's a funny thing," he said sympathetically. "It's nothing about you. Do you follow me?"

"Then what can I do?" she said. Her head throbbed.

"Let me help you," he said. "Let's not go to that congregational meeting. You don't want it. I don't want it. Your husband shouldn't want it. He's being led by advisers who don't care about him or for his reputation. But I care about *you*."

"I know," she said softly. "I know." A great calm settled around her like a cape. It seemed that this scene had happened before, had always been happening; that Milton, or somebody else like Milton, had always been standing over her, telling her what she must do for her own safety, for her own good, for the good of her loved ones. And always it was something painful, a thing she was not expected to be able to understand. She was expected to sacrifice and that was all. It was so familiar and so impenetrable that she could not be afraid.

"Give it some thought," he said. "I have confidence in you. But don't take too long," he warned. "There's so little time left, I'm sorry to say." He walked to the front door and looked back at her. "Lock this after me, will you? You really shouldn't be here in an open house." He went out.

Dizzy, burping, head pounding, she got up and went to the screen door. She watched Milton go to the street and climb up into his car. She latched the screen. She clenched her swelling hands. Her distance from the scene was evaporating. What should she have said? What clue had she overlooked? What were the words Milton wanted from her? Perhaps she could have mended everything. Her hands shook. She should call Bobby's house now and report to the men. But she was afraid of Shoe's anger, of Bobby's; of Norman's ridicule. She should have known what to do. But what? A person with experience would have known. A person of intelligence would have known. She stared through the screen. Outside somewhere in the summer darkness, a cat stuck in a hedge yowled like an abandoned baby.

21

The first Jew to set foot in New Saxony, Illinois, was Meyer Levy. That was the local lore. He came in 1899 to peddle his brooms and brushes to the German-speaking housewives and farmers. They laughed at his Yiddish but they understood him and they did business. In time he bought what came to be known as Levy's Woods. It was a vast flat cornfield with a privy near one boundary where a house had been and burned down and a decaying elm whose roots extended beneath the privy. In these fields, then, he settled and prospered under his vine and fig tree, along with his flocks and herds; which is to say that his wife, Sarah, kept chickens. They added feather dusters to his line of merchandise and made twig brooms during the long winters. They built a house for their family and started a vegetable garden and put up a grape arbor like all the villagers, but in their ignorance of real farming the cornfields gradually gave way to a woods, of a scrubby sort, that sprang to life of itself.

They never learned the names of the trees. There was no time. Their ten children grew rapidly; New Saxony slowly. Old man Heimerdinger, who had sold Meyer the cornfield, lived to see young Samuel Levy marry his daughter in church. Then he closed his eyes. By 1940 there were Levys who belonged to the New Saxony German Lutheran Alliance; to All Souls; the Community Ethical Society; and even to Our Lady of Saxony. A widow now, Sarah Levy continued her annual migration to Chicago for the High Holy Days, and the shochet, the ritual slaughterer, still came from the city every two weeks to kill four chickens for her.

During the Hitler period there was a little trouble, not too much. Some misguided toughs came up from the city to paint a swastika on the doors of the broom factory and to throw trash through old Sarah's front window, which now faced directly on the sidewalk of Main Street. A certain Meyer Levy, son of Samuel and a communicant at Our Lady, clarified matters. He and his friends, a number of them boys sensitive about their German heritage just then, appeared at Grandma Levy's with some iron tools from the factory and other implements of peace and half killed the city boys. But it was after the war that New Saxony underwent its real transformation.

No one knew how but suddenly there were highways from the city and the train became a commuter train and the fields were called developments. Every day the moving vans crossed the flat lands bearing their loads of French Provincial or Danish Modern. Meyer Levy was an adult and he went into real estate. And Levy's Woods, that forsaken cornfield with a privy at one corner, became La Vie Wood with ornamental gateposts at the entrance and a sign there: "A Residential Community. Keep Out"; and there was a waiting list.

To honor the original Meyer, this Meyer Levy set aside a portion of the acreage to be used for a synagogue. He had two first cousins in business with him, each also Meyer Levy, but Jewish, who laughed at him. It took a Catholic, they said, to think of a thing like that. But all of them had loved Grandma and to honor her husband's memory all three became founding members of the new New Saxony Synagogue. To honor Grandpa and because they admired the rabbi who was organizing it: Rabbi Joshua Rosenstock.

Now Myra and the children approached the synagogue in La Vie Wood crushed together in the car. Bobby and Shoe had gone earlier. It was the evening of the congregational meeting. Except for Joey, the oldest, who had to work emergency at Cook County Hospital that night, all the children had come to be with their father in case, in case . . .

"This is the last time in my life I'm going to synagogue," said Etta angrily.

"Oh?" said Myra. She looked at the big flushed girl next to her on the back seat. "You just became a Presbyterian?"

"I never will either," said Nathan, scowling at the wheel. "Screw 'em. I hate 'em. Let 'em die."

"Don't let Daddy hear that," warned Myra. "You'll break his heart."

"*We're* not breaking his heart," said Etta. "When I think of all the shit, even just this Christmas in Israel, the way they followed us, remember, Mommy?"

All of them talked at once. Etta had touched a nerve.

"Bar Mitzvah, so naturally he had to miss my graduation . . ."

"Yeah, but you didn't have to invite them all to your own Bar Mitzvah, like I did . . ."

"And the mean comments when Joey went to Harvard . . ."

"Oh, Harvard! We couldn't even have a nice dress . . ."

"They even bothered you on sabbatical," said Etta again. "Remember, Mommy?" she said eagerly. "How they popped out of caves, out of the Dead Sea the time we went swimming? We even met them in mosques! And always unloading their weirdo kids on you, Mommy. Using you for a rest stop and a sitter."

"Something special bothering you, kid?" asked Aaron. He twisted around in the front seat to look back at the red-faced Etta.

"Up yours," she said. "Your father's getting fired, archaeologist. Maybe nobody told you in your cave."

"I think we'll win, honey," said Myra, belly contracting.

"Mom," said Aaron calmly. He reached behind him with his long arm to touch Myra's calf. "We'll still always be a family." The others went on with their complaints. "We'll still always eat." Myra leaned forward to kiss his young cheek. Aaron liked to measure skulls, arrange fragments of pottery. He was an innocent.

"They stole our father from us," Etta was going on. "Those bastards. And now look!"

The older children tried to draw away from her. Myra put her arm across Etta's shoulders protectively. She craved a drink. But all the girls had trailed her around the house, watching her, making her change shoes, put on earrings. And with their fluttering and suggesting, their gossip about the drama professor's girl friend and what the philosophy professor said about the chances of making a living at it, she had lost the opportunity to be alone for a moment and have a drink. She listened to them argue and complain now and wiped her eyes, half laughing. "Oh, kids, what life would be without you . . ."

The synagogue parking lot was full and all the small streets of La Vie Wood were clogged with traffic. Nathan parked in Faigy Greenwald's driveway.

"They'll know our car," said Myra. "I can't walk too far. I don't feel so hot." She held out her hands. "I'm shaking! Isn't that ridiculous?" She laughed.

"Let's just get it over with, Ma," said Nathan. He pulled open her door.

Aaron helped her climb out of the crowded back seat. "Mom," he said quietly, "what can anybody say that will matter to us? It'll be all right."

Suzy Warmflash called from the street. "Myra! Kids! Wait up!" She hastened over to the Greenwalds' driveway. "Nice to have pull, isn't it?" she said. "Ordinary people have to walk from God knows where." She looked at the children. "Are you big!" she said. "What do you feed them, Myra?"

Nathan said, "We'll go ahead and get you a seat, Ma." He started away, the others following.

Etta hung back with Myra. "Mommy, should I walk with you?"

"I'll walk with her," said Suzy. "You want to be with young people. Go ahead." She took Myra's arm.

"Go ahead, Etta," said Myra.

Suzy patted Myra's hip. "How did you take that off? I'm dieting myself to death and she loses weight! Is that fair? Actually," she confided as they began walking to the synagogue, "I'm on a new diet. Is it wonderful! The whole idea is that it's expensive. You have to love yourself, especially when you're dieting. Am I walking too fast for you?" she said. "Because it actually gives you pep, energy, when you take it off this way. I eat lamb chops, lobster . . . I eat by myself, before Harry comes home. It's so expensive. But look at this," she said proudly. She held the waistband of her skirt away from her body. "And this old Chanel, I haven't been able to get into it for ages. And it's a shame, because she's a classic, you know, it's an investment."

Myra walked, looking at the ground. Her mind was vacant. "I haven't seen you in a while," she said.

"Myra," said Suzy, "we'll still be friends, won't we? Our talks, our nice times, I think of them fondly. Can we have lunch soon? I'll go off the diet," she offered.

Myra choked. "I . . ."

"I'm sorry we have to go through this," Suzy said quietly. "Look at me, Myra, before we go in." They stopped and faced each other several yards from the crowds at the synagogue entrance. Exhaust fumes were in the air. "Why not go in and tell Shoe to announce he's resigning? Give yourselves a break, Myra. It'll come to that anyway. Why let him prolong the agony? And we are still friends, Myra dear. Don't think you've been deserted."

"I do," choked Myra.

"Honey!" said Suzy. "Honey, everybody loves you and Shoe both." She laid the backs of her bony fingers with their many rings against Myra's cheek. "Go in and tell your husband what he's probably waiting to hear from you. That it's never too late to be smart and what does he need this for?" She pointed to the people struggling to enter the building. She knitted her brows. "I'm afraid for you, actually."

"If you're afraid, then stop it," said Myra hoarsely.

Suzy laughed, an open girlish laugh. "*I* can't! That's for Shoe to do. Will he spare us this ordeal or must we go through with it?"

"Go inside, Suzy," said Myra.

"I see. Well," she sighed, "we still have a lunch date, don't we?"

"Go inside."

22

Inside, in the quiet of the high-ceilinged white sanctuary, Bobby and Shoe sat together in a pew. "Sit tight, Rabbi," Bobby said tensely. "The sanctuary is more appropriate than the social hall. Let it be the place we already established for the meeting."

Sunny Winegarden put her smooth head into the room. "Better come in the social hall, Rabbi," she said pleasantly. "We can't very well start without you." She was violently thrust aside. Suzy Warmflash appeared in her place, legs shaking with anger.

She shouted, "Get out of there, you two! This is the sanctuary! You know what that means? A sanctuary?" Saliva flew off her protruding front teeth with each sibilant. "You know what that is? It's a holy place! Get out!"

Shoe and Bobby rose and walked deliberately toward Suzy. "Lady," said Bobby in a controlled voice, "this is a rabbi." He put his freckled hand on Shoe's sleeve. "Do you know how to address a rabbi?"

Suzy stared venomously at Shoe, her emaciated face shining with an inner light. Her silvery hair shook on her forehead. Looking straight at Shoe, she stood on her toes and slapped Bobby's face. She darted into the crowd in the social hall.

Shoe was stunned. He opened and closed his mouth. Bobby silently touched his cheek with his fingertips.

"Leave," said Shoe rapidly, finding his voice. "This isn't right. That slap was for me. I'll handle this alone now. I'm sorry. I'm terribly sorry."

"No way, Rabbi," said Bobby cheerfully. "Don't take it so hard. Now," he said with energy, "I better see what I can do to get some of those people out there inside. This can take all night." He strode to the outer doors where Mimi Seltzer, in all her obesity, consulted a great ledger one name at a time, challenging the people trying to come in. Kevin Nussbaum, white robes flapping about his dirty feet, marched steadily back and forth across the entrance, muttering to himself. Suzy Warmflash screamed at him, saliva flying, "Go demonstrate in Chicago, you Communist! This is New Saxony!"

Faigy Greenwald kissed Shoe. With brimming eyes, she said, "I've been on the phone for weeks. Rabbi, I say we've got a good chance!"

"Calm yourself, Faigy," he said. "We'll talk, we'll discuss . . . you'll see. We all have to live together after tonight."

Lena Bloom and Billy got out of their seats to shake Shoe's hand.

"I'm thinking of your father tonight," he told Billy softly.

"Nussbaum's out front," said Billy with disgust. "Did you see? The white dress? Creep. Madman. He was a lunatic even back in high school." Billy stared fiercely at the milling people in the aisles. "I hate these people."

"Billy," Shoe said. "Them is us."

They heard Milton's amplified voice. "Be seated, people. We have very important business tonight." Milton Winegarden rested on two cushions to make himself visible behind the microphone. He was flanked at a long table by Harry Warmflash and Irving Seltzer. A dozen men sat behind paper cups and pitchers of water, facing the rows of seats. Bobby and Norman Dorfman came up the center aisle with armloads of folding chairs. They quickly set up a new first row facing the table and gestured for Shoe to be seated with them.

Myra was pushed up to the front of the room. She pulled a chair out of the new front row and set it even further in front, putting herself between the men at the table and Shoe. She looked over her shoulder at him. "How are you?"

"Fine," answered Bobby. He pushed closer to Shoe. "Where are the kids?"

"I don't know," she said vaguely. "You know I persuaded him to get active?" she said with disbelief. She stared forward at Milton. He smiled broadly at her, teeth bright.

"You told me," Bobby said, looking through his briefcase.

"I thought it was wonderful," she said. "A man could overcome his handicaps and be a good, contributing person . . . But he can't," she said in a changed voice. "He's a dwarf," she said. "That's still all he is, inside and out."

"No philosophy tonight?" said Norman plaintively behind her.

Milton struck the table with his gavel. "Can we come to order?" There were shouts. "This seat is mine!" Chairs were dragged across the shining black tile floor. "Open a window!"

"Mr. Chairman," said Shoe, rising, "if I may suggest the sanctuary . . . It has better ventilation. It's already terribly hot in here and there are people here with heart conditions."

Harry Warmflash laughed. He leaned forward. "Look out for your own health." Milton gaveled.

"Who are these people?" whispered Norman.

Shoe kept his eyes on the table as he described them softly: "They represent different interests, I guess; the very old man is the president, a symbolic figure, really . . ."

"Uh-huh, the money." Norman nodded.

"That effeminate one, I can never recall his name," Shoe continued softly. "Winegarden you know; the lawyer, Warmflash; Seltzer, has some big business . . ."

"Big business ain't here," said Norman.

Shoe moved restlessly on his seat. "What's the difference? When should I speak? I want to get started. My kids are here."

"Hold on, we have a plan, you know," Bobby said acidly. He poked Myra's back with a pencil. "You helped make it too. We are going to invalidate this meeting, remember? And we have questions about who's here and who's being kept out." Bobby grinned. Mimi and Suzy were shouting at someone at the door. "Then there's the contract," he said with relish. "I chew them up and Norman gives the big speech. So we can't get carried away, none of us," he said, looking at Shoe. "Please be patient, Rabbi. You'll have your chance."

Milton pounded the table with his gavel. Women cheered.

Bobby jumped to his feet. "Doctor, I want it known"—he pointed to the side aisle—"I have a court reporter here."

At the table, the girlish man looked up. He indicated Shoe with his little finger. "Why is he here with lawyers?" he inquired of the air. "And, Mr. Etkind," he asked, "why are you making a record? Are you taking us to court?"

"We are making a record to have a record," Bobby said.

"Anyway," broke in Faigy Greenwald's husband, "he has a life contract. So that's the whole story."

Milton gaveled again. He had already taken off his jacket and was displaying the wet armpits of his shirt. "We will proceed."

"The rabbi must preside," said Bobby.

"At what?" asked the girlish man.

"At this meeting, idiot," said Norman in his booming voice.

"What then, your funeral?"

"The rabbi, who is leader, must preside," said Bobby.

Harry Warmflash took charge. He pulled the microphone by its cord over to his place. He glared at the front row. "Barnum and Bailey," he said, his voice rough and enlarged, "take this circus away."

"Yes!" screamed Mimi Seltzer. "No lawyer tricks!"

"Jeez," said Norman, effortlessly raising his voice. "This happened to me years ago," he said from his seat. "Right in the middle of my summation, somebody in the back of the courtroom gets up and hollers, 'Jew! Jew!' But Jeez," he said witheringly, "even I never looked to see it in a shul! What the hell is this, Warmflash?" He set his huge feet firmly to the shining black floor.

"This meeting is a nullity," interrupted Bobby in a formal voice. "The rabbi, as leader of this congregation, has not been allowed to preside." Shoe looked up at him expectantly from his seat. Bobby sat down and dove into his briefcase. "Nice," said Norman. Myra was bewildered.

"The chair will proceed," Milton said frostily. He pulled the microphone closer. He scowled. "You know, I never expected to be at this kind of a meeting," he said testily. "I thought we would focus on other matters once we put up our building. I thought we would be growing and putting all our energy into that. The town was growing; the churches were growing. I asked myself: Why not us?"

Lena Bloom's shy young neighbor spoke timidly. "Sharon Gitlin," she breathed. "Could you possibly stand on your chair, sir? We can't see you in the back."

"We made systematic inquiry," said Milton. "What was the trouble? And from every quarter came the same reply," he intoned. "The rabbi. His deficiencies have stunted us."

Norman laughed aloud. "Watch it, Dorfman," threatened the girlish man. "Or we'll have you thrown out."

"Oh, please don't hurt me!" cried Norman, pretending to cringe and wringing his hands. Bobby went red. "Sorry," muttered Norman.

"We decided to look into the rabbi's duties, one by one," said Milton. "I will have a speaker concerned with each of these duties, to describe the long history of the rabbi's resistance to the wishes of the congregation. The rabbi claims to have been surprised by our action. I will prove the untruth of this assertion. I will prove there has been dissatisfaction over a long period and that he knew it."

Greenwald stood. "The chair is supposed to be impartial, not be giving the arguments."

"I am impartial," replied Milton quickly. "The president," he indicated the half-dozing old man at the table, "has honored me by suggesting I chair this very important gathering. But I will have speakers for every point I will make in my report."

"You are making charges," said Greenwald. "It's not a report at all."

"Here," said Milton, promptly, heroically. He shoved his folder in front of Irving Seltzer. "I'll take myself out of it. This is an important report!"

"Good," said Irving. "I'm growing moss sitting here."

"This has nothing to do with personalities," insisted Greenwald. "You can't break a lifetime contract no matter how you dress it up."

In his comfortable way, Irving said, "I don't know of any meeting where you can't give a report." There was applause. "Don't you want to know what the meeting's about?" The applause grew. "And you don't have to holler and demand," he said, peering over his bifocals at Greenwald. "We'll also hear from the rabbi, as it's right. But so far, what have we heard except for lawyers shooting off their mouths and some personal remarks that didn't belong here at all, and I'm sorry about that, Rabbi," he said, looking in Shoe's direction. "Now let's get something done, eh?"

Mimi Seltzer screamed. She stood at the rear and almost howled. "It's boiling! It's late! We have to get up tomorrow! Let's just vote and go *home!*"

There was laughter and applause. Near Mimi, a man arose and appeared to speak quietly to his sleeve. "There are norms of discourse," he said, picking at a speck of tweed. "Madam," he said to Mimi. "There are environments where your disruptive behavior would be dealt with quite differently." Mimi turned away angrily.

"Can't control your wife, Seltzer?" remarked Harry, amused, at the table.

"Nope," Irving said calmly. "And when I want comment from you, I'll tell you."

"Tannenbaum," called the man near Mimi. "Colleague of Professor Winegarden at our college." Milton flared, then paled. "I'm in mental health," continued Tannenbaum. "Now," he said with authority, "you can't vote at all tonight. You must have adequate notice in advance of a meeting to hire or fire. That's our constitution. You didn't do it and you can't go to a vote tonight."

"We thank you, Dr. Tannenbaum," said Harry.

"So do we adjourn?" asked Faigy Greenwald's husband.

Harry laughed coldly. Myra looked behind her and saw several couples tiptoeing to the exits. Kevin Nussbaum, outside, marched on.

Old Isidore Le Bowitz rose in the center of the room. He rested his hands on his plaid wool hips. "There are too many attorneys and too many attorney types around here," he said mildly. "And I say that as an attorney. The less we deal with legalisms, the happier we'll all be. This is a synagogue!"

"Thank you, Iz," said Milton, gaveling.

"Wait awhile," said Le Bowitz. "I want to know why I haven't seen a copy of the rabbi's contract. For that matter, I never got a copy of this famous proposal to terminate. Am I expected to make a decision without these documents?"

"I'm going to have to rule you out of order, Iz," said Milton, uncomfortably.

"Wait awhile," said Le Bowitz, unmoved. "This is a synagogue, I say. We are all friends here. Yet where is common courtesy, I say? Where is reason?" He stared imperiously around the room.

"Appreciate your reminder, Iz," said Milton, perspiring. "Now, Irv. Please?"

"All right," said Irving. "We have permission to read you a letter tonight, to begin with." Bobby wrote furiously on his pad. "Such and such address, I'll skip all that . . ." His eyebrows rose. He adjusted his tie and touched his throat as he read to himself.

"Just for curiosity," said Norman carelessly, "what's the date? What's that?" Norman cupped his ear. "Hah, Seltzer? I don't hear so good. This letter is ten years old? Hah?"

"Yes," said Irving.

"I'm not sure we all could hear you," bellowed Norman. "Ten years old, this letter!" he shouted. Bobby made notes.

Irving read a sad letter of resignation from the synagogue. Mrs. Shapiro was sick. Mr. Shapiro was sick. They had needed surgery, both of them. Her mother died. The children broke their limbs at an unnatural rate. A tree fell on the house. "The rabbi's cavalier attitude," read Irving.

"Does she blame you?" Myra asked Shoe, incredulous. She twisted around to look at him. He shrugged. Possible, his shoulders said. He patted her back. "It will be all right," he whispered. "Soon I'll speak."

Her breath came short. She was filled with resentment. "Is this what we've been waiting to find out? That you kill people? Make them sick? That you throw down trees on their houses? Is this what I've been so afraid of?" Her voice was rising.

"Quiet," said Bobby sharply.

Irving's voice rose to the peroration. "The rabbi failed in those duties at the matrix—"

"If she wrote that, I'm Shakespeare," said Myra loudly.

"Shh," said Bobby, grasping her shoulder tightly. "I'm serious."

"Matrix," she repeated sullenly. "And I've been so scared . . ."

"Will the rabbi get a chance to respond?" demanded Greenwald.

"He'll answer, he'll respond," said Irving impatiently. "You think he wouldn't?" He felt angry without knowing why.

The men at the table fought each other to speak first. The microphone took on life, its black cord writhing and flipping along the table as the men there struggled for it. "This is a synagogue!" cried Isidore Le Bowitz vainly.

Ruby Feiner threw himself on the black cord. "Died," he said somberly. He choked the writhing microphone. "Where was he?"

"Our little problems," said Eugene Templeton through his teeth, "aren't all that serious." He fingered the small silver face of the microphone with rapid hands.

"Coma," said Ruby Feiner. He dried his eyes.

"And how do you think I feel," moaned Manny Ganz, "when the rabbi's daughter won't speak to me tonight, that I've known her all her life?"

The Rosenstock children drew closer together at this. They stirred their long limbs where they sat together on the floor and set their backs to the wall. "I did so speak to you!" shouted Etta, face flaming. "I told you to get away from me!"

Shoe struggled to rise. Bobby held him in his seat with rigid, powerful arms. "Bobby!" Shoe's eyes went bloodshot. "For God's sake! Let me at least protect my children!"

"Wait," ordered Bobby, face crimson.

Milton had taken back his report and was reading in high excitement. "And the rabbi must work," he read in a quivering voice, "to enhance our sense of Jewish self-worth."

"I don't need the man to enhance me, myself," cut in a heavyset man.

"Meyer Levy?" said Harry, squinting into the lights to see. "I rule you out of order."

"And where do you get the right to rule me anything?" said Levy, turning red. "Who made you a judge in Israel?"

Jackets were off and ties were torn open. The temperature rose further. Women stepped out of their shoes with swollen feet. A furtive, sheepish few slipped out to the parking lot and away. Milton looked anxiously around him. "Let us hear the rabbi!" roared Greenwald.

"Of course he'll say he loves us," retorted Ruby Feiner, his bronzed cheeks sunken. He squeezed the microphone. "I don't doubt it," he said indignantly. "Who would the rabbi be without us? We have fed him and clothed him, sent his children to fancy schools where people a lot richer don't send their children . . ."

"Bobby, for God's sake," said Shoe. Bobby held him fast.

"And how're you going to pay for this breach of a contract?" demanded Greenwald. "Not with my money, you won't!"

"There will not necessarily be a payment," Harry said coldly.

"Oh, I see," shouted Greenwald, enraged. "Cheat him and rob him too!"

"This is a synagogue, I say," Le Bowitz' voice rang out. "Mr. Chairman, let a reasonable man say something. Maybe we can learn something."

"Good point," said Milton. "Simmer down, everybody." He peered at a list before him. "I see Mr. Etkind signed up first to speak. Mr. Etkind?"

"I will reserve my comments," Bobby said. Shoe ground his teeth.

"No sir, Mr. Etkind," said Milton joyously. "If you don't speak now, you'll have no rights."

"Please, sir," said Bobby icily, "some semblance of due process."

Harry lay a restraining hand on Milton's arm. "You've got it, Mr. Etkind," he said.

Milton nodded to a small, curly-headed man in the crowd. "Then I'm going to call on our good friend, there, Fritz." The man rose and limped forward slowly to the table. "I know we do not agree," Milton went on. "But I honor him and revere him, and I want him to have his opportunity so that we may all work together in the future in amity." Milton all but bowed as Fritz pivoted about in front of the table to address the crowd.

"Ah, money," sighed Norman. He looked at Myra with a resigned smile.

"I am what is now known as a Holocaust survivor," said the small man gently. "My name is Fritz Newman. I wasn't born Newman—that's what I became." He paused. The hall was becoming relatively quiet. "I jumped off a death train and ran on my broken legs into the forest to hide. I was fourteen and I said to myself: if I live, I go to America and I become Newman." He smiled. "God was good to me." Shoe gazed at him somberly. Myra leaned forward to hear better.

"The rabbi is second to no other human being I have ever met," Fritz said. "Without his help . . ." He broke off and wiped his eyes. "And I am not the only one. So many have told me their stories."

People were sighing and looking at the wall clocks. They fanned themselves with newspapers. Milton had opened his folder and was reading to himself. His lips moved and he scratched absentmindedly between his fingers. Harry Warmflash took notes. One of the men at the table combed his hair.

"Yet the minute of his departure for his well-deserved sabbatical, his lifetime contract was on everyone's mind. They wanted him home, you see. They felt rejected. They begrudged him his leave, not because he had failed to perform his duties, as we are going to be told"—Fritz glanced behind him for an instant at Milton—"but because they didn't know how to do without him, how to shepherd along their families. A personal vendetta began. I'm sorry to say this . . ." He turned to the men behind him.

"No, go right ahead," said Milton. He waved his small strong hand. "This is a free country."

"Good," Fritz said. He faced the crowd once more. "I object to this termination proposal and here is why. He was a founder. He has a lifetime contract and we must honor it. And he wasn't even here! I sit on the Board and I, myself, cannot tell you how we moved from a budget discussion to somehow, suddenly, firing him!"

Fritz became agitated. "Undermining him! Calling on this one to tell him that one's complaints! Making him a scapegoat for everybody's troubles! This synagogue will be destroyed if we break this sacred lifetime contract. We will be split apart. Vote down this proposal! We must again be united under the fine leadership of Rabbi Joshua Rosenstock! I thank you." Fritz limped away from the table to loud applause.

"Thank God," said Myra.

"Fine," said Milton, holding the microphone. "Now as to my report and my speakers—"

The microphone slid away from him, apparently of itself. Manny Ganz rose at the end of the table, mopping his withered face unhappily. "Excuse me, Doctor," he said. "But I just couldn't . . ." He wiped his upper lip. "A scapegoat of our rabbi? God forbid," stated Ganz. "We have problems, very true. With our health, with our children . . . So is this the rabbi's fault? Did anybody ever say that? God forbid!"

Milton broke in. "Manny, I know you have a laden heart. And I assure you, you will have your chance. But there is my report which takes precedence, so that the congregation may know—"

Once again the microphone moved along the table on its own, its dark cord undulating like a snake. Milton rubbed at his neck in frustration. "Templeton," announced the man who captured it. His voice faded in and out as he moved his sleek, closely barbered head. "Destroyed?" he said between his small teeth. "People who say we might be closing down if we fire the rabbi? These are timid, frightened people. Let 'em go! This lifeboat is small. I know all about survival, it's my business. In fact," Templeton said, baring his teeth, "I've even given the rabbi some financial advice. I charge for this, I told him, but I won't charge you. And he's done pretty well."

There was shocked, scattered laughter in the hall. Myra hung her head. "How dare you?" erupted Faigy Greenwald's husband.

Milton gaveled.

"I do dare," said Templeton. He lounged in his chair. "We'll survive. Without him."

"I appeal to the chair," shouted Greenwald.

Milton gaveled. Templeton sat up. "Greenwald, I have built this room you're sitting in tonight." He smirked. "I'll give over this mike right now to the guy who gave more."

Milton gaveled and reached for the microphone. It was snatched away. "I haven't been called on, so I'll hurry," said a young man in a striped T-shirt. He laughed impudently at Milton. Myra and Shoe watched dully, confused. "How can this place survive?" asked the young man. He held the microphone close to him. He gestured to an impassive Templeton, leaning back and picking at his cuticles. "He gave this room? Well, I'm also in the investment business and I'm not impressed."

There was a burst of appreciative laughter. People nudged each other and repeated what the young man had just said. "And this big money he gave, it's tax-deductible, so it only cost him something like half," said the young man. There was applause. "All right, how *can* this place survive?" asked the young man briskly. "The gentleman from Germany is certainly leaving if the rabbi goes. Wasn't that your impression, ladies and gentlemen? And maybe he's got a lot more to give away than our friend, Templeton, here. I wouldn't be all that surprised." He grinned.

"Or say our man, Templeton, stays only if the rabbi's kicked out." He laughed. "They won't both stay. Because our man, Templeton, he doesn't like to be overlooked. He's not used to it. Either way, folks," the young man smiled complacently, "you'll go broke. You need everybody. You might as well give up and sell to a church tonight." He turned with disdain to the table. "None of you big planners could figure that out?" He chuckled and patted the microphone cord. "What a pathetic bunch. I resign." There were cheers and prolonged applause. Someone rang a cowbell.

"What is happening?" said Myra aloud. Lena Bloom reached forward and patted her hand. "I told them people would just resign," said Shoe. "Wait," warned Bobby.

Old Isidore Le Bowitz stood. Milton gaveled. Le Bowitz stood calmly, waiting to be heard. "This is a synagogue," he said strongly. "Shame on you all! A little seriousness! A little respect, if you please!"

"And we're talking about the welfare of an entire family," said Faigy Greenwald, agitatedly approaching the table. "Oh, Irving! Why are you on that side of the table?"

"I don't endorse every jackass up here," he replied, flushing. "But I still do believe that the congregation has the right to do as it wishes."

"Oh, Irving, you didn't used to be a fool," Faigy said, weeping nervously. "Your friends there will be laughing at you soon enough."

"They're not my friends," said Irving huffily. "This is community service."

"This is breaching a contract!" shouted Greenwald, beside himself. "How can I make you understand?"

"Everyone who wants to speak will get the chance," said Milton in the uproar. His shirt stuck to his fiery back.

Ruby Feiner struck the table with a trembling forefinger. "We all know how we feel," he said. "Let's end this comedy and vote."

"But friends, this is not a beauty contest," thrust in old Isidore Le Bowitz. He came up to the table and handled the microphone easily. "This is a synagogue, I say. This is not the way, friends—shouting and cursing and charges that are absurdities. I'm older than most of you. I know. I was living here when the rest of you were still sitting on the great West Side or worse," he said haughtily. "And I'm a founder. And I'm afraid we'll close this synagogue I helped to found if we vote, no matter which way it goes. Thank you very much, I'm an old man; I don't want that distinction. There's no emergency," he said, persuasively. "We've lived twenty years with our rabbi; we can live a little longer with him. Table, I say. Table this resolution. We'll investigate properly, I say, and then we'll go to some form of conciliation. This is a synagogue!"

"I'll second Mr. Le Bowitz' motion," called Lena Bloom.

"There is no motion on the floor," said Harry.

"I make a motion, then," Lena said earnestly. "I move to table this proposal." Billy looked up at her strained face.

"Hold on now," said a female baritone. "I see no reason we can't hold a meeting and take a vote if we see fit. We're adults."

"Your name?" asked Bobby, looking around.

"I'm the mother of your fellow member, Mrs. Suzy Warmflash," answered a trim, blue-haired woman. "You younger people better realize you're not that young anymore." She swung her intricate earrings. "You must run your synagogue."

"I'll be damned," said a shocked Greenwald. "Members were locked out and she gets in!"

"Honor thy father and mother," snapped Suzy. "Don't you know the Jewish religion?"

Harry pinned his wife with a cold eye. "Milton," he ordered, "assert yourself."

Milton gaveled, a pained look on his face. "People, this is an amendment we're discussing . . ."

"No, no, no," Harry said, deeply annoyed. "We are going to vote on whether to table. I better explain." He inhaled. "Ladies and gentlemen, if you vote to table this resolution, if the resolution to terminate the rabbi goes down on the table, we will then proceed to frame another one. So if you vote to table, understand that."

"But that doesn't make sense," said Lena Bloom. She got to her feet. "I moved to table because I want to drop the subject for the time being, as Mr. Le Bowitz suggested, and go to a better way of resolving this issue."

"Hear, hear!" cried Le Bowitz.

"We can go on discussing this proposal," said Harry without emphasis. "Or we can frame a new one. It's entirely up to you."

Shoe was breathing heavily. Myra hung her head.

"This is a mockery of us all," said Lena solemnly. "I will not participate."

"Thank you," said Milton. "Next speaker."

Billy Bloom burst out, "You people suck! Who wants to belong to a place where you belong? Do you people know what the rabbi did for my father? Do you?" Billy rushed out to the vestibule to hide his tears. His mother sat back and closed her eyes. Myra put her face in her hands. As though a strong wind blew through a dry cornfield, people were moved to get up as Milton called after Billy vainly. "I'm sure you have the condolences of the entire congregation," Milton called after him. "I'm sure I speak for all of us." The people moved about; they stumbled restlessly in the hot hall. A group of women ran to the kitchen to cry; a ring of men to squat and confer behind the glass showcase filled with silver. The congregation palavered in the hallways, the men's room, near the children's stage.

Manny Ganz grabbed for the microphone. "I don't want there to be bad feelings here!" he cried. "Don't think we decided on this lightly! I haven't slept or eaten," he moaned. "I don't think there's been a normal bowel movement on the whole Board in months!"

Old Le Bowitz stood with effort. "Mr. Ganz," he said softly, "I beg of you. This is a synagogue. And Mr. Warmflash, sir," he said wearily, "you have given the entire legal profession a black eye." Milton gaveled. Le Bowitz failed to react. "I thought this was a synagogue," he said. "I thought I was at a congregational meeting." Milton gaveled. Le Bowitz went right on. "I want respect, reason, law. I'm ashamed to tell you," he said rhetorically. "When I was young, I was ashamed of my grandfather—my zayde, if you know that word. His shul was a filthy little storefront with spittoons . . ." He looked about the disorderly social hall. "Uncivilized, I said." He shook his head in self-reproach. "The old fellows'd swing a chicken in the air . . . with all their sins on the chicken's head . . ." Le Bowitz ran his arthritic hand through his thick white hair. "Uncivilized?" He drew himself up. He laughed angrily. "This! This is uncivilized. You're like a lynch mob. You've got a kangaroo court going here. This is a Soviet show trial. And you're not satisfied with a chicken; you want a human sacrifice." He stared in great weariness at the men at the table. They returned his gaze quite stolidly. "You ought to be ashamed of yourselves, you men, but I don't know if you're developed enough to have a sense of shame. I resign. With regret. But there's no option." He pulled his old wife to her feet and led her to the doors. He turned back to the table. "I only regret I didn't wake up sooner."

Manny Ganz spoke shakily. "People, I will still love you if you vote for the rabbi. It happens to be the kind of person I am."

Shoe began to rise, breathing hard, smoothing his tie, composing himself to speak.

"I call the question," said the girlish man at the table hurriedly. "Let's vote."

"Now I will speak in the rabbi's behalf," Bobby said firmly, standing next to Shoe and gripping his arm.

"Let us hear the rabbi," insisted Greenwald.

"Rabbi," said Milton, half off his cushions, body on fire, "would you like to avail yourself?"

Shoe looked at his lawyers. Bobby tightened his grip.

"I'm trying to be patient," called Milton.

"Wait!" cried Faigy. "A man's life is at stake!"

"We're going to a vote," said Milton crisply.

"The rabbi," persisted Greenwald.

"I'm ready," said Shoe.

"No," said Bobby harshly. "There's nothing to be gained. Don't dignify these proceedings. You'll have your day in court."

"Norman?" asked Shoe, turning to him.

"I don't see how you can harm yourself," Norman said soberly. "It won't help. We'll have to see them in court."

"That's all right," said Shoe. "I'll speak."

Myra sat erect, hands in her lap, numb as though she sat in a hailstorm. She clenched her hands, gritted her teeth. The original Meyer Levy's cornfield had not been more exposed, more without shelter. Shoe said, "I'll speak," and her numbness vanished. She was in terror. "Don't, Shoe, don't. Don't!"

His face went wooden. He flicked her shoulder with his fingers. "Then let's go. If I can't speak, I'm leaving." He started away by himself down the littered aisle.

"Wait!" she said. "Don't you want to see how it comes out?"

Bobby drove his pencil hard into her back. "Go with him."

"Go, Mrs. Rosenstock," said Norman. "They got no case, but we lost," he said kindly. He sat back and put his enormous hand over his eyes.

23

Billy Bloom was crying in the vestibule. He struggled to pry a brass nameplate off the bronze founder's plaque on the wall. "It's my father's name," he sniffled as he worked. His fingers bled. "My father doesn't want to be here."

"Billy . . ." Shoe said helplessly.

Kevin Nussbaum sat in the doorway, still keeping his vigil. He held a rosary on his thigh.

"Akiva," said Shoe. "Put away the rosary. The outfit I can take but put away the rosary," he said wearily.

People came out to the Rosenstocks, swirled around them, kissed them, cried, tried to take Shoe's hand. He stepped away to the long dark driveway. Myra hurried after him. "Can I take your arm?" she said. "I feel funny, like my head is miles from my feet."

"Did you ever eat today?" he said angrily. Cars were passing them in a patient line, stopping at the stone menorah at the head of the drive, then leaving.

"I must have," she said.

The children sat perched like birds on the car in Faigy Greenwald's driveway. "Just get in," she said. "Don't say a word. Let's just go home." She got in under the wheel. Shoe pushed in under the wheel as though she were invisible. She said nothing, slid over next to Etta, who got on her sister's lap.

They drove the dark way in silence. Shoe braked at a stop sign and fell into thought. "I should have spoken," he said. "I shouldn't have listened to you."

"You can go now," she said. "No cars coming."

"Why did I listen to you?" he said, voice rising. "My friends wanted to hear me. I owe it to them."

"Dad," said Nathan from the back, "there's somebody behind us. You have to move."

"I'm half tempted to go back now and tell them," said Shoe.

"So go ahead," said Myra. "I only told you what I think. Go ahead if you want to dance like a bear for these unspeakable . . ." She choked.

"You ganged up on me," he said wonderingly. "Why did I listen to you?" He put the car in gear and moved toward home. They saw lights in the house.

Myra said, "Oh, Lord, who's here already? Didn't they stay to vote?"

"What's the difference, Myra?" Shoe parked.

"Daddy," Etta said in a frightened voice. She put her elbow in Myra's chest and placed her cheek next to her father's. "Daddy, I'm sorry. I'm so sorry, Daddy. I flunked French."

"Oh! You baby!" her sister said viciously. She threw open the door. "Get out of this car!"

"Jesus, Etta," said Nathan.

"It couldn't have waited?" asked Myra.

"That's all right, baby," said Shoe. "I flunked too. You all saw Daddy flunk tonight, right in front of everybody. It's all right. Nothing is forever." He kissed her ear. "Now go in and put the dog in your room. I don't want him jumping on the company."

Joey stood in the dark backyard. "Mom? Dad?" he said. His voice was uncertain. "I got away early . . ." The family was getting out of the car slowly, brokenly. "Dad?" His voice wavered.

Shoe came up to him. "I'm glad you came, son." He embraced him. "Mommy needs you." He let go and walked to the back door alone.

"Mom?" said Joey.

"Go in," she said in an old woman's voice. "You'll talk to Daddy tomorrow. Don't ask him anything now." She went past him without touching him. Joey stood bewildered.

"I'll tell you what happened," said Nathan.

"What'll you say?" demanded Etta hysterically. "What, counselor, that justice was done?" She threw herself at her oldest brother. "I flunked, Joey," she cried. "Oh, Joey, I'm so sorry!"

Tears appeared on Joey's fair, stubbled cheeks. "They did it, then," he said.

"I don't care," said Aaron. "I don't care at all." He kicked a flowerpot across the yard, then seized his toes in pain.

The dining room was crowded. Fritz Newman was there, having run all the stop signs and traffic lights to be there before the Rosenstocks. Faigy Greenwald had brought wine and put it on the table.

"Friends," called Fritz. He raised a plastic glass. "Friends, I propose a toast." Everyone gathered at the table. "Long life, good health, love and friendship for our rabbi," he said.

"L'chayim," said Shoe. "Thank you, Fritz." The Rosenstock children slipped away. Shoe set his glass down and went alone into the living room. He sat in the armchair in the dark.

Fritz followed him, limping rapidly. He bent over the chair and put on the lamp. "I'll tell you something, Rabbi," he said. "I'll give you advice like you would give to me." Shoe looked up at him. "Don't do anything you'll regret later. Give yourself time to think. And remember how many friends you've got."

"You put me to shame," said Shoe. "I'll be all right."

"We go home," said Fritz. "I have to be early to work tomorrow." He limped back to Myra in the bright dining room. "Take care of him, will you?" He held her hand.

"I guess I will," she said resentfully. "Why should this night be different from all other nights?"

"We call you tomorrow," he said.

"Fritz," she said, "you're so wise, maybe you'll tell me why I am so ugly to my friends? Forgive me."

"You know what I think? Perhaps we will be the better for this. Good night, rebbitsin, we love you."

Bobby and his wife arrived, flushed and voluble, colliding with Fritz. Bobby looked around for Shoe. "I gave him the papers tonight," he boomed into the living room. "The midget. After you left.

We'll see them in court." He turned to Myra. "I'll have a drink. Not wine."

"You had papers ready?" asked Myra. "You knew?"

"Myra, you must tell me where you got these cute paper napkins," said Faigy, surveying the table. "Don't the children look terrific? I can't believe how grown up they are. And I want to see your snapshots from Israel," she sped on. "Oh, Myra, Myra, I'm so miserable!" Tears stood in her eyes.

"Have a drink," said Myra, moving away from her. "Have a drink."

"Now listen, Mrs. Rosenstock," said Dr. Tannenbaum, waving his glass. "Don't get lost in fantasies of revenge. Don't you and the rabbi start plotting. Turn the page and look to the future."

"You're right," Myra said.

"What I don't see," said Tannenbaum to the others, "is how the rabbi ever did get anything accomplished with that gang around his neck."

"And look how, for a thing like this, they could work together," sniffed Faigy Greenwald. "What do you make of it? Winegarden's such an attractive person? Such a natural leader?"

Tannenbaum emptied his glass and shuddered. "What a bunch of defectives at that table tonight. Their parents rejected them and they were right!" He filled his glass again. "At the college, we have *some* control over that dwarf Winegarden. Here, he runs amok. I'll get him if it's the last thing I ever do," he said. "I swear it."

"He's a fairy," said Meyer Levy. He had just come in, unable to remain at home. He helped himself to wine in the silence that followed. "He's got drives we don't understand. I say he wants to bring in the boyfriend, that little faggot rabbi we had all year."

There was deep silence. Norman Dorfman said, "Granting that what you say may be the case, Levy, it's not the explanation. We all know these people, Doctor," he said to Tannenbaum. "Don't you remember from when you were a kid, there's always one kid that's only happy when he makes somebody cry?" He sipped at his glass of water. "We grow up and they run the shul." He looked gloomy. "Oh, the poor rabbi."

"Goddamnit," said Tannenbaum. "Why does any man want to be a rabbi anyway?" He looked angrily at Myra.

"I don't know," she said. "He seems to want it, though." She looked around for a cigarette. She was tired and kept on talking only because she was already talking. "You're the experts," she said to Tannenbaum without much interest. "You psychiatrists. Why does a man want to be a rabbi?"

"Beats me," he said. He shook his head. "It would make an interesting study."

Shoe came into the room. "Did you ever hear the one," he said, "about the rabbi who got sick? And his Board voted to wish him a speedy recovery, ten to eight?" He laughed strangely. Myra laughed to cover his laugh. "Did you ever hear the one about the rabbi, he's begging in the street, he's destitute, and they ask him, 'Why do you insist on being a rabbi?' 'For the honor,' he says." He laughed again. "I got a million of 'em. A million." He went back to the living room alone.

"I think," said Tannenbaum after a moment, "I'm going to get some oily rags and lay them around the foundation of that place. I'll burn that goddamn building to the ground, goddamnit!"

"Good," said Meyer Levy. "Me and my cousins never gave that land so Winegarden could be a little king. Burn it down and we'll pick up the land from the bank for a song. What do you say?" He looked around the table. "There's room on that property for a dozen, fifteen homes. We'll build quality homes, not drek. We'll cut the rabbi in on it so he'll have something for all his work. What do you say?"

The silence was absolute. Myra drank wine, lit a cigarette. "Oh, Meyer," Faigy Greenwald finally said.

"He wants to build his temple," said Norman Dorfman quietly, returning from deep concentration. "That's why he wants to be a rabbi, Tannenbaum," he said solemnly. "To build his temple." He looked at his shoes.

"He already built it," Faigy said. "What do you mean?"

Blushing, the gruff Norman said, "Don't be obtuse, Faigy. He wants to build his temple." He pointed upward. "For all of us; for the Jewish people." He looked mortified.

"Oh, Norman, you're so sweet," said his wife. She touched his burning face.

"Well," said Faigy. She took a deep breath. "Right now, we have to help Myra put her kitchen in order. I'm not leaving you to clear up after us," she said, overriding Myra's protest. She went into the kitchen. "What?" she cried, so that everyone in the dining room fell silent. "What? Who left this mess? This is incredible! Myra, get your children in here this minute or I'm going upstairs after them!"

"Help me, Bobby," said Myra softly. She sank against a chair by the wall. "Shut her up or I'll slap her." She pushed the hair off her forehead.

"Come on, everybody!" shouted Bobby instantly. "Let's go home! Let these people get some rest!" He threw sweaters and jackets around the dining room. "Faigy, get out of there! They have to go to sleep!" He went to Shoe in the living room. "Good night, Rabbi," he said, clapping him on the shoulder. "I have to be at the airport first thing in the morning. Should have been in California today."

"My dear friend," Shoe began.

"How can we thank you?" Myra interrupted. "Bobby, when I think how we really didn't even know you before this happened . . ."

"No, no, no, you two!" He laughed. He was exhilarated. "We'll see them in court. We have a lot of preparation to do. Don't try to get rid of me yet! Come on, everybody," he yelled. "Let's go. Go home!"

The Rosenstocks were left alone. The lights glared. The house reeked of wine and smoke. "Let's go up," he said. "Enough."

"Go ahead, Shoe," she said. "I'll just clear away a little." She badly wanted to be alone.

"The dog, the dog," he said. He pointed beneath the table. She saw the dog hunched forward, vomiting on the floor. "My God, will this day never end?" he said in despair.

"I'll take care of it," she said. "He must have gotten into the garbage. Go up. I'll clean it up."

She stroked the dog's back as he lay panting on the floor. She knelt next to him, soothing him as she wiped the floor with a pile of paper napkins. "It's been a long day for the poor doggy, hasn't it?" she purred. "The poor doggy is upset too. Don't worry, Mommy will clean it all up." The dog thumped his tail on the floor and drooled. "My poor dog."

Shoe came down the stairs. "Etta's in our bed," he said. It

sounded like the saddest story in the world. "She's fast asleep. I didn't have the heart to wake her. I'll lie down on the couch." He was pale. His eyes were sunken.

"Yes, go ahead," she said.

He lay down on the faded sofa in all his clothes and began to snore immediately. The yellow lamplight poured into his open mouth.

Myra put out the lights in the kitchen and dining room. She took the seat cushion off the armchair and put it on the floor next to Shoe's head. She stepped out of her sandals and pulled off her panty hose. She switched off the lamp and lay on the floor alongside Shoe. "Here, doggy," she called softly. The dog came slowly to her, his mouth stuffed with her panty hose. She patted the floor. "Come here, poor boy." She touched his head. "Poor boy, he'll feel better. Mommy and Daddy will take care of their doggy. They always do." The dog slumped next to her, groaning. She held his silky ear in her hand. "Now let's guard Daddy."

A forgotten burner in the kitchen glowed red as they slept. The crackers grew limp on the table. Half-empty glasses stood on the mantel. The moon came in the window, white, dispassionate; and flowed over them like cream, like an ointment.

My dear brother,

Just a note to let you know that I was, indeed, in attendance at your synagogue last night for the congregational meeting. But I couldn't get in. The people at the door were wild. I wore my collar so there would be no question of my voting. I explained that I wished to be there to witness to your good works in the community, nothing more. But I was turned away. I went back to the end of the line they had established and waited till I reached the front. It was like the old days in Alabama when we were training ourselves in non-violent confrontation. I went back in line three times but when I was denied the third time the trinitarian aspects of the situation became clear to me and I left. May they be forgiven their shortcomings.

Call me, brother, when you feel up to it, and we'll have a drink. You have a great future before you, I know it in my soul. We'll think about it together.

In Christ,
Winn

Dear Joshua,

It's always good a letter from you. Momma and I looked forward to a visit when you came home from Israel, but what can you do? You'll come when you can. What the goyim do to us, we can stand it. They don't know no better. They eat meat with the blood in it and it makes them like that. But another Jew, he can give you a stab right where it kills you. That's what it means it's hard to be a Jew.

You got a beautiful family, let them live and be well, and you got Myra, one in a million, and you still, thanks God, got a Momma and a Poppa with a thousand dollars put away which we don't need it, it's yours. From here it'll be a hill up climb, but so what, what are we born for? We live, we struggle, we pull and drag our pekl, and we bless God we're here and it's no worse than it is. If you'll look around and see what the next one is carrying, you won't exchange your troubles for his. What you're having is an old story with the Jewish people, I'm sorry to say. From the time of Moses. They don't like to be told. They don't want to look up to anybody. Each one wants to be the king. Good luck to them. Who knows what we'll have to go through in times to come? We'll all need each other again, God forbid. Meanwhile, kiss the family and write soon.

                                                                       Poppa

Dear Rabbi,

I feel just terrible about what happened. I grew up in an Italian neighborhood and the other kids used to run after me and call me Christ killer. It never bothered me. I would tell them—you know me. You know my mother and father. Would we hurt anybody? But after the congregational meeting, I said to my kids, "You know what? Maybe we did kill Christ."

What a disgusting experience. They told me I was out of order, remember? Was that an orderly meeting? They told me I was hysterical. That was true. I'm a very hysterical woman when such things are going on. But there was no way to deal with those animals. I feel very helpless. Just know that we love you.

Faigy Greenwald and family

Dear Rabbi ~~Rosenman~~ Rosenstock,

The placement office is in receipt of your vita. Thank you. The boss asks me to remind you that no one of your age has been able to make an upward move, or even a lateral one, in the last five years. However, there are openings in New Zealand, and in two congregations in Australia as well as a part-time position in Curaçao. We are taking the liberty of forwarding your vita to them without waiting for your permission in writing since you must be anxious to make plans. Keep in touch with the office.

> Faithfully,
> Joy Geduldig
> (for Rabbi Samyonov)

24

The summer ground forward like a machine, mowing down one day at a time. The Rosenstocks' lawn yellowed as they waited for their day in court. The bolts and screws in the old redwood picnic set loosened and came out. The table and benches became a pile of kindling.

Etta was in summer school taking French for the second time. Joey had a good job, a salary that satisfied him, in the emergency room. He agreed to suspend the idea of leaving medical school. Postcards arrived from the other children from the summer camps where they labored, teaching basketball, Hebrew, jazz dancing. The Greenwalds went on vacation to the Upper Peninsula. Lena Bloom took Billy on a visit around the country to relatives, leaving all their addresses and her schedule with Myra. Myra secretly read want ads for mature women who were needed to address envelopes at home or who could sell by telephone.

Shoe collected sworn statements, unearthed old letters and synagogue bulletins to prove his performance in the past, spoke daily to Bobby in preparation for the hearing. He had moved his things out of the synagogue on a lonely, brutally hot day and said good-by to Matthew, the custodian, who hung about pretending to be busy with work of his own, trying to help. The front hall of the house was stacked with cartons of books and papers that neither Shoe nor Myra knew where to put. Brushing off a cloud of dog hair from the top box one day, Shoe had pushed open the flap and there—there was the life contract he had never been able to find for Bobby. He called Myra into the hall. "Look," he said.

"Don't show it to me," she said angrily. "Throw it away."

He laughed at her. "No, I'll give it to Bobby for his scrapbook."

The summer wore on. A fresh breeze with a touch of fall in it came into the room one morning, waking Myra. It ruffled the dog's fur as he slept at the foot of the bed. The dust on the windows gave a diffused brightness to the room that Myra enjoyed. She lay still awhile. It was very early. Then she rolled over and hung her body over Shoe's. She touched her nipples to his crinkled eyelids and laughed softly.

"Good morning!"

Without opening his eyes, keeping the rest of his body quite still, he raised his hands to her breasts and licked his lips.

"Time to get up," she said, laughing. She backed out of the bed. "Rise and shine!" She went into the bathroom.

Shoe stumbled in, tripping over the dog. "Do we have to get up?" he asked. "Can't you spare me a few minutes, lady?"

"Take your shower," she said. "It's late. I'm all dressed." She was nude. "I haven't got time."

"Must be tough, leading such a busy life," he said sleepily. He pushed open the shower curtain, threw down the stockings drying on the rod, knocked over an open bottle of shampoo, and stepped into the shower stall.

"Am I your personal servant?" she said.

"Uh-huh," he said. He stuck his head out of the shower. "I have you sexually enslaved. You're helpless."

She laughed and went to the kitchen. She looked in the refrigerator: half a moldy cantaloupe. The dog wagged his tail. "You I can feed," she said, petting him. She started the percolator. Shoe came in, hair dripping.

"I forgot I didn't go shopping," she said. "We could go to a diner."

"Let's just take the coffee outside," he said. "What a great day out there."

They pushed two broken chairs against the sunny wall of the

house. "Oh, lovely," she said. She tipped her face to the sunshine. "Honey, how long is life? Let's enjoy what we've got."

"Did something happen I don't know about?" He looked at her.

"No." She sipped the coffee. "I just woke up and looked at the sunshine. Here's this glorious, glorious, glorious day and we're alive for it." She lifted her arms to the sun. "We still have a life contract, honey, from God. Milton Winegarden doesn't know a thing about it." She looked around the scattered yard. "I want to cook today and polish up the house. You go out and buy us a flat of petunias to plant out here."

Shoe got up. "You're not as dumb as you look, lady," he said. He stooped to kiss her lips. The dog jumped between them, licking both their faces. "My rival," he said, scratching the dog's head. "I'll go get the paper before he tears it up. Then I shall return to you," he said grandly. "My wanton . . ." The dog jumped between them again. Myra laughed and stretched out on the dry, warm grass. Shoe went around the corner of the house. He returned and handed her part of the paper.

"Do I have the obituaries?" she asked, squinting at him in the bright light.

"Yes," he said. He sat down again on the broken chair. "Please, just read it to yourself. Leave me out of it."

"Why?" she said, laughing at his uncomfortable expression. "You know very well I'm not killing anybody. I'm just keeping up."

He hid his face behind the paper.

"I'm not bringing it about," she persisted. "I refuse to be ashamed."

"You ought to be ashamed," he said, pulling the paper around his face. "Don't tell me about it."

"Shoe, Shoe," she said, sitting up suddenly. "Shoe! Gabe Becker!"

"What?" he said, shocked. "But we just talked! Remember, when I called him about the Nussbaum kid? It wasn't very long ago."

"He died last week," said Myra, reading. "This is an announcement. Funeral's over, everything."

"Maybe he had cancer," said Shoe. "Oh, poor guy. He *told* me he was going to the hospital. I should have *understood*." He pulled at his light hair. They both rose.

"I'll call her right now," said Myra. "I'll tell her you'll come to see her. I'll see if there's anything I can do."

Shoe followed her inside, the dog close behind him. Shoe put his arm around her as she stood, stricken, by the phone.

"I'm going to get you the petunias." His voice trembled. "Whatever happens next, first I'm buying you your flowers." They embraced in silence. "Go ahead, call her," he said.

25

Before she called Gabe Becker's wife, Myra prepared. She set out an ashtray and a pack of cigarettes near the sink. She took out a bottle of scotch and a paper cup and put them near the cigarettes. She checked the water in the dog's dish and went to the bathroom. In the bathroom mirror she inspected her lined face. Finally she went to the phone and called Rose Becker to offer her condolences.

Rose Becker asked, "Do you need money?"

"What a world," said Myra, pouring herself a drink. "Look how I call you to give you my sympathy and you offer me some of your widow's mite instead. People are so different, Rose. You have no idea." She ran water into the sink and began to scour it. "Listen, how are you doing? That's why I called. I want to know how you are and if I can do something for you."

Rose sighed noisily. "The pain is severe but I can fight it. What's so sad is that Gabe didn't have the strength. The pain was too much. He wasn't strong enough to face life. He couldn't focus on the beauty and draw from that."

"Rose," said Myra doubtfully, "could Shoe have helped? Did you know it was so bad? I wish you had called us."

"How could I call you? I couldn't add to your burdens. When Gabe talked to Shoe, it was one of the last things he found the strength to do. He wanted to help. And we had just visited a new doctor, as a matter of fact. He gave us a little hope, at least I thought so. Outlined a course of medication and some other therapies I won't go into. It wasn't good news but there was a basis for hope."

"And?" Myra dried her hands and sat down on a step stool. She reached up to the counter for a cigarette.

"And I was driving him home, we weren't saying much, he was very weak and tired, when he got out at a light by the park and walked away. That was the last I saw him alive."

"Oh," said Myra. "Oh, Rose . . ." She poured more scotch into her paper cup.

"When the police called me, I already knew," said Rose. "Myra, it wouldn't have made any difference if I had watched him every second. He would have found a way. That's depression. He wanted to stop living."

"Oh," breathed Myra. "Poor thing . . ."

"Yes, a lot of people say that. I don't know . . . Gabe never shared his feelings much with others. Only I was elected for that."

"And I thought it was a disease. . . ."

"It was," said Rose. "Depression is a disease."

"Oh, Rosie," said Myra all at once. "Oh, Rose, living with a man who doesn't want to live—what heavy work! I see you did your best, for years and years, probably," she said with authority. "And nobody realized what you had to do. Now you're entitled to a rest. Oh yes, absolutely," she said. "You're going to live for yourself now. Absolutely entitled, oh yes," she said. She swallowed the burning scotch. "People do not realize."

"You're very sweet to call me," said Rose, touched. "I'm going to try. I hope I can do it," she said shakily. "I don't sleep. Nightmares I wouldn't even want to describe. I've got this bronchial thing . . . I think he wants me," she said darkly. "Maybe he didn't want me in life, but he sure wants me now."

There was a brief silence between the women.

"Rose," said Myra sternly, "no melodrama. Please, Rose. You'll try it and you'll do it. You just need a rest and who wouldn't?"

"I don't know how I'm going to do without you two," said Rose.

"Why should you do without us?"

"Don't tell me you're staying on in the community where they did you in?" Rose sounded incredulous.

Myra stood up and started the water in the sink again. "Yes, we are." She scoured.

"Is that really what you want?" Rose Becker was amazed.

"I don't," said Myra shortly, "but my husband does." She split the skin on her fingertips as she bore down and scoured. "I prefer him to live, though many wouldn't," she said bitterly. She wiped her eyes with a kitchen towel. "He's even talking about starting a new congregation. Do you believe it? It's like a Jewish joke," she said in despair. She gulped another mouthful of the scotch. "Listen, Rosie, I'm not going to load you down like this. Everybody has troubles. We're all right. I wanted to ask how you are and to do anything I could for you. So does Shoe. He sends you his love. And I have a little research project for you when you feel up to it. But first, get a rest."

"What? What is it? I don't want to rest. Let me help you. It'll be good for me."

"All right, but you can back out any time."

"Myra, what is it?"

"Well, you must know a lot of people over at the college, like in the mental health department . . ."

"I guess so," said Rose. "Gabe was connected with it from the start."

"Well, I keep hearing little bits and pieces about the place. From a literature man here and a sociologist there. I just keep getting whiffs, little whiffs, that something over there at the college stinks. About Milton Winegarden. Nobody wants to say too much. But either Milton was fired and later rehired in some new capacity, maybe something lower on the scale; or there was some kind of scandal that was hushed up. It might be racial but I can't be sure what it is. There's some kind of cover-up and Milton Winegarden's involved. What did he do? I wish I knew."

"I see . . . ," said Rose. "There was, there was . . . something about six months ago. Doesn't that correspond with your sabbatical?"

"Yes!" said Myra excitedly. She stubbed out her cigarette. "My

God, Rose! You might be the one! With the key to just what I need!"

"I'll find out what I can tomorrow," said Rose. "Now I have to get off. I'm sorry, Myra, but I have a patient due in a few minutes."

"Do you have to be made of iron?" demanded Myra. "A patient? You don't have to be Superwoman. I don't think it's good for you."

"You're a little piece of the rock yourself, you know," said Rose affectionately. "Now let me go. I have to do something with my face. It isn't nice a psychotherapist should look like a battered woman."

"I want you to know I don't approve," said Myra.

"And I thought of another lead for you," replied Rose easily. "Dolly Rabin's husband was very active last year in some interdepartmental stuff at the college, he was busy with Milton somehow. Talk to Dolly. If anyone knows, it'll be her. She's some kind of administrator there. All right, good-by." She hung up abruptly.

Myra went outside with the dog. Together, they lay down on a dying patch of grass by the back door. I've got to put this yard in order, she worried to herself. I've got to clean the house. I haven't done a thing since we came home but talk on the phone. But there's so much to do, she thought, now Dolly Rabin to catch up with. . . . Myra went cold. Dolly Rabin's husband was another suicide. Rose hadn't even mentioned it. It was like the most natural thing in the world. What is it with these shrinks? thought Myra. What do they do to them at that college? It's like a pogrom. She stared up at the clouds. Suicide, all kinds of deaths . . . Gabe should be gone and others still live . . . and why did Milton live . . . to do evil? . . . She chewed on a blade of grass.

The woman next door pushed through the hedge and stared down at Myra. "Could I speak to you a minute, Mrs. Rosenstock?"

"Sure," said Myra, not stirring.

"I'm sorry to trouble you, Mrs. Rosenstock," the woman said aggressively. "I called the synagogue but they told me unfortunately you own your own home."

"What is your problem?" asked Myra, flat on her back, looking at the sky.

"It's just that I'm afraid my little girl is going to become an anti-Semite, that's all," she said. "You should be concerned about that."

"Oh?" said Myra. "Why?"

"It's because of the way you keep your place. My children look over here and see the way you and the rabbi live . . ." She looked around the overgrown backyard. "Your place looks abandoned. It invites burglars."

Myra sighed impatiently.

"You'll be on your way soon enough," said the woman. "Everybody knows. I just thought I'd make a neighborly suggestion."

"Good fences make good neighbors," said Myra, lying immobile. "Ever hear that?"

"Don't you quote me the Bible," the woman said vigorously. "I think I know my Judaism as well as you do."

Myra got up. "You're absurd," she said. "I have nothing to say to you. You're the one making an anti-Semite of your daughter. You're doing it to me, I'll tell you that."

Shoe drove in. He stepped out of his car and dumped a full ashtray on the grass. He reached down to the floor of the car and raked out a shredded wad of old paper with his hands. He dropped it in the driveway. Then he took a sweater off the front seat and polished the windshield with it. He came toward the women. The neighbor turned rapidly and shot through the hedge to her own home.

"What's with her?" he said.

"Nothing," said Myra. "You wouldn't believe it if I told you."

"The petunias are gone," he said. "Too late in the season. I bought you some mums, they're in the trunk. God willing, we'll see them bloom in the fall." He put his arms around her.

"We'll see them," she said grimly. She stood back from him and looked into his tired face. "I want to tell you about my talk with Rose," she said.

26

The following day a pallid Dolly Rabin gazed across the cafeteria table at Myra. "I've got to get back to the office," she said. She rested her palms on the sticky white Formica. "I have a lot of work to do, thank God. It's all that keeps me going."

"How are the kids?" asked Myra. The faculty cafeteria, all tile, was noisy with clashing silver and china. Every footstep in the busy room was amplified by the ceramic floor. She leaned forward to hear Dolly.

"We've all needed therapy," said Dolly drearily. She let her hands relax and sat back. "That's what families of suicides have to do. One man takes a shit and a whole family is covered with it. He left us to cope."

"Well, I won't keep you, Dolly," said Myra. "So there's nothing to all I've been hearing about Milton and the college?"

"Rumors are rumors, Myra. Don't believe everything you hear," Dolly said unpleasantly. "I would know. Look," she said, standing up and straightening her waistband. "Isaiah Summers is a black guy. He's Milton's chairman. He wants to pull Milton out of all his highfalutin courses and give him remedial English to teach, the most poorly prepared kids. Well, Summers is in charge. But he doesn't know how to run the department. He's in over his head. Nothing wrong with him a Yiddishe kop wouldn't cure. But he'll catch on in time. So there's tension, so what else is new? A professor got insulted? Call the papers!"

Myra kept her seat and looked up at Dolly, thin, tired, so distracted with sorrow. Myra pitied her. Quietly, she persisted. "I just hoped there would be something that Shoe and I could use. It's just for us, Dolly," she explained. "We're not accusing him of anything. He's not going on trial. No harm will come to him from anything I find out. It's just that I'm trying to create a background for myself, Dolly," she said intensely. "It's for *me*. So I can sleep nights. I'm trying to find out what happened. What happened while we were gone?"

"Nothing," said Dolly lifelessly. "One man doesn't make such a difference. An institution has a life of its own. It goes on. Look at your Milton Winegarden. He's still on a leave of absence, extended it all summer. You think it makes any difference?"

"He is?" said Myra. "I didn't know that."

"And we really work here in the summer," said Dolly. "He went fishing, I guess. You think it makes any difference?"

"I didn't know he was on leave," repeated Myra.

"He was struggling with a submerged homosexuality," said Dolly, sitting down abruptly.

"Oh?" said Myra carefully. "Really? Oh?"

"Yes," Dolly said, brooding, wiping the table with her paper napkin. "I'm working it through with my doctor. He says he couldn't make his peace with it even if I had been willing. Which I would." Her eyes filled. "I would take my husband back this minute, with all his problems. I loved him. But he didn't think enough of me to trust me." She wiped her eyes with the dirty napkin.

"I see," said Myra. She stirred her coffee, watched the liquid swirl around the spoon. "I suppose you're satisfied with your doctor." She sat back. "You know, Dolly, you'll feel better. With treatment, without treatment, you're made of the stuff that lasts."

"In the fullness of time," said Dolly distantly.

"Sure," said Myra. "It takes time." She laughed a little at herself. "I was confused for a second there. I thought you were talking about Milton or this Summers, his boss." She patted Dolly's hand.

Dolly pulled back her hand. "Summers?" she said. "Hell, why would I judge Summers? He's alive, isn't he? He has that much sense.

And he cleaves, as they say, unto his wife." She made a face. "So who am I to put him down?"

"I see what you mean, Dolly," said Myra. She groped for her purse on the dirty floor. "Stay well. I know you'll be all right. My love to your kids. And I guess I'll tell Shoe there's nothing for us to look for over here in the college."

"You can look, as far as I'm concerned," said Dolly indifferently. "You don't fool me. I know what you're after. You come and pretend all this sympathy and all the while you want to trap me, and get me to admit there was something between my husband and Milton Winegarden, just because some people are saying that. I expected more of you."

"Dolly, I assure you—"

"Mrs. Rabbi, Mrs. Mother of the Year, Mrs. Perfect," said Dolly harshly. "Snooping around accusing a dead man, getting me to talk . . ." She stood up again. "You can tell Shoe from me that whatever happened happened in his own backyard. Maybe he's not being altogether straight and honest with *you*," she said bitterly. "Maybe you should question *him*. You can tell your husband from me I think he's grasping at a very slim reed," she said, eyes glittering. "I'm sick to death of blaming the college, blaming doctors, blaming professors. I'm sick to death of blaming." She looked hard at Myra. "I'm sick to death. Shoe must have dug his own grave."

27

Rabbi Joshua Rosenstock, in chinos and a T-shirt, prowled the baking, bleaching Main Street of New Saxony. The wide, absolutely flat old street was deserted. The shopkeepers stayed inside near their air conditioners, sipping cold drinks. Shoe walked along talking to himself. He stared through a plate glass window of the dry cleaner's store. A woman seated at a sewing machine waved to him and gave him a thumbs-up sign. She clucked in sympathy as he passed.

"Here he comes," said Meyer Levy to his cousins. The men looked out at the street from their desks. All three Meyer Levys looked alike; they shared the Levy cross bite, the fine black hair, the bulbous nose.

Meyer Heimerdinger Levy, the Catholic one, heaved himself up. "I'll go talk to him," he told his cousins. They nodded.

"Invite him in," said Meyer Cohn Levy. "To cool off."

The third one said, "He sure looks bad."

Shoe stopped and looked across the street at the Korean grocery. He watched the grocer come out to the pavement with a crate of apples. His tiny wife followed. Together, they began creating a pyramid of yellow apples in front of the store alongside a display of plums, peaches, nectarines. Is it already time for apples? Shoe asked himself. The Korean couple worked silently, in harmony, sweating abundantly.

Meyer Levy stepped out of his office. "Never saw you before in a T-shirt," he said, clapping Shoe on the shoulder. "Looks good."

Shoe looked at Meyer distractedly. "Oh, say there," he said. "Yeah." He looked down at himself. "Well, why not? Don't always have to look like the angel of death, do I?" His eyes were red-rimmed and tired. "That's one thing they don't tell you in rabbinical school," he said. "That you'll have to look like an undertaker the rest of your life."

"Come on inside," invited Meyer. "Ice water."

"No, I can't," said Shoe. "Got a few things to do." He remained where he was on the hot sidewalk. "Just look at them, Meyer," he said, watching the Koreans. "Makes me think of my folks."

"They can work, all right," agreed Meyer, looking.

"They had a little store, you know," said Shoe. "My folks. Needles and thread."

"Umm," said Meyer.

"And buttons, elastic by the yard, things like that," Shoe went on. "Fourteen hours a day, every purchase less than a dollar. Together all day long." A yearning look came to his weary face. "We lived upstairs. And you know, Meyer," he said, "they never had to ask anybody for a damned thing. Never needed a favor. Never needed a damned thing from anybody. Independence." His voice shook.

"It's hot out here," complained Meyer. "Come in."

"I still have them, thank God," said Shoe. "They're retired. They still like to work in the store. They help out the new owner sometimes."

"God bless them," said Meyer. "Why don't you come inside?"

"My father can look any man in the world in the face," said Shoe. "Like that fellow, probably." He pointed to the Korean. "Only rabbis . . ." He took a breath to steady his voice. "Only we can be knocked loose by any wind that blows. . . ."

"Rabbi, last night, at the meeting at your house?"

"Yes?" Shoe looked at Meyer intently.

"It was good," said Meyer. "You got a lot of wonderful friends. I enjoyed myself," he declared. "I think we can start a dynamite congregation. As long as we got you," he added. "Now come inside and say hello to my cousins. They want to join also."

Shoe waved across Meyer's shoulder to Meyer Cohn Levy and

Meyer Weissbrodt Levy but stood his ground. "Can't. Busy." He paused. "Tell me," he said, "how did Myra seem to you?"

"Why, fine," said Meyer, disconcerted. "Wonderful woman. Who doesn't like Myra?"

"Would you like to know something?" said Shoe energetically.

"Let's get something to drink," said Meyer with faint hope.

"She gave me holy hell for that meeting!" Shoe stared at Meyer with something like triumph. "You wouldn't think that, would you? You wouldn't think that I'm supposed to get permission to hold a little get-together in my own house, would you?" he puffed.

"She's been through a lot, I guess," said Meyer, embarrassed. "I can understand how she feels."

"No, you don't! No, you don't, Meyer. Would you believe me if I told you she wants to get out of here? She wants to move to this cabin her mother left her up in Wisconsin?"

Meyer was very uncomfortable. "Maybe it's a time for a little thinking, like," he said. His shirt grew wet with perspiration.

"Oh no," said Shoe. "Introspection is a luxury I can't afford, Meyer," said Shoe angrily. "I've got to work and this is my work. What does she want? I should stay home and be a mommy's helper? And she'll go be a supermarket checker or something? What's she trying to do to me?"

"Rabbi," said Meyer desperately, "I'm married three times. What do I know?"

Shoe drove on. "She has no conception of money, I tell you! Ask her who's going to pay the college bills. You know what she says?"

Meyer waited.

"Says we've done all we can." Shoe's face looked stern. "My immigrant father sold thread. And he educated me and my sister. And I'm going to let my kids down? Never!"

"I'm sure you're gonna win at your hearing," said Meyer. "You'll have a few bucks. And before you know it, the new congregation will be self-sustaining . . ."

"You know that mimeo machine?" Shoe interrupted. "That Fritz Newman brought last night? You saw. You saw how he broke his back getting it into the dining room. He's giving it to me, to help us get started. And she says she won't have it!" His blue eyes searched Meyer's. "Explain this to me."

"Women are different from us," offered Meyer. "Emotional. She don't mean it. She's not sore at you, Rabbi. You know who she's sore at. Well, Jesus Christ, so am I!"

"All I said was that the cabin in Wisconsin doesn't have enough room for my books," said Shoe. "You know what she said? She said, 'Don't be such a Jew.'" He laughed bitterly. "If she wanted an Irish bartender, why didn't she marry one? What does she want?"

"Rabbi, it's two hundred in the shade," said Meyer. "Why not take a swim in my pool this afternoon? Take the wife and go over my place. You'll have it to yourselves. Relax. Cool off. Do you both good."

"Ah, Meyer," brooded Shoe. "Mine own vineyard have I not kept. My poor wife. Raised six kids, kissed everybody's rear end for twenty years, and look what I did to her. She's got a right to be sore."

"It's not my place to say this," said Meyer reluctantly, "but I'll tell you again she ain't sore at you. You know that. She had a shock. So did we all. But she'll settle down. Let her see some money after the hearing. After all, that's what it's about. You can't get your job back. But when she sees the new bunch shape up, she'll be her old self. She ain't as strong as you, that's all, she don't bounce back as fast. Now come inside and have a cold drink."

"The old Main Street sure is different," said Shoe abruptly. He looked down the street, as straight and white and dry as a bone. "Remember when all the elms were still here, how leafy it was? The shade in the summer? Do you remember it, Meyer?"

"I was born here," he answered. "I remember. Everything changes."

"The sun sets; the sun also rises," said Shoe. "You're a philosopher."

"Not really," Meyer said modestly. "We all gotta live."

"I want to," said Shoe, face contorting. "I want to go on."

"That's the spirit!" said Meyer. "Come in and see the cousins."

"I better go," said Shoe. "Thanks for listening to me. I'm afraid I really let you have it. I'm sorry. I made you into my pastor."

"You couldn't say anything nicer," said Meyer. He returned to his office as Shoe continued down the street. "There goes a man walking straight to a heart attack," he told his cousins.

"He looks bad," agreed one of them.

The third Meyer said, "There are men in this town dropping like flies every day from business worries. Do they think the rabbi's not human? Don't they realize they could kill him? Why the fuck aren't they paying him? Why are they going to court?"

"Jesus, Mary, and Joseph," said Meyer H. Levy. He sat down hard at his desk. "How I wish that wife of his would come in with us. We could throw a sale or two her way." He watched Shoe mumbling to himself as he walked. "He needs to put something in the bank."

"What about this new shul?" asked his cousin.

"Oh, my dear Christ," Meyer said. "A big six people showed up for the meeting. Six people can't support him. I'm telling you," he told his somber cousins, "a guy that age, if he's unemployed, he might as well croak. There's nowhere to go." The three Meyers attacked their paperwork.

Shoe entered the post office. He peered through the dimness at the young woman behind the high counter. He cleared his throat. "I'd like . . . some change-of-address cards," he said. Tears came to his eyes.

"Yes, sir," said the young woman, turning away. She reached for the forms from a stack behind her. "Here you are," she said softly. "I wish I was moving," she said. "I'd go to California."

"Really?" said Shoe. "Why California?"

"Oh," she said dreamily, "you'd like it, I'm sure. You can swim all year round . . . and play music . . . what a great life."

Shoe's hands trembled slightly as he accepted the cards. "You make it seem very appealing, young lady. Have you lived there?"

"No," she said. "I've never been anywhere but here."

"Here is very nice, too," he said soberly. He tried to smile. His gaunt, pale face looked ghastly in the dim post office. "I'm sure a wonderful young person like yourself has much to look forward to. Right here. Often we don't appreciate what we already have." Tears welled up again. "Well, thank you very much," he said stiffly.

The young clerk watched Shoe walk slowly through the heavy bronze doors. Then she cried on the blotter in front of her, getting ink on her cheeks. Her supervisor came out of the glass office in back.

"What's the matter, Mueller? Getting your period? Again?"

"Oh, Miss Leuthardt," she sobbed, "that was Rabbi Rosenstock!"

"So?"

"He didn't recognize me," she gasped. "I was in Brownies with his daughter Etta."

"That's a while ago," observed the supervisor. "You've changed, dummy. Nothing to cry about."

"He took a whole pile of change-of-address cards! He doesn't even know where he's going!" cried the girl. "And he looks so sick!"

"These things happen," said the older woman.

"Back when my father was alive," said the girl, "when we were in Brownies, me and Etta, the whole troop went once to visit their church. And Rabbi Rosenstock showed us everything, even these real old scrolls they keep; and he was so respectful, I remember, like we were grown-ups. And then he took us outside, and he stopped the ice cream truck, and he bought ice pops for every one of us." She wept. "He looks so sick. I'm afraid he's going to die."

Dear Rabbi,

Your name was given to me by my own rabbi here in Cupertino. He says you can help me to arrange moving my father's body from back there in Chicago out here to me. It's very inconvenient to have him so far away. If I want to speak to him I have to go to the local cemetery where my sister-in-law's mother is buried to send him a message. My rabbi is against disturbing my father but he says, if I really insist, you should take care of it. Please let me know the fee and when I can expect my dad.

Thanking you in advance,
Rena Abbady

Dear Rabbi,
If it's any comfort to you, my family and I will never walk into a synagogue again. What they did to you is a disgrace to our people and a scandal for the goyim to enjoy. My wife made me join and I admit the children got a lot out of knowing you but I warned her these petty people were not for us. Professional people, doctors, lawyers, to decide they want a younger man just on a whim and you can go whistle? This is religion? I'm no lawyer but if you ask me it was a crime and I want no part of it.

I hear you are going to court. Pardon me for butting in, but what can you win by going to court? The best possible outcome is you will get a few dollars in compensation and then they'll knife you again. They'll find a way. I would run from them like from a fire. You're an intelligent man. You can make a living some other way. I wish you all the best.

Respectfully,
Velvel Fox

28

As the summer's day began, the Winegardens were quarreling. "What do you want?" asked Milton, exasperated. He longed for his coffee and they were still upstairs. "Sunny, what is it you want? I feel like Freud. What does a woman want?"

"I want you back again, Mr. Freud," she said hotly. She whipped the crewelwork spread over the king-sized bed. "I want our life back the way it was before you became such a big man in the synagogue. With all this rabbi business, I'm just a caretaker now. This whole house, all your appointments, correspondence. Double-talking for you at the college, covering up for you when you didn't go to class last term." She beat the pillows up and slipped them into their covers. "These people you're so involved with, they're not our kind. My family's been here a hundred years. We're not about to start being pillars of the synagogue or some such. I've been willing to help you a little, but this world is much bigger than this. Leave this parochialism to these inadequate . . . dopes."

"The hearing date has been set," he placated her. He pitched a pair of shoes into the walk-in closet. "Then we're going on a cruise with the Warmflashes and forget all about this. Try to be patient till then."

"Yes?" she asked. "You already know the results? I wonder why we need a hearing, then."

"Oh, Sunny," he said. He raised the brocaded shades exactly to the center of each leaded window. "Have a heart, Sunny. Give me a break. This could never have been brought off without me. They needed someone expert in interpersonal relations."

They left the bedroom and walked down the back staircase side by side, jostling one another.

"I'll make the coffee," he said.

"No," she said. "I don't like how you do it." She pushed him aside and got to the sink first. She turned on the water. "You make a mess."

"Soon we'll be sailing in the Caribbean," he said, standing close to her. "Keep your mind on that."

"My mind is on it," she said, measuring the coffee with a copper measure. "A week spent talking to that dolt, Suzy Warmflash. Fashion. Hairstyles. And you in important conference all the while with the great attorney Warmflash. I suppose you think I'll have a good time."

"What's your idea of a good time?" he said impatiently. "What do you want, for Christ's sake?"

"I want," she said, turning her puffy face to him, "to go to my Audubon meetings again, without being called out by you on the phone. I want to be ready to take part in the Christmas bird count. I want to raise orchids with you like we were going to. I miss my chamber music nights. Your Jews have swallowed us up."

"Just a little longer, Sunny," he said.

"And Suzy goes on and on about her genius son at Michigan. Who cares? Milton," she said, mouth contorting, "I don't mind any more not having children. I just want you. I want you back again."

"Wipe off that counter before it stains," he said.

"And I want you to get back to work," she said loudly. She slammed the pot on the burner. Milton winced. "You had no business taking a leave of absence from the college. You were already in trouble with your chairman. And now you stretched it out all summer long because of your wretched meetings with your friends. And where are all your private students?" she cried. "Where are they? They may be poor readers but they're not that stupid. They caught on sooner than I did." She sat down in the breakfast nook. Milton sat opposite. "They know your mind is elsewhere. It's become an obsession with you. Get rid of the rabbi. Bring in Rabbi Yossel." She slapped the shining table. "I never required you to earn a living, Milton. Daddy's money is sufficient. But you *do* have to work. I insist." Milton was silent. "I plan to resign from the synagogue, myself," she said viciously. "I don't know about you. But at this rate you won't even have the money for dues, much less cruises and all this vulgar showing off for your new friends."

"Is the coffee ready?"

"See for yourself. Don't take my good cups. Use the earthenware."

He poured the coffee. "Sunny, go out today. The change will be good for you. And I'm having a meeting here with Harry and Irving. It's important," he said hastily.

"And why must you have all these get-togethers up in your study?" she said angrily. "You let them track up the whole house and litter the stairs. You let them smoke. You should sit them down in the kitchen where they belong, like my mother would have done with people like that. And I don't like to have them peeping at my things and going through my closets. What do you do up there, anyway? Everybody is allowed up there but me."

"Nobody's looking at your things, Sunny," he said patiently. "We just like it up there, that's all. It's like a club."

"Sometimes I feel like a widow," she said sulkily. "I'm so alone when you're up there. I feel lonelier with you up there than when I'm all alone. You're very cruel to me, Milton." A crafty expression crossed her swollen face. She set her heavy breasts on the table between them and reached for his hand. She put his short fingers on her nipple. "Let's go upstairs, Milton. We'll play awhile." She smiled crookedly. "We'll go back up and play, you know? We'll do that thing with your finger and your big toe, you know?" She whinnied.

Small Milton looked at small Sunny, squat and buxom, and fought down the impulse to belch. He saw that Sunny's chin was sprouting a new long hair. He patted her breast. "Sunny, are you through with your coffee? Go out. Go shopping. Do something. I don't dare, Sunny. I'm like an athlete before a big game. I've got to have my mind clear for our strategy meeting."

"No," she said clearly. She sat back. "This is my house. My father paid for it when you couldn't pay for a cup of coffee. So don't you send me anywhere." She stood up and put on an apron. "I'm going to polish my copper. I want to be here to watch your friends and see they don't steal anything. All night, even in your sleep, you talk to them, or to Yossel, while I'm right there beside you. Oh, I'm going to keep my eyes open."

"Oh, Sunny, please go out, Sunny," he pleaded. "I have important business to look after."

"Bastard!" she shouted. She flung the copper measure at him and pulled off her apron. "I'm not going to beg you for a little attention. I'll go. Better worry if I'll come back."

"Oh, look," he said, stooping. "You put a dent."

"Bastard," she said, the tears flowing. She opened the door to the attached garage. "You better clean up this kitchen good." They heard the front door chimes ring. "Answer it," she said. "I have to go out. My husband told me to leave." She slammed the door. Milton went to the front of the house.

Harry Warmflash stood on the brick path in front of the door, looking at his watch. "Can we make it fast?" he said as Milton opened the door.

"Come on up," said Milton. He led the way to his study.

"I've got a good man in mind," said Harry to Milton's short legs as they climbed ahead of him. "As I project it, we'll never get all the way to court at all. This fellow I have in mind to represent us, he'll put the fear of God into Rosenstock!" He laughed. "I've seen him operate."

Milton unlocked his study door and led the way in past a potted tree and huge, potted ferns. He flicked a wall switch that turned on concealed air conditioners.

"I won't have time for the details," said Harry. "You'll have to work with this lawyer," he said warningly. "We're going to have to show nonperformance over a long period of years."

"Well, it's true, isn't it?" demanded Milton. He put his fingers inside his belt and scratched.

"Milton," said Harry patiently, "simple assertion won't do it. We're talking about money. It's not like the congregational meeting. For a judge not to award him money, you have to have real testimony and hard evidence. I thought I explained that."

"But I thought you said we'd never get that far," whined Milton.

They heard chimes downstairs. "That'll be Irv," said Milton. "Watch yourself, what you say now." Harry returned his gaze with hostile calm.

Irving came in, short of breath, in blue and white checked slacks and a blue golf shirt. He took off his white cap and wiped his brow. "Scorcher." The other two did not respond. "All right," said Irving finally. "What are we meeting about? How much to give him? I say settle. Give him three years' pay over a five-year period. It's fair." He waited. "The congregation'll buy it," he said. "What do you say?" he asked.

Harry Warmflash consulted his watch. "Have to run." He looked strongly at Milton. "Milt can fill you in. I've got a good man in mind to represent us, he owes me a favor. We'll have no bargaining position, Irv, if we just go ahead and make your proposal now. We have to shake him up first. I'm going." He departed abruptly.

Milton broke into stinging perspiration. "Irving," he said with an ingratiating smile. He exposed his yellow teeth. "I know you'll support us. Of course," he said, patting Irving's knee, "we all want to do what's right. It's a matter of psychology."

"Pay the man off," said Irving. "Let's get finished with this thing."

"I couldn't agree with you more," said Milton mildly. "Unfortunately, there comes a time when we must be advised by experts. If you're sick, you go to a doctor. And you listen to him. Am I right, Irv?" Irving sighed. "Well, that's our situation," said Milton. "Now I am reliably advised—" he said. He got up and wandered about the vast room, picking his way past the overpowering potted trees and plants, and touching his art objects as he walked. He stopped and stared into a mirror above the exposed sink. He touched his pebbly, mottled cheek. "I am advised that you don't go and make your last offer at the outset."

"Doc, who do you think you're talking to?" said Irving. "Ain't I the one in business?"

"Naturally," said Milton. "Precisely why we want you on our team. Can't do without you and your counsel, Irv. Couldn't get along without you."

"Do what you want," said Irving huffily. "I got work waiting for me. I'm not going to back out now, don't worry. But I would like to see an end to this."

"I am going to speak to the rabbi myself," said Milton.

"He needs the money," said Irving. "He'll take a fair offer."

"Don't be too sure," said Milton. "Emotion has clouded reason, I'm afraid. However, I'll try."

"I have to go," said Irving, rising. "But listen to me, Doc. Offer him money. It makes the world go round and he needs it. Let's not drag this thing on. We all got lives to live."

Dear Rabbi,

I enclose a letter which will interest you and maybe some other people. Don't worry about holding onto it, I made copies. You see, I'm getting to know you! I don't know where this rag comes from. Norman Dorfman gave it to me. He claims he found it slipped underneath his back door yesterday evening. I'll see you again on the weekend. We have a lot of work to do.

Bobby

Dear Rabbi Yossel,

I've been giving some thought to our joint program at the synagogue next month. We want to make sure it's an adequate showcase for your talents and to get the ball rolling well before Rosenstock gets home.

As to topics, if I get the message today, in politics: no Jews need apply. Regarding social unrest, a big interest with Rosenstock, by the way, do the shvartzehs care about what happens to us? It's their problem. As for an appeal dinner for Soviet Jewry, frankly, I think our people have reached the point of total resistance. There's always going to be a crisis somewhere.

I've been thinking about psychohistory and what we might bring to it, each from our own disciplines. Although I'm ordained myself, I've never wanted to function as a rabbi. I like to keep it a thing apart. I was referring to myself in my role as a lay analyst. We might be able to do a good program. I've been reading Freud on Da Vinci again and feel enthused. There's *Moses and Monotheism* but, frankly, it's been done to death. Rabbi Akiva'd be a subject of great moment for us, I think. I feel a remarkable contemporaneity in a man who leaves a simple shepherd's existence, driven by a hunger for learning. Think of it: He leaves his wife to fend for herself for seven years (the magic number) and returns to great honor. He stops the welcoming procession to lift his humble wife from the crowd to sit beside him. It has such a modern ring, don't you agree? It's like The Astronaut Returns. What impels a man to do it? What kind of woman would he have chosen who so honors her husband's psychological imperatives? And can they go on from there to a so-called normal life?

This would lead to a consideration of just what a normal life is supposed to be, especially by our Jewish lights. Which is where you could come in. We experimented with this at my Jewish Life Center and, with you added, it can't miss. Perhaps we may find that our traditional idea of a man, a woman, children, bound together, unable to stretch, to expand, to grow, may not be as traditional as we think. I look forward to preparing this with you.

May I say without, I hope, embarrassing you, Yossel, how much I enjoy our mutual explorations? I feel we can take much, one from the other, can dip into the well we each possess, and slake our thirst mutually. I was an only child and feel in you both brother and sister.

The congregation will be very much inclined, frankly, toward keeping you and letting Rosenstock go, after they see what you have to offer.

Shalom,
Milton

I don't mean to dictate to you. If you don't like the above, give some thought to these topics:

> Male Menopause
> Was Freud Really a Jew?
> Should Women Be Rabbis?
> Crisis Management for Today
> The Case Against Unthoughtful Reproduction

Give me a ring and we'll talk.   M.W.

Is he nuts, Rabbi, or is he nuts?
Bobby

29

"And that's not all," said Bobby. He faced the rabbi, who slouched in his faded living room, a sheaf of papers in his hand. Bobby laughed briefly. "Don't ask me how he did it," he said. "But Norman came up with a letter of agreement with this Rabbi Yossel. They got him pretty cheap. Threw in Milton's used Caddy. This whole thing was concluded while you were over there in Jerusalem. Very nice . . ." He bit the insides of his cheeks and waited for the rabbi's response.

"We'll be telling it to the judge," said Shoe thoughtfully. "I hope I can handle my testimony." He looked bleak.

"You?" demanded Myra. She came in from the kitchen with a broom in her hand. "You can't handle public speaking? You don't know how to talk in front of a judge? You'll just open your mouth, and they'll be sorry they ever started this. What a disgrace! Thank God we got a Jewish judge—it's such a disgrace!"

"You just never know, Myra," Bobby said. "I'll ask them questions, I'll ask your husband questions. The truth will come out, I assure you. But you just never know. I want to ask you both: Do you still want to go through with this? It can be painful. You've already been through a lot."

"Yes," they both said.

"I'm going to tell that judge," said Shoe grimly. His face went dark. "They have the gall to call for my income tax records; they try to get the bank to open my records to them; they threaten to sue me for interfering with their conduct of synagogue business. Wait till I tell that judge!"

"And I say no, Rabbi," said Bobby, red-faced. "No and no and no. You're not going to deliver some big speech. You have to let me do the talking. This is a game, and that's how the game is structured. Get up and denounce from the pulpit if you want, but you can't do it in court. This isn't the movies. We have to do it the proper way. You get up and rave, and we can forget it. You won't see a dime."

Shoe stood. "Forget the money a minute. I have a right to speak. I have a right to tell the judge what kind of drek we're dealing with. He can't know. He wouldn't imagine it. They're an anti-Semite's delight!" He was panting. "Bobby! I've got to speak up! I haven't said a word all this time. Myra hasn't said a word. We don't let the dog bark! It's intolerable!"

"What's wrong with him speaking, Bobby?" asked Myra, instantly angry. "He's not a dummy. What are you afraid of?"

"All right then," Bobby shot back. "Speak! You know what'll happen? The judge will say, 'Fine, say what you want. But you lose.' Will that satisfy you?"

"I don't care," said Shoe. "Money isn't everything."

"Rabbi, Rabbi!" shouted Bobby. He pulled at his earlobes. "You won't say that the next day! Believe me!"

"Shoe . . . ," said Myra.

"All right, all right," he said. He ground his teeth. "Maybe I'll just kill that little putz. I'd like to kick his ass, if I could get down that low."

"Good, Rabbi," said Bobby beaming proudly. "Keep up that anger. It'll be useful. But let me direct it, please."

"And maybe it'll all be settled, honey," Myra said. "And you'll go right back to work again."

"Myra," said Bobby in a loud and cranky tone, "the hearing is to prove that you are entitled to a lump sum of money because your contract has been breached. Don't you understand that yet? The judge can't put you back on the job. You can't compel people to employ you! You can only make them comply with their agreement with you, which says they owe you if they break the contract for any reason."

"No," she said resentfully. She dropped the broom. "I didn't understand. You talk about so many things. Did you understand, Shoe?"

He nodded, angry, withdrawn.

"Well, so I didn't," she said. "Is that a crime? So I'm stupid."

"So be stupid, My," Shoe said. "But be quiet."

"Children, children," said Bobby blushing, "we're all nervous. But just remember that judges don't like you to argue with them. They know what's good for you, and they tend to get a little angry when you don't recognize that right away." He chuckled. "Winegarden's hung himself. You can't hire your friend and then proceed to trump up a case against the incumbent. I don't know how Warmflash let him do it. But all I know is Winegarden's going to walk out of there with his head between his knees. If he can walk at all. Myra," he said with a big grin, "serve us a drink! I'm going to leave you people alone till after Rosh Hashanah. Give you a rest from your crazy lawyer. There must be an easier way to make a living." He threw back his head and laughed.

"The news must be good," said Nathan, entering the room. He carried a briefcase and several books.

"Good, it's not," said Shoe to the floor. "But soon it'll be over."

"Honey," said Myra, greeting him, "I'm so glad you could come home!"

"Lawyer!" shouted Bobby in greeting. "What are you studying?"

"Contracts, mostly," said the boy. "Not too interesting. You learn that contracts don't mean all that much." The boy looked surprised as his father laughed. "Oh, I get it," he said.

"We're going to get your father some money," said Bobby loudly. "It's all we can get. At least you'll have time to get yourself together, Rabbi," he said turning to him, almost pleading for approval. "At least you'll have bread on the table."

Myra brought in three water glasses of scotch. She handed Nathan a Coke. Bobby's words brought her a vision of a long-braided bread on her table, a chalah that gleamed the length of her table. She saw a feast. Shoe took his glass from her and stepped away, staring into the sealed, dirty fireplace. "Then what'll you do, Rabbi?" asked Bobby, holding his glass.

Shoe said, "Do? I already did it. I'm starting a new congregation."

"That's my father," said Nathan. He drank half his Coke.

"Good for you, Rabbi," said Bobby. "I just joined." He looked at Myra. "I must be nuts!" he shouted.

Myra went to Bobby and took his red face in her hands. She kissed his cheek, his lips, the other cheek. She looked into his eyes and kissed his cheek again. "Stay and eat with us," she said, touching his red hair. She picked up his hand and held it against her face. "We'll eat Behemoth and Leviathan."

Bobby looked at her, bewildered. Was she already drunk? He held both her hands in his and looked at Shoe. "She's a Bible scholar? Is this Bible talk?"

"Why not?" said Myra. "Aren't I a rabbi's wife?"

Bobby let her go and raised his glass. "Here's to you both. What'll we toast?"

"I don't know," said Shoe. He looked at his glass.

"Say *l'chayim*," said Myra. "It means life, Bobby. What more can you ask for?"

"No," said Bobby. "Here's to winning." He drank.

Myra said, "That's more important than life? I don't think so."

Shoe was growing flushed. He walked deliberately to Myra, dragging his feet on the threadbare carpet. He put his free hand heavily on Myra's crown and began to sing in Yiddish. "Oy, what do you understand, you philosopher?" he sang tipsily. "With your small, catlike mind?" She touched his lips with her little finger. "Come here," he sang, "to the rabbi's table." His dry lips trembled. "And learn a little wisdom."

Bobby backed away a step from them. Nathan watched them all, drank his Coke. There was a silence. "You can't carry a tune," she said.

"You look exhausted," Shoe said.

"No, you do," she said.

"No," said Shoe.

"Winning, Myra! Winning, Rabbi," repeated Bobby doggedly, red in the face. "There's no life without winning."

Myra shrugged and drank. Shoe turned away to the fireplace.

"Now we'll toast again," insisted Bobby. "Here's to you both, to your future. Let this be the worst experience of your lives."

"Give it to us in writing," said Myra with a catch in her voice. "We'll take the deal."

"Jews," said Shoe formally. He turned and faced them. "Jews!" he cried. "L'chayim!"

Dear Shoe,

You ask what kind of man I am. I could pretend not to know what you are talking about but I have too much character for that. I am, first of all, a man of fierce loyalty, even blind loyalty, but my loyalty has been trampled upon and laughed at. Why did you ever call me to be your substitute? Just because I was cheap? Because you know I need every cent I can put my hand on? I wish you had never called me.

Milton Winegarden has told me in confidence how he defended me and shouted you down at meetings where you belittled me and tried to undermine me. He told me for my own good, so I'd realize I'm worthy to have friends, as much as any man.

What kind of man am I? A question like that only degrades the questioner. You can only degrade yourself, Shoe. What kind of man are *you*? Your world is collapsing around you and you want to drag me down with you. You want some private Götterdämmerung. You think I'm fooled by you and your advice—how much to ask for and how to write the contract. Oh no, your Machiavellian machinations will not prevail now.

To the congregation, I say, "Speak up! Let justice well forth as waters; and righteousness as a mighty stream." I, too, have complaints against you that only rabbinic etiquette restrained me from making public. But for your own ears, let me say that the many meals I endured at your home over the years were a feast of bitterness for me. Did you two never think that it was salt to my wounds to sit with you, to have to play with the children and overeat, and then go to see my poor Blanche in the hospital, now addicted to methadone? That my own poor child has to live halfway across the country because she has no mother to care for her and a father who must eat at the tables of strangers? And the gifts you sent her, don't you know how you shamed me? Sending a child picture postcards and even stamps for her little collection—you love feeling superior, don't you? You need me. As long as you can look down on me, you know you're all right. Even your damned dog felt free to sit on my foot and laugh at me. Look at Yossel, he'd say. He doesn't even have the right to kick a dog. He's nobody.

But I'm getting on my own at last. Milton has been my savior in making this breakthrough. So, Shoe, although you meant it for evil, and just used me for cheap labor and to laugh at me, God meant it for good. God meant for me to meet Milton at a time when I was ready, emotionally, and for me to take over this congregation of yours and give them the leadership they deserve. I respect them. You never did, I see it now, any more than you ever cared about me. You stand aloof on the mountain and commune with God while down below people are in trouble.

Maybe it's not your fault. You've always had it too easy, Shoe. You'll get more human now. And maybe I can call on you now and then to substitute for me. Like if I take a vacation. I could talk the Board into it. Life is long and much can happen.

Shalom,
Yossel

30

"You must be out of your mind," said Harry Warmflash. He stood in front of Milton's gleaming bathtub and glared at him. "Where is Dorfman getting these letters? Did you write to Yossel? Last year? In Rosenstock's absence? Yes or no!"

"Let me elaborate, please, Harry," said Milton stiffly.

"Yes or no!"

"Yes, with an explanation," said Milton. His stinging skin was wet with sweat.

"Get a lawyer," said Harry.

"What? I'm astonished," began Milton.

"Get a lawyer," repeated Harry. "You're on your own."

"And why can't you represent me, assuming I need representation?"

"Get a lawyer, take my advice," repeated Harry. "Don't waste any time."

"I see," Milton said softly. "You're too emotionally involved with me, is that it?"

"I'd like a cheaper rabbi," said Harry. "That's as far as it goes. Get yourself a lawyer. Don't go to that hearing without your own lawyer. Or call it off and pay him out of your own pocket."

"You're joking," said Milton in reproach.

"Good-by," said Harry without emphasis. He walked out of the study and went down the stairs. "I'll let myself out."

The postman was coming to the front door as Harry came out. "The doc at home?" he asked.

"Ring the bell," said Harry. "He talks to you from a hole in the wall."

"Dr. Winegarden?" said the postman into the grill. "I have two registered letters for you? You have to sign?"

"Who from?" asked Milton, unwilling to walk down the three flights. "Maybe I'll let you sign my name."

"Heh, heh," said the postman nervously. "Um, they're both from Summers; Ize, Iz—something Summers."

"Be right there," said Milton, his heart moving in his chest.

"Have a nice day," said the postman, tipping back his cap as Milton opened the oak door. He handed over the letters. "Looks like another scorcher."

Milton waited immobile until the postman was out of sight. Then he opened the letters, still standing on his doorstep.

Dear Milton,
You will be receiving a copy of my letter to the Board of the College. I think it speaks for itself. May I wish you all success and fulfillment in the future.

Fraternally,
Isaiah Summers, Ph.D.

Dear Friends,
We look forward this year to a renascence of our original vitality and of our service to the community. To this end, I ask your support in the release of Dr. Milton Winegarden from his obligations to us at the College. Our essential capacity to function has been severely eroded. There is too much activity directed away from our central purpose. But we can make the comeback we all so desire by a pruning, however painful, of those whose primary dedication is elsewhere. I know you all join me in wishing Dr. Winegarden Godspeed and

success in his private endeavors. And I know we can look forward in brotherhood and joy to a year, many years, of achievement here at our Community College, where the wholehearted dedication of each professional to our students, our poor, and our community can make a difference.

In peace,
Isaiah Summers

"Like a pink slip," said Milton, going pale. "Like a fucking pink slip, like I'm some laborer," he said, going red. He tore the letters into shreds and went into the kitchen to send them into the garbage disposal, away from Sunny's relentless prying. He wiped off the spotless counter with a damp sponge. At a loss, he opened and closed the refrigerator door soundlessly. He picked up a saucer of wet coffee grounds by the sink and went out to his back lawn. He emptied the saucer over the roses and returned to the kitchen. There he filled a flat pan with birdseed and went out again to fill Sunny's bird feeders. Sunny was withdrawn and scarcely at home anymore. All her many chores fell to Milton. The phone rang. Milton took the call on the patio extension, one hand still occupied with the birdseed.

"Milt?" said Irving. "I'm out. Sorry, but take my name off everything."

"What's wrong?" asked Milton. He set down the pan and scratched his neck.

"I'm going to tell you one more time," said Irving, breathing fast. "Right along I've been saying pay the man off. That's the price. Make him emeritus, all those ideas you had, they're fine. But pay him something! I don't like this hearing. It's giving me the creeps. Did you know there was a congregation down South that went all the way to the Supreme Court with some fight about men and women sitting together? You never know how these things will turn out."

"Oh, but Harry assures me," said Milton quietly.

"Warmflash assures you borscht," interrupted Irving. "Don't tell me what lawyers say. Lawyers think a certain way. Like if they can prove the rabbi didn't really have a contract, we owe him nothing.

And if he did have one, he didn't fulfill his part of it. Nonperformance. I know all about it. I know better, believe me. We're kidding ourselves."

"Irving, come over," said Milton.

"You got to know how to roll with the punch, Doc," said Irving intensely. "You got to adapt when you have to. Look at me. I was in paper goods. Now I got a Christmas business, right? What could be simpler, right?" He laughed. "Wrong. These professionals don't know a thing about it. Like you, a professor, you got tenure, right? You don't know a thing about it. But things change out here in the world." Milton did not interrupt. "Today," said Irving didactically, "I cannot touch a crown of thorns. The Arabs want a price you wouldn't believe. And those olivewood figures for the creche? Forget it! The baby alone is more than the whole family used to be."

"Irv, come over, we'll talk. This is not precisely . . ."

"No, I'm out," replied Irving. "Before Yom Kippur, you'll go in front of a judge and you'll fart around about a contract and I already know a contract's not worth the paper it's written on. I had a contract, too, you know. The unions fixed me good with my contract." Milton sat down carefully on a white wrought-iron chair. "It's crap, Doc," said Irving. "The judge is going to say, 'Don't dray me around with documents. Hasn't the man been with you twenty years?'

"Pay the man off and be done with it!" cried Irving. "We'll still be making an economy. I'm afraid of appeals and God knows what. Did you know there was a rabbi in Hollywood who got millions? For some kind of a mixup about kosher cookies? We could be involved for years!"

Milton was perspiring again. The wrought iron bit into the backs of his hard thighs. "Irving, I wish you'd present your views to Harry and our lawyer. I don't want to do this alone."

"Not me," said Irving. "I'm out. But did it ever occur to you it's funny we had to hire a lawyer? How come with a hotshot like Warmflash right in the congregation we have to go outside and pay big money for it, yet? Is this economizing? Is he getting a kickback? And the rabbi's got lawyers for nothing! That Etkind says he'll stay with it as long as it'll take."

"Irv, why didn't you say something before this?" cried Milton, wriggling on the chair. "This is a hell of a time to back out!"

"I have tried," said Irving loudly. "Who can get a word in edgewise? Nobody wants to listen to me. I'm a plain man. No college. Not a professional." He paused. More quietly, he went on. "But this morning, I get up and I say to myself, 'You have to phone to El Salvador today for tinsel. You got Christmas tree balls waiting to be shipped in Yugoslavia. What are you fucking around with a few lousy grand for the rabbi? I got a man in Taiwan," he continued. "He's got me by the short hairs. One false move, I'm bankrupt. So in my position, my *precarious* position, I should cross a rabbi? And right before Yom Kippur? What am I, crazy?"

"You know," said Milton, settling back and crossing his short legs, "of course, you know—basically you're aware of the reason we went outside for a lawyer. Harry says it's unethical for him to appear as our attorney since he's a member of the synagogue himself, but he's given us worlds of time at no cost. I don't want you impugning his motives."

"I look at everybody's motives," said Irving. "That's my business. You sit in a college. You may think it's just buying and selling I do, but believe me, you have to know psychology to do business."

"Irving, you're feeling a natural trepidation, it's perfectly understandable . . ." Milton stroked his bare calf in an attempt to soothe the rash flaring there.

"Milton, I'm out. I wish you luck. I hope you win."

"*We* win," said Milton.

"No, to me winning is not to kill a rabbi. For the last time, I'm telling you. Pay him off. Make any change you want—it's our congregation, not his. But you have to pay your bills or you're out of business." He sighed. "Well, you won't do it. Call me and tell me what happened."

31

Milton looked with longing at the bathtub in his study. "First things first," he said aloud. The sound of himself filled him with pity, and he had to wipe his eyes. Why didn't they understand? Why were Harry and Irving leaving him to stand alone against the rabbi? And Sunny, his own Sunny? It was all very well for Harry to tell him to pay the rabbi from his own pocket. But with what? And now, to be kicked out of the College, his College, by that primitive, that unevolved . . . Milton trembled. He was being made into a wanderer, an exile, a refugee. What would he use for money? He owned nothing that was not also Sunny's. And what school would have him with the new term about to begin? He steadied himself with five regular deep breaths. The reason I'm so upset, he analyzed, calmer now, is that it hurts to be misunderstood. That's the real, basic reason. I'm doing this for them, for them. And they turn on me! "First things first," he said again.

He went to the gilt phone on the desk and dialed with his stubby, trembling forefinger. "Rabbi," he breathed.

"What do you want?" asked Shoe.

"Rabbi, Joshua," he said, "let's talk. You and I don't need lawyers to talk to each other, do we?"

"What do you want?" repeated Shoe.

"Rabbi," said Milton, "we've been maneuvered by others into positions that are not natural for us. We're friends. Why do we need a judge?" His breath came fast.

"Are you all right, Milton?" asked Shoe.

"Just give me your ear for a minute, Rabbi."

"Milton, if you're making an offer, make it," said Shoe wearily. "I'm very busy. I have to go to court soon and plead for a crust of bread from my former employers."

"No, Rabbi," said Milton. "Let's reason together."

"Milton, are you trying to drive me crazy?" said Shoe explosively. "Is this some kind of psychological torture? What *is* it?"

"Rabbi," said Milton, almost whispering, "what would you say to becoming emeritus?"

"Emeritus to what? That whorehouse?"

"No, no, Rabbi, be calm," said Milton. "It's an honor. You'd value it. I know you would."

"You're mistaken, Milton. Now leave me alone. I don't need your honors. You have no honor. And I don't need you to love me. My wife is with me, my children are with me, my parents always loved me. Leave me alone, will you? Talk to my lawyer if you're ready to talk about money. That's what I need, Milton, I think even you are capable of understanding that much. I have six children to support."

"Yeah, *that* you knew how to do," said Milton impulsively. He struck himself on the side of the head for punishment.

"Every one of them is in school," said Shoe, ignoring him, "and I'm proud of it. But I'm already on borrowed money. You owe me money and either you're going to give it to me before the hearing or after it. Talk to my lawyer and make a sensible offer. As bad off as I am, I wouldn't be in your place for anything. You'll have to live with all your destruction and justify it. I won't."

"Let's make it look better," pleaded Milton. "For the sake of the community. Let's not go on quarreling. How about a testimonial dinner? Would that be meaningful? With a purse presented to you? And we could put a plaque by the entrance; the Rosenstock Building? Wouldn't you rather do things that way?"

"I'll see you in court," said Shoe evenly. "If you want to speak to my lawyer before then, I'll give you his number. I don't blame you for being scared."

Milton heard him shouting, "Myra! Myra! Where's Bobby's phone number?" He gently hung up. He went to the mirror hung over the gold-trimmed sink and stared into it, cupping his hands around his face. The water lilies etched into the lower corners of the mirror framed him. "Old," he said. He sighed and coughed and turned away, blew his nose.

32

It was the morning of the holiday and Shoe finished his coffee standing by the kitchen sink. Sunlight came through the window and lit up the overflowing garbage pail and the unswept floor. His black suit attracted dust and dog hair as he stood there. "Let's go, Myra," he said, setting down the cup. "I must leave right now for the church."

"I'll be ready in a few more minutes," she said. "You go ahead. Take Etta. The rest of them already went ahead with the Etkinds in their van."

"I don't see why you can't be ready when I am," he said. "I'm going. Etta!" he shouted.

"She's waiting in the car for you," said Myra, wincing. "Will you please go?"

As soon as she heard his car pull away, Myra brought out a bottle of sherry from the pantry. "I'll get through today," she said to the dog. "Then tomorrow. That's how I'll have to do it." She drank from the bottle. The phone rang.

"Myra?" said Faigy Greenwald. "I thought I might still catch you. Darling, I just want to wish you a very happy New Year. Let this year be a better one for all of us. I think the new congregation has every possibility and I'm so glad Shoe wants to stay with us. We love you both, you know. So much."

Myra's eyes stung. "Thank you, Faigy. Happy New Year to you.

I'll see you at the church in a few minutes. I'm just about to leave."

Faigy laughed. "Yes," she sang. "Get me to the church on time." She hung up and the phone rang again. "Mommy? Etta."

"I know," said Myra. "What did Daddy forget?"

"His glasses," said Etta. "He says they're either in the living room or by his side of the bed or in the kitchen and you should bring them."

"Okay, I'll be right there," said Myra. She went up to the bedroom to look for the glasses. The phone by the bed rang. "What?" snapped Myra, picking up the receiver. "What else, Etta?"

"It's Suzy Warmflash, Myra," came the voice. "Happy New Year, dear, health and happiness to all of you."

Myra sat down on the unmade bed. The sherry boiled up in her throat. "I have to hand it to you for gall, Suzy," she said. "But I suppose it's nice of you. Happy New Year to you too."

"You see?" said Suzy. "I told Harry there'd be no hard feelings. I said to him, 'Don't start in with injunctions and all that legal business. Let me call my friend Myra, and we women will straighten it out.'"

"I don't follow you." The sherry burned in her chest.

"Yes, you do, honey. We just heard this morning that Shoe is holding services in the church over there on Manor Street. Now, honey, you should know we couldn't allow that. I'm surprised at you."

"You won't allow—?" She burped. Hot fluid came up her throat.

"You should realize that, honey," said Suzy. "You should know that anything a rabbi does reflects on all of us. Shoe can't do as he pleases. We aren't living in Palestine, you know. It makes it very awkward for us to have him over there in the church like some kind of counter movement. Now just explain it to him, will you, so Harry won't go tearing off to the police station? And you can tell Shoe," she confided, "that Harry has forbidden our little mutual friend, the professor, to say one single word today to the congregation." She laughed. "So it's fair, isn't it?"

"I'd love to talk, Suzy," said Myra. "Another day." She hung up. The phone rang at once. "I have nothing else to say, Suzy," said Myra.

"It's Etta, Mommy. Daddy says bring him two clean handkerchiefs."

"All right, sweetie. Now don't call any more. I'm leaving."

"There's a lot of people here, Mom," said Etta. "Daddy's feeling pretty good. Winn is here with him. He says he's waiting to see you. He's got a present for you."

"I'll be right there." She returned to the kitchen with the handkerchiefs. She opened the back door and let out the dog. "Happy New Year, my doggy," she said.

The woman next door called over the hedge, "Happy New Year!" and waved at Myra. Myra waved back, astonished, and went to her car. Something cracked loudly as she backed out of the driveway. She opened the car door and looked down to see that she had rolled over a bamboo rake. What pigs, she said to herself. She drove on. Six children and one husband and not one of them can bend down to pick up a rake. She braked and made a wide U-turn in the street, holding her breath, and sped back to the house. She had forgotten Shoe's glasses. The dog broke into a wild run as she went across the backyard. "No, no!" she cried as he raced toward her. He jumped up and put his paws on her shoulders as though centuries had passed since they had been together. He licked her face. "Stop, you idiot!" she cried, knocking him down. She rushed into the kitchen and saw Shoe's glasses by the sink, on top of his prayer book, also forgotten. "Oh, great," she said.

The dog trailed in, his tail as limp as his ears. He put his nose to her knee and stood motionless, eyes on her shoe. "I'm sorry," she said impatiently. "You know very well I didn't mean it. I'm just in such a damn hurry. Daddy's waiting." He wagged his tail. "You know I love you," she said desperately. "Can I leave now?"

She ran back to the car and drove over the splintering rake again. She could hear the phone ringing in the house. "Tough," she said. "I'm not available."

Winn waited in his study at the church with Shoe. A painting of Jesus with a lily in his hand hung on the brown wall behind him. He rose from his brown chair and reached for her across the brown carpet. "Myra, Myra," he said, beaming. "Happy New Year, my dear, you're looking lovely. I have something magnificent for you." He went into the bathroom off the study.

"Warmflash is trying for an injunction," she said in an undertone. Shoe leaned forward to hear her. "I guess we have time to get through the morning service before he really starts trouble."

Winn came out of the bathroom with a clear plastic box in his oversized hands. Through the plastic, Myra could see a monstrous purple orchid. "A corsage for you!" Winn cried with delight. "Surprised? I told the florist you'd be thrilled. I asked him for what we used to have back in the old days. I said, 'This is for a real woman, not one of your little so-called teeny boppers of today.' He had to order it especially for me. Seems it's out of fashion. A lot they know!" he cried, wriggling with pleasure. "Put it on, my dear. Let us see how you look."

Myra took the truly awful bloom in her hands. "I love it, Winn. I'm pleased to tears."

"Say, I'm a little jealous," said Shoe, standing up.

"Good, good, that's good," said Winn in transports of excitement. He capered about the brown room and came back to them. He stood between them and threw his hands across their shoulders. "By the way," he said, "don't worry about that injunction business." He walked to his leather-topped desk and sat down.

"Ah, my God, they never quit," said Myra. "There'll be trouble before the day is over. Let's just live an hour at a time."

"No, my dear," said Winn. "The matter arose last week—"

"But Suzy told me they only heard about this service today. . . ."

"Don't tell me she lied to you," said Shoe. He widened his eyes. "Not your pal, Suzy Warmflash."

"Yes," said Winn distantly. "And it was taken up with my chief vestryman and the chief of police, who conferred with me a bit. There won't be any trouble."

"What's your vestryman got to do with it?" asked Shoe.

"Oh, sorry," said Winn. "Forgot to mention it." He cast down his eyes. "He's the mayor." Shoe burst out laughing. Winn jumped to his feet. "Now, happy New Year, good people, and remember me in your prayers. Remind the God of Abraham of all the miserable sinners in His care. God bless you, dear people."

"I'm so ashamed, Winn," Myra said faintly. She put her face to Shoe's thick shoulder. "I'm so ashamed of the Jews."

"No, no, Myra," said Winn. "My dear, do you actually think this is about the Jews?" He encircled them both with his long arms and huge hands. "No, no, my dear, this is a story of human beings. Human beings and what they can do to each other. It's the story of mankind."

Myra drew away from the men. She kept silent.

"Thank you for everything, Winn," Shoe said finally. "I'd better be getting started."

"How does the orchid look?" asked Myra. The petals grazed her chin as she spoke. The pin scratched her collarbone.

"Oh! Absolutely magnificent! Happy New Year!"

They went to the chapel door and separated. Shoe mounted the steps to the high white pulpit. Behind him a faded American flag hung against the wall. As the sunlight touched the flag, the brass cross concealed beneath it glowed. Before the pulpit stood a square mahogany table covered with old lace. The Torah rested on the lace, wrapped in crimson velvet.

"He looks good, thank God," whispered Faigy Greenwald to her husband in their pew. "Thank God, it's all behind us now."

"The beautiful vases of rhododendrons," announced Shoe, "are given by Lena Bloom and her son Bil—William, in memory of their husband and father and my good friend, Dr. Charles Bloom. I also would like to tell you that I have received a number of contributions in Dr. Bloom's memory and honor, which will be used to make a gift to this church, which has extended such hospitable arms to us. All Souls has invited us to meet here for as long as we like."

A gray-haired man stood in the vestibule arguing with Nathan. "I'm a stranger here," he told the boy. "I must be allowed to attend. I'm a Jew." His body was tense and alert. "It's Rosh Hashanah. You have to let me in."

"Go right in," said Nathan.

"Don't talk to me donations, don't talk me money," said the man in a threatening voice. "It's a holiday."

"No, sir," said Nathan, grinning. "Just go in. Happy New Year."

"What gives you the right, young fellow, to just let any shnorrer inside?" the man said indignantly. "You just let people in off the street?"

"Yes, sir," said Nathan happily. "That's the way the rabbi is. You can go in if you want. If you don't want to, you don't have to."

"That's no way to talk to Jewish people," the man said. He glared at Nathan and went inside, still suspicious.

Fritz Newman distributed prayer books. He leaned toward the Etkind family, lined up side by side in a varnished pew. Bobby and his wife sat like bookends, pinning their sons between them. The boys were radiantly uncomfortable in their starched shirts.

"Here are your books, my friends," Fritz said. "You look like a perfect goyishe family, all you redheads together in church. Bobby, the rabbi wants you to help him with the Torah reading. Happy New Year." He limped away with the prayer books for the rest of the congregation.

Norman Dorfman yawned. "How long till we can leave?" he asked his wife. He hit her ribs with his elbow. "What time is it now?"

"This can become a wonderful congregation," said Dr. Tannenbaum, sitting next to Norman. "I know a number of unaffiliated Jewish guys at the college who should join us."

Norman covered his eyes with his hand. "Jeez, can you run a little check on 'em first? The idea gives me the chills. It brings little Winegarden to my mind, he should drop dead and roast in hell."

Marie Dorfman leaned across Norman and said, "Get them, Doctor. We want all the members we can get. Invite them. Don't pay attention to Norman. Norman," she said, pulling at his arm, "you get one mosquito bite, you never go outside again? That's not like you, Norman."

"I could take it, myself," said Norman, uncovering his eyes. "I was thinking about the rabbi."

There was a brick front walk leading to the front doors of the church. Outside, the Kligman family, arriving late, stood on the walk. Their son spoke to Etta, who was too restless to sit down in the church. "I wouldn't have recognized you, except that I saw you at the congregational meeting," the boy said. He blushed. "I'm sorry. I didn't mean to mention it."

"That's okay, Donny," said Etta belligerently. "We're not ashamed of anything we did. I'm proud of my father and he's proud of me." She looked the boy up and down. "I'll bet I wouldn't have known you, either. I haven't seen you, really, since sixth grade."

Donny turned his body away from his parents, who were studying the church landscaping. "Have dinner with me, Etta? Soon?" he said, just above a whisper. "Do you like French cooking?"

Etta looked closely at him. French? Was she being mocked? But all she saw was a shy boy she had known all her life. "I guess so," she said carelessly. "Anything's fine."

The service was beginning. Shoe said, "We open our prayer books . . ."

Myra was alone in the empty balcony. A little rash was developing on her neck, caused by the touch of the orchid. She looked around herself at the empty pews up there and at the tops of the trees, losing their leaves and scratching against the tall church windows, and stretched out full length in the pew. She smiled at the pale blue ceiling. Shoe's voice sounded strong, carried well up to her. She felt hungry.

Nathan looked out through the front entrance of the church. "Hey, Aaron," he called his brother softly. "Here he comes. Nussbaum."

Kevin Nussbaum strode quickly up the brick walk past Etta and the Kligmans with bells on his fingers. He came up on the shady church porch and looked around. His robe was white, his bare feet were filthy. "Filch, zilch," he mumbled. "Ring, sing."

Kligman came up on the porch. "You want some help, boys?" he asked quietly.

Aaron said, "No, it's all right. Our dad told us to expect him. Here, Nussbaum," he said. "Stand over here where it's sunny. You'll get too cold in the shade."

Kevin looked haughtily at Aaron and Nathan. "I know it," he said in an everyday voice. "You think I don't know it's September? You think I don't know it's Rosh Hashanah?"

"Sure, you do," said Nathan. "Our father told us you'd be here. Happy New Year, Nussbaum." The Rosenstock boys went inside the church with the Kligmans. Etta followed last with a regretful look behind her at the fall sunshine. Kevin sat on the porch's edge and let his bare feet dangle. He shook his arms rhythmically so that the bells sounded continually as he mumbled his mantra. He said his mantra and he repeated his "Hear, O Israel" several times with his eyes fastened on a parked Cadillac half a block away. "Winegarden," he said, working it into his chant. "Winegarden," he sang and shook his bells. "Winegarden."

"And now," said Shoe, on the pulpit, "we will begin. This marks the beginning of the beginning." The sun was in his eyes. His glasses were still in Myra's purse. The faces of the congregation were unclear to him. He looked out before him lovingly. He raised his arms. The sleeves of his black robe fluttered. "And now, with the permission of God; with the permission of the congregation; by the authority of the Academy on high; and of the Academy here below; we declare it lawful," he said mightily. "It is lawful to pray with those who have transgressed."

33

The Rosenstocks all came in the front door of the house, in honor of the holiday. They laid their prayer books on the bench in the front hall and dropped their jackets on the floor. They looked together from the dim center hall through the archway into the dining room. A ceremonially large silver bowl filled with apples was in the center of the table. The polished silver flashed against the white cloth as Myra switched on the chandelier. They looked at the apples; maroon flecked with ivory; faint yellow stripes on bright red; green apples, as green as the flesh of a honeydew melon. A silver bowl of honey stood next to the apples and an enormous long polished challeh lay on the table.

"Mommy's an artist," said Shoe. He went to the table, the family following, and broke off the end of the bread with his hands. He said the blessing and handed each one a chunk of the yellow bread. He took an apple from the heaped bowl and laughed easily as the mound collapsed and apples rolled across the table. The dog pounced on a fallen apple and slobbered on it. Milton Winegarden's Cadillac rolled by in front of the house, unnoticed.

Myra said, "If you'll each help me for two minutes, we'll get dinner on the table right away."

There was a sudden break for the staircase. Shoe and Myra stood alone in the dining room with the dog, who slowly wagged his tail.

"This family!" she said. They laughed. Shoe followed her into the kitchen, steamy with chicken soup vapors on the windows, the odor of burnt onion rising from the oven. She stood at the sink and ran water over a colanderful of tomatoes. He stood close behind her and put his arms around her waist, pressing against her.

"You were good," she said over her shoulder. "I don't know how you do it. You're always good, no matter what's going on." He turned her around to face him as Milton drove around the corner again, straining to see into the dining room from his car.

"Ma!" screamed one of the girls down the stairs. "Joey's here! The doctor! He's fast asleep like Snow White in my bed with his hospital clothes on!"

Shoe and Myra looked at each other. "Now I have everything," said Myra. "Happy New Year," Shoe said. He kissed her lips. Laughing, she stuck her tongue into his half-open mouth. The dog pressed at their knees, trying to get in between them. They pushed closer together.

Etta walked in wearing shorts and sneakers. "Don't you two know you've got young children growing up in this house?" she said, and the water suddenly overflowed the sink behind Myra, drenching the back of her dress. They broke apart. Myra frantically dropped newspapers on the floor to sop up the water while the dog paced excitedly across the wet paper.

Shoe shouted at the bottom of the stairs. "Come on down!"

Milton slowed up outside and leaned across the front seat, trying to see into the house.

They sat down to the soup, the chicken, the carrots in honey, the noodle pudding. The boys belched. The girls objected. Everybody asked Joey questions. The heap of dirty dishes in the kitchen grew and Etta took care to scrape the chicken bones together on a dish out of the dog's reach. Shoe sliced apples as rapidly as a machine and accepted the family's compliments. Honey lay in blobs and strings on the cloth as they passed the bowl around and dipped their apple slices in it.

"Boy, I love this," said Aaron lazily. He leaned back in his seat. "Why don't we eat like this all the time?"

"Poor boy," mocked Shoe.

"Does anyone stop you?" demanded Myra.

The dog jumped to the door, barking loudly. "Who?" said Myra. "Who would have the nerve?" Her face reddened. "Who would dare?" She went to the door and opened it, stood speechless by the open door. Her hand, which still held a streaked linen napkin, moved to her face, then to her throat. A silent moment passed. The family became quiet and turned toward her.

"Who is it?" called Shoe. "Welcome, come in," he called. "A good year! Why are you standing there, Myra?"

She dropped her napkin to the floor and went to the kitchen without a word. Milton Winegarden, flushed and itching with tension, stepped into the dining room. He kept his hand in the pocket of his tweed jacket. Etta got up so abruptly she knocked her chair over. She rushed through the kitchen and out to the backyard where she began to weep loudly. The other girls went out to her.

"*Shana tovah*," said Milton quietly. He smiled minutely at Shoe.

"What do you want, Milton?" said Shoe, keeping his seat.

Milton said nothing, stared stupidly about the room, taking in the remains of the feast scattered on the table.

"You want some honey and apple?" said Shoe. He sat, powerful and relaxed, hooking his armpits over the posts of his chair. "You want a cup of tea? Or coffee?"

Nathan left. He went to the kitchen and viciously pulled a dried, baked noodle away from the side of a casserole dish. He popped it in his mouth. Tears came to his eyes as it scraped painfully down his throat. Never, he vowed to himself. Never will I eat shit. I'll be rich. I'll never eat shit like Daddy. He heard Etta crying in the backyard, the other girls trying to soothe her, whimpering themselves. "Will you shut up out there?" he yelled. "You women!"

Joey was upstairs, crying. He threw himself across his old bed. What use was it? Was it possible to cure anything at all? This ugly little cretin was like a rampant cancer; kill him here, he appears elsewhere. No, it was no use, there was no cure, no hope. Joey fell asleep, exhausted after twenty-four hours on emergency.

"You want some schnapps, Milton?" persisted Shoe. A smile he suppressed kept coming to his mouth.

Aaron unconsciously imitated his father, sat back with his armpits hooked over the back of his chair, at ease. "What is it?" he said gently. "What do you want, Dr. Winegarden?" with that same smile playing on his face.

Myra was morbidly drawn to listen at the dining-room window. She stood in a tangle of blighted lilacs and said through the screen, "Don't give him anything of mine. I mean it!" She was through. She tried to think of how she would break it to Shoe. But there was no way she could go on living with him. Not with a man who allowed every reptile and creeping thing to enter her home; never mind that it was a holiday, never mind that he exposed her children to these base creatures, hardly human beings, but to offer this scaly being his hospitality! No, she was through. She could not recall a single moment of happiness; no, never. She brushed at her eyes, at the cobwebs sticking to the diseased lilacs, which stood, really, for the condition of her whole life, and she sniffled. She peered in at the disgusting little Winegarden. Why did he keep his hand in his pocket that way? Was he going to stand in her dining room on Rosh Hashanah and play with himself? She slammed back into the house.

"What do you want, Milton?" she screamed, only it seemed to come out in her ordinary voice, and he seemed to take it as an ordinary question.

"I want . . . ," he answered softly and looked around him. He looked like a sleepwalker, unaware that he is on the edge of a cliff. He caressed the pistol he carried in a plastic sandwich bag in his pocket and left it where it was. He felt absentminded. He felt as though he watched a character named Milton Winegarden on a stage. He wondered what Milton Winegarden would do next. He heard himself from far back in the theater. "I want . . . ," he said dreamily. The player had forgotten his lines. He held the pistol against his wet palm. He wondered abstractly if the moisture would affect it. He went toward Shoe, fixing his eyes on a patch of dry skin on Shoe's forehead.

Myra jumped. With great aversion, she took his tweed-covered short arm between her fingertips and led him back to the front door. He went with her as in a sleep, smiling hazily. "That's all, Milton," she said firmly, feeling nausea. "Go home. Good night, now." She pushed him gently through the door and slammed it at his back. She whirled back to Shoe and Aaron. "Stop laughing! What's funny about it?"

"Oh, Ma," said Aaron. "It was just getting good."

"Got any cake?" said Shoe. He went to the window to watch Milton climb up into the Cadillac and pull away. "Wonder how it went over there today? At the synagogue," he added, as though Myra would not understand.

34

Milton came into his dim kitchen in the still house. He saw a note from Sunny on the refrigerator and ignored it. He dragged himself up the stairs to his study, tired, very tired. He unlocked the room and went directly to the mirror over the sink. The furrows around his mouth were dark and deep. He saw a rocking chair out of the corner of his eye and turned to look at it. A surprise from Sunny? Not in the best of taste.

His mother materialized in the rocker. Her apron was smeared with chicken blood and chicken droppings. It was stuck all over with pinfeathers. "What are you doing here, Momma?" he demanded. "You know I told you to stay away from me."

She held out her stringy arms to him. "Moisheh, Moisheleh," she said. "Never a letter, never a phone call, son?"

"Leave at once," he said coldly. "Please leave."

"Son," she repeated angrily. She shook a blackened, chapped market woman's fist at him.

"Stop bullying me," he said. "I'm a Ph.D. doctor. Get out." The old lady sat motionless. "Take a look at this," he said. He dropped his pants and stepped out of his shorts and faced her.

She threw back her gray head and laughed. "Ha, ha, ha," she cried. "Ho, ho, ho. You think I'm impressed?" She drew up her rough woolen skirt and exposed herself. A long penis hung to her knees like a dark, mottled sausage. "You think you'll impress me, shmendrik?" she said. "You'll try to impress a judge with that little wienie?" She flung a handful of pink and blue chicken intestines from her pocket at him.

He jumped, rejuvenated. "You can't catch me!" he said in excitement. "Nyah, nyah, you can't catch me!" He neatly whipped a designer bath sheet across himself like a toreador and stepped out of the way of the flying intestines with the mincing steps of a bullfighter. "Olé," he shouted. "Beat it!" He did a fast waltz clog over to the mirror. He saw without looking directly that the old lady was disappearing. He stared again into the mirror. "Oh, Carmen, I love you," he said. He snatched a plastic flower from the block of room deodorant, shaped like a flowerpot, which stood on the broad ledge of the sink. He jammed the wire stem in his ear. The pain was staggering. He held to the dolphin faucets with all his strength while his head roared. Something trickled down his earlobe. He avoided the mirror. His sadness and fatigue were returning after the moment of challenge.

He dropped his tie and shirt to the floor, keeping his tweed jacket over his arm. He withdrew the pistol from the pocket and ran his itching fingers over its contours within the plastic bag. "Oh, Yossel," he exhaled. "I only wanted . . ." He began to pace his study, nude and crooked forward. He put the pistol into his concealed wall safe, where the permit was. He slammed it shut. "What did I want?" he whined. "Was it so much to ask? Oh, Yossel . . . bigger men . . . if we were bigger men . . . Oh, Yossel, I only wanted . . ." He felt his forehead for fever. His body felt painfully bent. "A bath, I need a bath," he said restlessly. His skin was flaming and erupting. He ran water in the tub. Straightening up his husky small body, he pulled the flower from his ear and suffered a terrible wave of dizziness. It passed and he began a slow, shuffling fox-trot back to the mirror with Yossel in his arms. "Save the last dance for me," he moaned. He let Yossel go and pulled open the mirror to study the white shelves built in behind it. He took a grape lipstick from a lacquered, Chinese box and wrote with it on the wall.

"Tell Yossel," he wrote.

Then he wrote, "Sunny: Best regards."

He giggled. He went back to the medicine chest and, with that earlier sense of watching a character named Milton Winegarden on a stage, he watched this character take down a glass apothecary jar filled with blue pills, each with a pink belt around the middle.

The first handful went down dry. Then the actor took some with water; a scoop with hot, a fistful with cold, for variety; till the bottle was empty. The tub was filling. He climbed up on top of the toilet tank. "Remember," he said in a little boy's voice, because evidently the actor now thought he was a child, "only Superman can fly." And then the deluded actor raised his arms anyway, to fly over tall buildings, and leaped, and belly flopped into the full tub. The water flowed heavily over the edge as Milton quivered, face down in the water. He breathed deeply, deeply content, and began to die. In a few minutes he fouled the water.

Still running from the mouth of a golden dolphin, the water seeped through the floor to the bedroom below, staining the carpet and the crewelwork spread and lifting the veneers off the period furniture. And still Milton's body bobbed and swayed in the tub. The water continued downward to the dining room. It trickled down the crystal pendants of the chandelier and into the huge Ming bowl in the middle of the table. The bowl filled and toppled over, spilling water across the mahogany and cascading to the flowered carpet beneath. A ball of dust picked up speed and raced with the water beneath the swinging door to the kitchen. Soft crumbs of wax lifted off the kitchen floor and hardened in the fast-moving stream. The water ran under the door out to the attached garage. As it flowed over the sill the burglar alarm was activated. It rang steadily in the silence of the house.

35

"It has to be Rosenstock," said Irving Seltzer that night. "The one and only question is who's going to call him."

"I still don't see it," said Mimi. They sat in Sunny's dining room beside the big coffee maker she had brought over. The house was full; people talked quietly and ogled the water marks everywhere. They stepped fastidiously on the spongy rugs and made no mention of them. "Just because Yossel is off sucking his thumb somewhere," said Mimi righteously, "it doesn't mean we have to go back to Rosenstock. There must be another rabbi in the world to do this funeral."

"Sunny wants it that way," said Irving, clenching his hands. "Isn't that enough for you? The main thing is, let's get it over with. I'll call him if you won't."

"Be my guest," she said with a shrug of her great shoulder. "I wouldn't make that call for a million dollars."

Irving dialed from a needlepointed chair. "Rabbi?" Mimi heard him say. "You heard, I guess? Yes, well, the funeral is tomorrow naturally, and Sunny wants you, if you'll be kind enough."

"Of course," said Shoe. Mimi was by now listening on the kitchen extension. "I will. Only I'm not sure that Sunny will be comfortable with it. I wouldn't want to upset her further. Have you heard her say she wants me? Directly?"

"Take it from me, Rabbi," said Irving.

"Well," said Shoe doubtfully. "Just put her on, would you? I'll speak to her for just a second."

Sunny rose from a chair at a distant window to take the phone. "Hello, Rabbi," she said flatly. "It's true. I want you to do it."

"Sunny," said Shoe, "I'm sorry—"

"Never mind, Rabbi," said Sunny. "I see things more clearly now. It was him or me."

Shoe cleared his throat. "Do you own a grave, Sunny?" he asked.

"It's all taken care of," she said. "I'm burning him. This time tomorrow he'll be in the oven."

"Sunny," he said, "I want to give you my sympathy—"

"Just do what you have to do," she interrupted. "I have to get it over with. There are no survivors but me. Friends . . ." She laughed. "Don't knock yourself out. Just do it and then we'll burn him."

"All right, then," said Shoe. "I'll be at the synagogue tomorrow. Myra sends her love."

"Sure," said Sunny. She hung up. "I think I'll give Rosenstock a thousand dollars," she announced. "No more calls," she told Irving as she left the room.

Mimi returned. "I hope she's not cracking up," she said, rolling her eyes. "A thousand dollars! For what? To stand there?"

"Enough, for God's sake," begged Irving. "Is it your money?"

"Speaking of which," said Mimi, "I better get my rear in gear and do whatever shopping I can tonight. She wants me to cater tomorrow. You think it's safe to lay out the money, Irving? Rich, rich; then they don't pay. It wouldn't be the first time. What do you think, Irving? Two hundred bagels enough, Irving? Look up the bakery number, Irving."

"Look it up yourself," he retorted. "This is a house of mourning. Have you no sense at all?"

"And what exactly is wrong with our Rabbi Yossel?" Mimi asked. She was making a shopping list.

"I don't know *exactly*," he said with sarcasm. "He's had to be hospitalized. They say he collapsed. I don't know what that means, do you?"

"It means we have to start looking for a new rabbi," said Mimi briskly, looking up from her list. "It's all for the best. We need to make a fresh start." She rubbed her hands together.

Faigy Greenwald left her plate of honey cake on the warped dining-room table and hurried home to phone the Rosenstocks. "I'm sorry to be the one to tell you this, Myra," she began. She hesitated. "But you'll have to know . . ."

"Thank you, Faigy," said Myra. "We were already called. She wants Shoe. I can't understand it."

"Who can?" said Faigy. "Who knows what anybody wants? I don't understand anything. Poor thing."

Myra went back to sit in silence next to Shoe on the old sofa. She put her head against his shoulder. He held her hand. Upstairs, someone was taking a shower. A stereo played in the girls' room.

"Tortious!" shouted Nathan, throwing a ball at the dog. The dog raced across the yard. "Contumacious!" He laughed till the tears came.

Etta said, "How do you ever learn all that stuff, Natey?"

Joey came outside. "Think that's tough?" he bragged. "Do you know how many bones there are in the foot alone?"

Myra smiled on the old sofa. "I can't believe it," she said after a time. She stretched out with her head in his lap. "This has been some day." She smiled upward. "It's too good to be true."

"Oh, Myra," said Shoe. He pulled his thighs away from her and moved over. "Oh, Myra," he said, scowling.

"It's like an answer to my prayers," she insisted.

"Oh, don't, Myra," he said. "Death. Death." He stared at the floor. "And to have to do that funeral tomorrow. God only knows what will happen."

36

They stood facing each other in their front hall. Shoe was in his black suit; Myra stood barefooted, braced against him, angry and gaunt in her oldest blue jeans and a tattered sweat shirt of Joey's. "Go," she said. "But don't you dare tell me to go."

"What'll you do this afternoon?" asked Shoe quietly.

"You think I need funerals to keep me amused?" she said. She tightened his tie. "Although this one I might like. But you say the casket will be closed, so where's the fun of it? If I could see the little creep dead, I might be tempted to go." She looked at him. "Don't answer me. Don't say a thing," she said.

"Myra," he said, "a Jew has died. A man is dead."

"So?" she said.

"I have to go, Myra. It's my duty. Obligation."

"So go then, good-by. I swore I'd never set foot there again and I won't. I said I'd never speak another word to those people and I'm not even tempted. You go if you want. I'm not telling you how to feel." She put her hand on the front doorknob. "Good-by."

"It's not that I want, Myra," he said unhappily. "I want you to understand. He was a Jew. He died."

"Well, why didn't he die a long time ago? That's what I'd like to know," she said shrilly. She shook the doorknob. The dog leaned disconsolately against her leg. "A man they find dead from pills in a bathtub full of turds; he had to live to be your judge? And the police find a pistol in a safe in his room? What else will they find? Tarantulas? He had to live to say you aren't worthy of him?" She reached over and tightened his tie further. The dog ran into the dining room and got under the table. "Give him a respectable end, if you insist, and let's forget him! Thank God he killed himself and not you, you simpleminded, childish, naive . . ." She shook his tie. "You're going to do it, so quit wasting time, as the prostitute said." She let go of his tie and walked toward the kitchen. "Maybe I'll wash my hair. Do something meaningful."

Shoe loosened the tie, picked a single dog hair off his leg, shook his head hopelessly, and left the house.

The synagogue parking lot was packed. Instead of using the main doors, he went inside through the school wing. The keys were still on his key ring. He saw the custodian in the hall.

"Rabbi, Rabbi," said Matthew, pumping Shoe's hand. He was Shoe's height and just as burly. His white hair stood up and his black forehead was creased. "Sure is good to see you. I knew I'd see you here again."

"You're looking good, Matt," said Shoe. "It's just for today, you know, for the funeral."

"Amen," said Matthew. "And hallelujah. The man is gone."

"Matt," said Shoe, "I just realized I came without my robe. Can you let me into the study? I'll borrow one of Rabbi Yossel's."

"Follow me, Rabbi," said Matthew. He led Shoe to the janitor's closet and unlocked it. There, hanging above the deep sink, was a black pulpit robe Shoe had forgotten, in a clear plastic bag. "Had it cleaned for you and all," said Matthew smugly. "Knew it was just a matter of time, O Lord, and you'd be back. I'm ready." He pushed aside his mops and took down the robe. He presented it with a flourish. "Amen, here it is."

Shoe was moved. "Thank you, Matt. I'll just be here today, you know, for the funeral."

"God *rest* him," said Matthew energetically. "Amen."

"Family okay?" asked Shoe.

"Bless the Lord, oh, my soul," said Matthew. "How's the missus?"

"Fine," said Shoe. "She won't be here today, though."

"Uh-hunhh," said Matthew through his nose. "Ah-hanhh, women . . ."

Shoe inhaled to ready himself. "I guess I have to go into the sanctuary. I'm damned if I know what to say." He looked at the custodian.

"Twenty-third Psalm's right nice," offered Matthew.

Shoe grinned. "I swear," he said, "they ought to give you the job."

"Lord, no!" exclaimed Matthew. He held up his hands. "Look upon me in mine affliction; have mercy, O Lord!"

"I'll see you later, afterward, Matthew. . . ."

"The Lord bless you and keep you," the custodian said, eyes moist.

"Hello, Rabbi," said a man, offering his hand before he reached Shoe. Matthew walked away, looking busy. "I'm a distant cousin of Sunny's. Thought I'd say hello before the service and thank you. You're a really big man to do this for us. A gent."

"Can you make any suggestions," said Shoe, holding onto the man's hand, "for the eulogy?"

The man laughed. "Rabbi, I was his best friend, probably, and I'd have to say he was a no-good sonofabitch. Oho, I tell you, we're all waiting to see what you'll say."

"Great," said Shoe. He walked with the man into the overheated sanctuary, pulling on his robe as they went. The large room was buzzing. Silence fell as he walked the aisle alone to the dais. Several people stood as he passed and offered a handshake without speaking. Shoe climbed the three steps to the lectern. He felt relaxed, at home. He looked at the crowd. He knew almost every person present.

"Friends," he began, "friends . . ."

"Oh no, here we go again," moaned Mimi in her pew. "We're *not* his friends. Can't he get that through his head?"

"*Will* you shut up?" said Irving in a furious whisper. "I see Myra coming in." Mimi shrugged her weighty shoulders.

Sunny Winegarden sat in the first row, dry-eyed, in a tweed jacket and jodhpurs. Her boots caught the autumnal sunlight as it flashed across the varnished coffin lid.

"Friends," Shoe said, "we are gathered here to express to Sunny . . ." Sunny gave a slight start. Her cousin put his arm around her. ". . . and to recognize, not for the first time, that our life is as grass. As the grass that withers, as the flower that fades . . ."

Mimi squinted in the bright light flashing off the coffin. She whispered, "That casket is so big. . . ." Irving touched her hand.

"It is a gift," said Shoe. "Life is a gift. But one that is not ours to keep. We only have it a little while. . . ."

Irving began to cry quietly. Mimi looked at him, shocked.

"We must endeavor so to live . . ." said Shoe.

Irving wiped his cheeks with his palms. "We've done wrong," he sniffled. "Milt's dead, the rabbi's half dead, just look at him; Sunny's a widow. Is this what we wanted?" He looked at Mimi with red, swimming eyes. She gave him a handkerchief and looked away, staring again at the large coffin. Why did Milton need such a large coffin? She pictured Milton in it, bloated and swelling, like a sponge in water, pressing at the sides of the coffin. Was that it? Her stomach rumbled.

"We have been following the life of Moses," said Shoe, as though there had been no struggle, no interruption, no congregational meeting; as though no hearing lay before him, now without Milton; as though he still were rabbi of this place. "In recent readings, we saw how Moses became the leader of his people and how he took them out of Egypt, the land of their enslavement. You all know the story," he said in a reassuring voice. "Of the final and most devastating act of the Lord: the killing of the firstborn of every Egyptian family." He looked down at the great pulpit Bible. "'There was a great cry in Egypt, for there was not a house where there was not one dead.' And how the Egyptians then hastened the Israelites on their way because, they said, 'We are all dead men.'"

"I don't like all this talk about death," muttered Mimi, her eyes fixed on the coffin. She was troubled. Suppose it were someone else in there? Irving blew his nose and sighed. Mimi remembered how her father, a powerful, obese man, had at the end exposed to them the dainty person he carried in himself, how he had revealed the delicate man inside the large one as his strokes, his heart attacks, his cancer, had eaten him away. Now here was Milton, just the opposite, growing huge in this huge coffin. Death was such a strange matter.

"But later Pharaoh repented of his decision to let our people go," said Shoe. "He sent horses and chariots in pursuit. You all know what happened," he said. "'The children of Israel walked upon the dry land in the midst of the sea; and the waters were a wall unto them on their right hand, and on their left.' And what happened to the Egyptians?" he asked. "Moses stretched forth his hand over the Red Sea as God had told him to do and 'they went down in the depths like a stone.' That's what it says," he breathed. "And Miriam, the prophetess," he said, "Miriam took a timbrel in her hand and led out the women and they danced and sang." Shoe lifted his arms. "'Sing ye to the Lord,' they sang," called Shoe. "'Sing ye,'" he called out, his black sleeves fluttering. "'For He is highly exalted; the horse and his rider hath He thrown into the sea . . .'"

"Is he talking about drowning?" asked Harry, incredulous. Suzy clutched at her withered throat and leaned against him.

"'Thou didst blow with Thy wind, the sea covered them; they sank as lead in the mighty waters.'"

"This is unbearable," said Suzy, trembling. "It's not fair to Sunny. She'll pass out."

Sunny Winegarden sat quietly next to her cousin, attentive, squat and buxom, calm.

"And when Miriam led the women out to sing and dance in triumph at these miraculous events—miraculous!—we are told that the angels of the Lord rejoiced also." Shoe paused. "And the Lord reproached them," he said softly. "'My creatures are drowning,' said the Lord. 'Will you then rejoice?'" His voice broke. "Will you then rejoice?"

Irving wept loudly. Mimi felt stunned, unable to hear clearly or to see the great casket only a few yards from her seat. Faigy Greenwald put her head down on the back of the seat in front of her and sobbed. "I love that man, I don't care what anybody says," she cried into her forearms.

"Will you then rejoice?" repeated Shoe, eyes glistening. "The dead praise not the Lord. God desires not the death of the sinner," he said. "God wants His people Israel to live. He wants His people to live and flourish in righteousness. He wants us to turn from evil and live!" He looked over the casket at the people before him. "And now we will have a moment of silent prayer and meditation. You may wish to read the twenty-third Psalm in our prayer book or to pray whatever prayer your heart may prompt." He took his seat on the dais, his body wet with sweat. His red plush armchair had been recovered. The new plush dragged at his robe. He saw Myra sitting alone in the back, within a ring of empty places, in black, weeping. She looked more widowed than anyone. His eyes filled.

On the outer steps of the sanctuary, Kevin Nussbaum crouched, shuddering with fear and fasting. His bare feet were bleeding. His muslin robe was muddy and stained with blood at the hem. He pressed himself to the wall of the synagogue; he huddled against it. "Please, please," he said to himself. He tried to see inside through the glass sidelights by the doors but saw only his own reflection. "No," he muttered to himself, shuddering, trembling. "Life and death are one. It's all the same thing."

Shoe rose. Inside the synagogue, they all heard Kevin Nussbaum outside, beginning a chant and moaning aloud. The hearse drove up to the front doors. They could hear the curses of the hearse driver as he tried to get Kevin to move. "And now the Kaddish," announced Shoe.

The sanctuary emptied quickly after the memorial prayer. The casket was wheeled out. Shoe walked around slowly on the platform in the silence. Outside, Kevin was struggling to plant a marigold in a crack in the asphalt driveway. Shoe walked to the Holy Ark and opened it. He stared at the Torahs inside, glowing in their velvet mantles: red, purple, royal blue. Their gold and silver embroideries caught the red glare of the Eternal Light hanging above. He could hear the cars starting outside in the parking lot. "It's still beautiful," he said quietly. He closed the Ark doors and stood there, his hand on the brass catch. Myra came up to him on the platform, wiping her eyes.

"There's a boy crying out there, Shoe," she said. "He needs you. Let's go."

"I built this place, Myra," he said. "They can't take that away."

"I don't care if they make it a Howard Johnson's," she said. "Oh, Shoe," she burst out, "Shoe, you must hate me." She put her arms around him, beneath his robe and jacket. She held his warm and sweating body. "I love you," she said, crying. She put her face to his neck. "I love you so much. Please don't hate me." She drenched his collar with her tears.

"Me?" he said, astounded. "Hate you? Myra!"

"Shoe, Shoe," she said, crying. She clutched him tightly. He stumbled backward, catching his heel in the hem of his robe. He wrapped

Myra in his arms and fell backward into his pulpit chair, holding her against him. He closed his eyes to the glow of the Eternal Light. "No, no, Myra, don't cry," he whispered. He held her to him, felt his heart beat against her.

She pressed even closer. "Shoe," she begged. She looked at his face. "Never leave me. Promise you won't leave me." She sprawled against him. "Don't die."

He strained his body to his wife's. He raised his legs and wrapped his thighs around her, tearing his robe. He held her with arms and legs, hot, sweat and tears mingling. "Never, Myra," he said. "Never. I promise."

EPILOGUE

Sunny fixed her face in the bathroom mirror. She could hear the front door opening and closing downstairs as the callers began their exodus. The house had been full when she returned from the crematory and the stream of people had continued till long after dark. She turned away from the mirror and ran a housekeeper's habitual eye over the bathroom. She snatched a checked sport shirt off the doorknob in haste and went to Milton's closet to hang it away. She stood in the closet doorway looking dully at all Milton's small clothes, so methodically arranged, so fragrant. . . . She tossed the shirt inside on the floor and closed the door.

She passed the flowering indoor garden in the upstairs hallway. Someone had placed a potted African violet, oversized and dark with variegated leaves, in among the other plants. A card was stuck to the clay pot: "In Sympathy, Dr. Isaiah Summers and the Entire Staff of the College." Sunny wondered how many had felt free that day to go up and down her staircases, to pry and to look. Perhaps she should have her locks changed. New Saxony was not what it used to be. She started down the broad stairs.

Through the banister railing she could see the great wasteland of her living room, empty now but for Mimi lumbering across the still damp carpets, collecting crumpled napkins and used cups and saucers. There were mounds of cigarette butts in the shining interior of the fireplace and in all the planters and flowerpots. So much for asking people not to smoke, she thought. A scorched odor hung in the still air of the stairway; Mimi's cheese puffs had burned up during the funeral while the teenage help played croquet outside with Milton's set.

"Go home, Mimi," said Sunny from the bottom step. "I'll finish up."

"As soon as you eat something," said Mimi, looking up from her gathering. "Irving's in the kitchen and the Warmflashes stayed on. We'll keep you company while you eat." She took Sunny's unresisting arm and walked her to the kitchen. "You'll just taste . . ." she said in a voice of comfort.

"I don't think so," said Sunny, her throat dry. "Maybe I'll have a little Postum. . . ."

"Here we are!" said Mimi, bright and busy, prompting the Warmflashes. "We'll all sit with Sunny and have a bite!" Mimi was deeply afraid of the moment when Sunny's peculiar composure would break, deeply hoped to be gone before then. "Sit, Sunny!"

But Sunny walked to an overhead cabinet to get a cup. She sprang back, repelled, as she looked inside. Discolored water filled the top cup of each little stack of cups. The floral shelf paper was stained and sticky. A few brown drops of water rolled forward and dripped slowly onto the counter. Without a word, she dragged over the stepladder.

"Here! No!" said Irving. He went to Sunny. "I'll take care of that. It's not for you to do. Not today."

"Let me, let me," she said quietly. "I have to put things right."

All Irving's long-dormant fatherly feelings were awakened. Whether because Sunny was so small or whether it was the pity he felt for her, a childless widow—was there anyone more alone?—Irving wanted to cradle small Sunny, comfort her, do something for her. "Sit down and eat a little," he said. "Do it for me."

"You have to eat," said Suzy Warmflash in a threatening voice.

"No, she don't, no, she don't," said Irving quickly, skipping around, playing the clown, protecting Sunny. He moved her to the table and sat down himself. "We're all gonna eat and Sunny will watch us." He grinned. His ears glowed red behind his white sideburns. "Mrs. Seltzer!" he shouted. "Mr. Seltzer is hungry! What you got to eat?"

Harry Warmflash took his cue and sat down deliberately. He pulled at Suzy's hand. "Sit down too, for Christ's sake. I'm exhausted. And I'm hungry, damnit." Harry and Irving helped themselves from the platters of pastry on the table.

"Taste this!" cried Irving as though he had just thought of it. "Sunny! Take one bite of this strudel! You never ate anything like it!" Sunny took a small bite, eating from Irving's open hand. "What did I tell you?" he said proudly. "I wouldn't be surprised if you could eat some more." He would have held Sunny on his lap if he could have followed his impulse. He fed Sunny a few raisins, a morsel of bread, a sliced pear, all the while clowning, talking, distracting her like a baby.

"Thank you, Irving," Sunny said quietly. "I guess I was a little hungry."

"I haven't seen you eat all day," observed Suzy.

All of them looked at the tabletop. The silence became prolonged. Irving sighed greatly. "I don't want any stranger at my funeral," he said. "Rosenstock did a good job."

"What's your hurry?" asked Mimi. "You're young yet."

"No, I ain't," he answered. "We ain't. Rosenstock ain't. We used to be but no more."

Suzy touched the gems on her fingers and the gold at her throat in anxiety. "Don't," she said. "I don't want to talk about it."

"I think we have to ask him to come back," Sunny said quietly. She sat alone, a couple on her right, a couple on her left, she alone at the table's head. "I know I want him back."

"An inspiration, Sunny," said Irving with approval and an extraordinary effort at restraint. "Been thinking like that myself. Harry?"

"I'm willing," Harry said calmly. "The money we have lost . . . The people who walked out to follow him . . ."

"Not to mention the ones that just dropped out, period," said Suzy.

They all looked at Mimi. "I can get along with anybody," she said hastily, defensive. "At least with him, we'll know what we're getting. A new man, who knows?"

"Well, I'm pleasantly surprised to hear you all," said Sunny, gain-ing authority. "Give me a cup of coffee, will you, Mimi?" She looked at Harry. "I think you could write to him for all of us and tell him we want him to come back. You can keep it simple. Just tell him that."

Harry said, "Umm, to be entirely proper, I suppose I would write to his attorneys, offer to meet with them, go over the contract . . ."

"And there won't be any award to pay," exclaimed Mimi. She set the cup down hard in front of Sunny. "That's a big help right there!"

"Don't write him a lawyer letter, Harry," said Irving. "With all respect to you, that won't work. Just write him a human letter, like, with charity for all, with malice for absolutely nobody . . . like that. . . ."

"Tell him to be magnanimous," said Suzy. "After all, in a way he won."

"But tell him you'll let Etkind look over the contract, to sew it up as tight as he pleases," said Mimi eagerly. "Because, God knows, I'm never going to go through something like this again!"

"I don't know what came over us," said Irving thoughtfully. "Did we think we could do it right this time? Not make mistakes? Not get older if we got a new man? Were we trying to turn back the clock? Oy," he said, shaking his head. "I know I don't want a stranger at my funeral."

Sunny's spoon made a harsh noise as she turned it against the side of her cup. "Just tell him, Harry," she said, voice breaking, "just tell him we need him and we want him. Just tell him we love him, Harry," she said. "That's what he wants to know." The first tears were coming fast, at last, the first healing tears.